Reviews of *The Mission*:

'Mission impeccable . . . A triumphant success . . . Robert Bolt's lucid script brings pathos and drama to the complexities of Church and Empire . . . Thank goodness films like this are still made' – *Sunday Times*

'A Mission accomplished in triumph . . . It met thunderous applause at viewings by 1,000 film critics from around the world' – *Daily Mail*

'Mission accomplished . . . A considerable feat of film-making . . . The film is epic in scale, totally sincere in its intentions and full of a sense of horror at the ways the Indians were eventually betrayed . . . Very definitely something to see' – *Guardian*

'The images are spectacular . . . Bolt's cunning tale of clashing imperatives – church versus church, conscience versus realpolitik, Christian love versus righteous anger' – *Financial Times*

Robert Bolt was born in 1924 and spent his early years teaching at a village school. It was when he was writing a nativity play for his pupils that he decided he wanted to become a playwright. He went on to have twelve radio plays accepted by the BBC. He gave up teaching when his play *Flowering Cherry* achieved a successful London run and his internationally acclaimed play *A Man for All Seasons* had opened at the Globe Theatre.

In 1961 he began his long collaboration with film director David Lean when they worked together on *Lawrence of Arabia*. Their films together included the Academy Award-winning *Dr Zhivago* and *Ryan's Daughter*. His other film work includes an adaptation of his play *A Man for All Seasons*, which also won Academy Awards, and in 1972 he made his only venture into film direction with *Lady Caroline Lamb* which starred Sarah Miles. His other stage plays include *Vivat! Vivat! Regina* (1971) and *State of Revolution* (1977).

After a period of illness he resumed writing for the screen in 1984. The resulting film, *The Bounty*, was described by a critic on the *Sunday Times* as having the year's best script. He was then approached to work on *The Mission* by Fernando Ghia, its producer, who felt that Robert Bolt 'was the only person able to give the mass of material a dramatic structure . . . capable of enhancing what history has concealed beneath a wealth of other information.'

ROBERT BOLT

The
Mission

PENGUIN BOOKS

Penguin Books Ltd, Harmondsworth, Middlesex, England
Viking Penguin Inc., 40 West 23rd Street, New York, New York 10010, U.S.A.
Penguin Books Australia Ltd, Ringwood, Victoria, Australia
Penguin Books Canada Limited, 2801 John Street, Markham, Ontario,
Canada L3R 1B4
Penguin Books (N.Z.) Ltd, 182–190 Wairau Road, Auckland 10, New Zealand

First published 1986
Reprinted 1986

Filmset in Times (Linotron 202) by
Rowland Phototypesetting Ltd, Bury St Edmunds, Suffolk
Printed and bound in Great Britain by
Cox & Wyman Ltd, Reading

The Mission

Rodrigo Mendoza was fourteen in 1725 when the rowing boat of his father, Alvaro, was found floating in the harbour of Cádiz at dawn. One oar was jammed between the rudder and the thwarts, and an empty flask of wine was stuck in the bottom. Alvaro had fallen into the slack waters of the harbour in the course of a lighterage job. A few sacks of grain were still waiting to be ferried out, so César Matías, the lighterage boss, loaded them on to his own boat and rowed them to the waiting *Grosso*. In answer to the inquiry where Alvaro was, he shrugged and indicated the waters of the harbour.

He knocked on the door of Rodrigo Mendoza, taking off his hat as he told the boy that his father was dead. The orphan went indoors and came out carrying his younger brother, Felipe, aged three. Then he went down to his father's boat and carefully inspected it. He set his brother playing, accepted a cigarillo from César and listened to him.

'I offer my condolences on the death of your father.'

'I thank you.'

'The boat is yours,' César went on, with a wave of his cigarillo.

'True,' said the boy.

'You, of course, cannot handle it yourself.'

'I can try.'

'Who will look after Felipe?'

1

'I will.'

'Listen, I have decided to give you ten dineros for the boat with licence.'

'It is worth twenty.'

'No, no. Say twelve.'

Mendoza looked down into the boat and then up at the *Grosso*, a three-masted *aviso* in the harbour. 'Had he delivered all the corn before he fell in?'

César said, 'I finished it for him.'

'All of it?'

'The last part.'

'Thank you,' replied Mendoza. 'It is good to know that when a boatman is claimed by the waters of this harbour, he is not forgotten,' he said, and looked away. So César had to give him the full payment for his father's work.

Mendoza lifted his brother off the pebbles. 'I must have time to turn over in my mind my father's death.'

'Naturally.'

Mendoza bought a piece of cheese, bread, a flask of milk and some wine. When he had shuttered the heat out of the cavernous house, which his father had paid for by the week, he gave all the milk and half the bread and cheese to Felipe. After saying a prayer for the dead, he settled himself at the foot of the wall, looking up at the window, while Felipe ate his meal. He then turned over on his side to sleep. As the walls became dark and the window became bright with stars, Mendoza reviewed his situation.

He had not liked his father. His mother, Catalina, had been different, but death came for her while she was giving birth to Felipe. Thenceforward his father took no notice of his two sons but found solace in the bottle. All Mendoza's affection was turned towards his small brother, enfolding the child, while Felipe regarded him as the ultimate authority and adored him.

Now that his father was dead, he could stay on here with Felipe and earn a living by lighterage, but this would mean that his brother would grow up untaught, as he was himself. There was another possibility. He might leave the child with the Sisters of San Fernando and seek his fortune overseas. He decided to interview the Mother Superior tomorrow.

He took the wine flask and snuggled down into the rock-hard bed, pulling the woven sacks about him, overwhelmed by his own decision. Maybe it would be best to be a lighterman. That would provide a respectable living for them both. But next morning he went to the Hospice of San Fernando.

'The question is, can you afford it? We make a charge here, alas,' the Mother Superior told him. 'What is your trade?'

Why not say he was the son of an aristocrat from up in the hills? It would not matter a whit then, not being able to read. But his mother had told him it was wrong to lie, that way perdition lay. He said, 'I am a lighterman.'

The Mother inclined her head. 'A lighterman!' she thought. 'Ah me!' 'We charge fifteen dineros a year,' she said.

Mendoza's face grew stiff. He counted on getting twenty dineros for the boat. This would leave him with five dineros to start off his life abroad. He inclined his head. 'That is all included?'

'Did you not hear me? Fifteen dineros.'

'I will place them in your hand tomorrow.'

'How?'

'I will do it.'

'Where shall we put Felipe if you cannot keep up with the payments?'

'There will be nobody here to protect him. You can make him your gardener.'

The Mother Superior tried not to smile. 'The young!' she thought. 'All the world seems a straight path to them.' She leant forward and said, 'What are you going to do yourself?'

'I intend to go abroad.'

'Ah, abroad!' she thought. 'That might be different.' 'You have prospects?' she inquired.

Mendoza nodded his head; his boat provided him with prospects.

César offered him fourteen dineros for it.

'No,' said Mendoza, 'twenty.'

Having seen Mendoza's expression, César said sixteen.

Mendoza shook his head. 'Twenty.'

César threw up his hands and walked away. In the evening he returned and said, 'Look, I have thought long about this. You are an orphan, with nowhere to turn your head. My price is now seventeen. Put your hand there.'

Mendoza ignored the hand. 'The price is twenty.'

César swore a mouthful of oaths and went away to his house, slamming the door. The next morning, before anyone else was awake, he said, 'Look, this is my final offer. If you do not take this, I retract all other offers. Eighteen.'

Mendoza said, 'Twenty.'

César gave in.

Mendoza placed five dineros in a strip of canvas and tied this tightly round his stomach, and then took fifteen dineros and Felipe to the orphanage. 'God be with you, Felipe,' he said, and kissed his brother farewell. Felipe understood, and the ancient stone walls of the nunnery were rent by a whole day and night of the child's weeping and banging his head on the walls.

Mendoza collected a small roll of clothes from his home, took one look round and shut the door. He went down to the harbour. There were three *avisos* just about to sail: the *Grosso* for Havana, the *Nuestra Señora del Pilar* for Vitória and the *Concepción* for Buenos Aires. He sat down against the jetty and watched the boats that came in and out to them.

At three o'clock came a large coach. A gentleman, two ladies and a young man got out of it and climbed, with much assistance, into a ship's boat. The coachman and a sailor lifted two big trunks in after them and the sailors, under the command of a boatswain, rowed out to the *Concepción*. In the afternoon the adults returned, without the young man. With one of the women in tears and the gentleman comforting her, they piled back into the coach and drove off. Mendoza put away his hunk of bread and waited.

At seven a long boat from the *Concepción* brought the young man back to the quayside, and Mendoza followed him. He walked into town with a sullen air and sat at an open-air eating-place, where he knocked his cup of coffee on to the ground; he was close to tears.

'Please,' said Mendoza and fetched another.

'Thank you,' said the youth.

'The *Concepción* is it, señor?'

'Yes.'

'A wholesome boat, they tell me.'

'Deplorable. Filthy.'

'Truly?'

'This is my first voyage.'

'Ah, señor, I understand.'

'You, I suppose, have been on many such trips?'

'Not on board the *Concepción*, señor. Many others.' That was not a lie. He had been on trips to the other side of the Gulf of Cádiz.

'You have been to Buenos Aires?'

'No, señor.'

'I am to be a business partner with my great-uncle in Buenos Aires.'

'Ah, señor, you have a long head for figures.'

'Alas, no. And two other persons will be sharing my cabin with me.'

'That is to be expected, señor.'

'Yes.'

'Would you like another cup?'

'Thank you.' The youth was gratified at having someone to wait on him. He said, 'You have a family in Cádiz?'

'A brother, señor. He is being taken care of.'

'I have no servant for this trip.'

'No, señor?'

'You could not be persuaded to take the trip with me, as my servant?'

'No, señor.'

'Why not?'

'How could I pay for my passage back home?'

'I will pay you for the trip back home.'

'I see. But pardon me, how much?'

'I would pay you two months' wages.'

'You make it very attractive, señor.'

'Four dineros, plus two dineros for the two months' wages.'

'But the captain may not have room for a servant, señor.'

'I, in my grandfather's name, will tell him.'

Two days later they sailed from Cádiz harbour. Mendoza's

last sights were of the bell tower of the Hospice of San Fernando, and of César rowing his dead father's boat.

The slow pitch and roll of the ship made Mendoza ill, but he obeyed the orders of the captain, the officers, the boatswain, the yeomen, the seamen and his young master, and never complained. He watched the pilot closely and cast his own eyes after his at the fluttering sails or at the stray currents of the ocean. Silent and withdrawn, the pilot alone knew where they were.

Week after week Mendoza waited at the *fogón* until all the sailors had finished their food before receiving his helping of salt pork and biscuits. He slept in the night alone among the reeking anchor cables.

The sailors began to look emaciated.

At the Canaries a ship's boy named Salvador came on board. He was about fifteen years old, with a slovenly face. Looking about, he saw no one but Mendoza beneath him, so whenever he had a foul job to do, he called Mendoza and made him do it.

When they entered the tropics, the captain allowed the two boys to sleep on deck in the bows. One hot night Mendoza opened his eyes to the slowly gyrating stars and caught the surprised face of Salvador a foot from his. Salvador grinned foolishly and took his hand away from Mendoza's waist, where he kept his money. Mendoza coiled his hands round the neck of Salvador and threw himself on top of him. The night watch came and looked on, for a fight between two boys was better than nothing. They were writhing about the deck. Salvador was roaring and blaspheming, but Mendoza fought with his mouth drawn back. He pressed his face near to the throat of his enemy, who went quiet and then screamed. Snatched into the burly arms of the watchman, Mendoza fought him. 'Jesus Christ!' the watchman growled, and threw the boy from him. So he was up and after Salvador again. The sailors gripped him and poured buckets of salt water over him. Only when he was two parts drowned did they give over.

They laughed uneasily. 'Holy Mother, who would have thought he had such a devil in him?' Salvador gave Mendoza a wide berth after that. Mendoza was not molested. He was not befriended either.

The pilot announced that Montevideo was just ahead, and they were all in the rigging when at last Mendoza saw the pale mountains loom out of the grey sea. Buenos Aires lay before them. They pulled right alongside the harbour wall, and a wide gang-plank was run ashore.

The young master paid Mendoza with a nod and a smile and went ashore, where he disappeared with his two trunks in the company of his great-uncle and a pretty cousin. They all got into a coach, and that was the last Mendoza saw of them.

Turning seaward, he saw strange vessels passing slowly in the distance, making stealthily for the far side of the bay. He could make out a harbour there, with four or five ships at anchor.

'What's that?' he asked a sailor.

'Sacramento.'

'What kind of ships are those?'

'Slavers.'

At the end of the day, when the officers and crew had all been paid and allowed ashore, he too was permitted down the gang-plank and made his way into town.

Wandering, he found himself in a public square which

offered the shade of some overhanging trees, and a stall which sold flapjacks stuffed with pork. He bought some and ate, seated near a fountain.

He admired the streets of recently built houses, the imposing, grandly decorated public buildings and the impressive churches. They were what he was used to. But he found the sun too hot, and everything lay beneath a pall of fine white dust.

The Spanish citizens seemed half smothered. Yawning, they began to make gestures which they lacked the energy to finish, as they sat in the square in loose waistcoats and unbuckled pantaloons.

There was also a group of natives, olive-brown, muscular and dressed in ragged garments, dozing in the shadow of a church. He peered at them narrowly, but they looked back at him uninquisitively.

Mendoza rose to his feet and went up to a little knot of Spaniards.

'Good afternoon, señores. D'you want a boy to work for you?'

'No.'

'D'you chance to know anyone who does, señores?'

'No.' Briefly they looked him up and down and then turned away.

Twilight began to gather in the twittering trees. Near by someone was playing a guitar. Mendoza sat down near the fountain. An officer from the ship came by, together with a man of about forty with a seamed face. Seeing Mendoza sitting there, he said, 'Here is a boy, if a boy will do.'

'Yes, a boy will do.'

The officer beckoned to Mendoza. 'This is my friend, Palacio.'

'Good evening, Señor Palacio.'

'How old are you?'

'Fourteen.'

'You can handle a boat?'

'He can handle a boat,' said the officer.

'I want a boy to come on a barge, to Asunción.'

'Asunción,' said Mendoza. 'I see.'

'It is two hundred leagues upriver. I am offering half a dinero.'

'One, señor,' said Mendoza.

The man laughed. 'One then! The barge is called the *Flores*. Cut along to the port now and tell the captain I sent you.'

The captain proved a dour old man who only grunted when Mendoza made himself known. From start to finish of the voyage that followed he never spoke a needless word. The barge was a ninety-footer with a huge spritsail and four long sweeps on either side, laden with ironware from Madrid. There were a dozen natives to raise the sail and, when the wind veered round, to lower it.

When they were under way, Mendoza took the helm. The captain watched him for a little and then, satisfied that the new hand could steer, sat down to peer myopically over the meandering waters. Mendoza had never seen such a broad river. Both banks were covered in tangled forest. He gestured at the muddy river: 'Big.'

'Yes.'

Mendoza nodded at the muddy water flowing past. 'A slow current.'

'Yes.'

He looked at the native crew. They were sunk in lethargy. 'What kind of men are they?'

'Guarani.'

'Guarani?' No response. At home in Spain nobody cared whether the captain was alive or dead. He was waiting to finish his days there.

One or two words floated back to them from the main deck.

'What language is that?'

'Guarani.'

'Are they from these parts?'

The captain pointed to the huge and silent forest which trespassed into the river.

'From there?'

'Up there.' He gestured far away up the river.

Mendoza watched them. 'They are stupid.'

'Yes.'

Each night they put in to the shore, at some place where the forest was cut back for about a mile and a village of three or four houses and a church presented itself, with big farms, mansions, fields of cattle, maize and orchards. The Guarani would build a fire and serve them maize gruel and fruits which they washed down with cheap red wine.

Mendoza saw three small towns on their journey, and then the vast forest would close back in, creeping stealthily into the water. On one quiet stretch their course took them near the trees. The Guarani crew peered into the trees and exchanged guttural words in an undertone, but then they saw Mendoza looking and resumed their blank expressions.

After five weeks a marked increase in the number of fishing boats and farms announced the approach of Asunción. At last, around a headland, the capital of the Río de la Plata hove into view.

They worked their way through crowded barges to the harbour wall, and the captain tied up and disappeared ashore. Mendoza looked at the Guarani and they looked listlessly back, so he sat down with them to wait. The captain re-appeared, ordering the Guarani to work at clearing the boat, and went away again. At length Palacio, who had journeyed to Asunción overland, approached Mendoza.

'Why are you hanging about here? You have arrived, is it not so?' he said.

'*Sí*, señor, but my dinero.'

'What dinero?'

'The dinero that you promised me.'

'I never promised you a dinero.'

'Señor, you gave me your word on it.'

'You have a paper?'

'A paper? No.'

Palacio wagged a finger, shook his head and said, 'There. You see?' and went off into the town again, but Mendoza followed and persisted.

'Señor, you have not paid me my wages.' He followed Palacio through the cathedral square, across the two or three fashionable streets and down a dark alleyway into the old part of town.

'Señor, you have not paid me my wages. Excuse me, señor – '

Palacio turned and looked up and down the alleyway. Then he dragged Mendoza into a courtyard and beat the boy soundly with the horn handle of his whip until he was semi-conscious.

'There, you see?' he said, breathless. 'You see? Huh? You see? See? See?' He went off.

Mendoza limped to a fountain and bathed his cuts. Then he searched the streets. In the evening he found Palacio dining in a restaurant, sitting below a high window. He went round behind the window and called, 'Señor, you have not paid me my wages. Excuse me, señor, one dinero – ' There was silence from the eating-place, and he called again, 'Señor, you have not paid me my wages. One dinero, señor. One dinero.' He heard the sound of a chair being pushed back and voices raised in laughter.

Mendoza quickly hid across the street. He watched Palacio search for him. Then Palacio paused and finally went back inside. He was greeted by laughter and a burst of stamping. Gradually conversation was resumed. Mendoza approached the window again and called, 'I will return for it, señor.' Then he sprinted off.

The following morning Mendoza, asleep in the square, was roused by the fluttering and hopping of the birds, and Guarani arriving with pitchers of water to prepare for the coming day. They said not a word at finding him stretched out there. A little later, however, the Spanish proprietor of a bakehouse appeared and began staring at him, so he made his way back to the harbour.

Dock workers were clambering sleepily over the sides of a careened merchant ship. Someone was cooking tortillas and fish. Mendoza bought some and enjoyed it.

Then he noticed an exotic group of men dressed in an assortment of garments, rags and strange quilted pants. One, sporting grotesque finery, with soiled ruffles and an earth-stained embroidered coat, looked as though he had arrived from some dilapidated court. There were also two blacks among them. They were armed with swords and pistols and a musket.

Mendoza asked the tortilla vendor, 'What kind of men are those?' One of the dock workers, who was leisurely eating a tortilla, looked up. 'Conquistadores. Have nothing to do with that lot. They take no notice of the law.'

Mendoza tidied himself and then went round the city of Asunción, knocking at the back doors of houses in search of work. The householders and their major-domos liked the look of him. At one place he was offered a job as a house-boy, at another a job as a gardener's boy, but when he inquired about the wage it was only half a dinero per month. He figured out with a stick how many dineros this would come to in a year, and it was not enough to pay Felipe's orphanage fee. He frowned thoughtfully and slept in the square again, amidst the distant barking of dogs and the roar of frogs from the river.

The next morning a voice woke him. He looked up and saw the man who seemed to have come from the courts of old Madrid standing over him.

'You want a place?'

'*Sí*, señor.' Mendoza scrambled to his feet.

'Then work for me.'

'*Sí*, señor.'

'Come.'

Mendoza followed. 'How much, señor?'

'Two dineros.'

'For how much time, señor?'

'Four months. Who knows?'

Supposing it were twelve months' work? 'Señor, four dineros for four months' work. And then, señor, the same for any time I work for you.' This would come to only twelve dineros a year, but he would find the extra three dineros for Felipe's orphanage fee in some other way.

'*Dios*, you strike a hard bargain.'

'*Sí*, señor. And half now and half when I have finished.'

The man stopped, and his narrow eyes flickered as though someone behind the lids were suddenly peering out.

'No,' he said.

'Señor, in that case maybe you will perhaps sign a paper?'

'What?' And then the man laughed. 'Why not?'

'What shall I call you, señor?'

'Victorio Paramín Tijare López Lusavida y Jermano,' his new master replied. 'Now come.'

Mendoza picked up the man's two muskets, pistols and travelling bag, and his own small roll, and followed him across the harbour. They entered a quiet warehouse where some fifteen of the conquistadores, including the black men, were assembled. Their voices rose into the high roof where birds were darting.

'Good morning, beloved,' said one of the black men.

'Greetings, Gaspacho.'

'Who is that?' asked Gaspacho.

'My boy.'

A laugh came from the group. 'Victorio's got a boy.'

The leader, Tiberio, entered. A middle-aged man, he was a trifle fat, with a face swollen by a suppurating disease. He looked at them and then turned to Victorio.

'Are these all you could find?'

'Where can I get more?'

'You, nowhere. Who is this boy?'

Mendoza answered, 'My name is Rodrigo Mendoza.'

'Call me "señor".'

'Señor.'

'We are collecting slaves.'

'Yes, señor.'

'It is against the law.'

15

Mendoza could think only of the twelve dineros a year, so he just said, 'Yes, señor.'

Tiberio shrugged. 'Come, then.'

Mendoza asked one of the men for a pencil and a shred of paper. Victorio made out a document, which Gaspacho read aloud. It seemed to match what Victorio had promised, so Mendoza stowed it away in the strip of cloth where he kept his dineros from the voyage and, carrying his new master's bags and weapons, followed the others to the riverside. He noticed that all the townspeople nearby drew ostentatiously away from them and turned their backs.

They embarked in ten forty-foot canoes, each crewed by two Guarani, and shoved off in dead silence. Looking back, he saw that all the townspeople were now turned towards them, watching them go.

'Why are they like that?' he asked the black man, who was in the same canoe. 'Why don't they wish us God speed?'

'They wish it, but they don't want to be heard wishing it.'

'I don't understand.'

'You will. My name is Gaspacho.'

'My name is Mendoza.'

'I know.'

So, with a slow murmur from the paddles, they set out on their long journey upriver from the capital city of Asunción.

The black slave-trader told them a story of the life he was leaving behind. Mendoza had heard many such accounts before but none as carnal as this one. And yet the conquistadores laughed! Then Victorio sang a song: it was a tale told by a heart-broken man of a suffering maiden. When he came to the end, they applauded him with cries of *'Formidable!'* and *'Elegante!'*

Gaspacho said, 'Alas. He will go back to the pavements in

Madrid when he has made enough money. But I? What can
I do?'

'You can go back between the legs of the little Madalena,'
said a man.

'She is dead.'

'Hey, Madalena is dead! How did that happen?'

'I did not stop it.'

'Then you can tickle the bum of her son.'

'I have done,' said the black man. 'It is a nice bum too, but
not as nice as Madalena's. I have only her son and the Guarani
now, to ease my aching.'

Mendoza asked, 'Are the Guarani servants or slaves, Gaspacho?'

'Better ask Tiberio.'

'Not slaves, but a special kind of servant,' said Tiberio.

Further up the river, where the forest had been cleared,
they passed a moored fishing boat. A Jesuit priest and a trio
of Guarani were sitting in it, and as they approached Tiberio
called out, 'Good evening, father.' Neither the priest nor the
Guarani seemed to have heard. They behaved as though there
were no canoes going by. Looking back, Mendoza saw them
still sitting without movement in their motionless boat.

Then came the mission. Mendoza caught his breath at the
size of it. They approached a long quayside with Guarani
children playing on it, two large barges and a host of canoes.
As they went past, the children stopped playing and watched.
There was a large cross in the centre of the wide square of
the mission and, on two sides of the square, row upon row,
the dormitories of the Guarani. Dominating everything, there
towered an astounding church, much bigger than any in Asunción. It was crowned by a grotesque carving, half angel and
half hooded bird, with an expression both threatening and

just. To one side of this were the spacious storehouses and workrooms and, to the other, the house of the Jesuits, two-storeyed and built of stone.

A Jesuit came down to the water's edge and shepherded the children away.

Enormous fields pushed the forest far back into the distance, with hundreds of Guarani placidly at work in them. They looked up as the conquistadores passed in midstream, and then down again.

When the forest had closed back upon the river, Gaspacho said, 'Did you ever see anything like that before?'

'No,' said Mendoza. 'They must be very holy men.'

'Very. Under them, all people are free. Even the Guarani.'

'The Guarani?'

'Yes. They own the land and the mission. But they want the Jesuits to rule over them.'

'Tiberio said we go to collect slaves.'

'A slip of the tongue. In the Portuguese territories they have slaves, but here we just have special servants called *encomienda*.'

'I see.'

'Do you? Explain it to me, then. For example, the *encomienda* are paid no wages.'

'They are slaves, then.'

'No, as I told you, *encomienda* are not slaves. It is very important to remember that there is a difference. They are paid no wages all the same. We go now to pick some up.'

'Where?'

'On the Portuguese side of the mountains, where they are slaves. But when we bring them back with us over the mountains, they'll become *encomienda*.'

'Where is the boundary?'

'Ah, who can say? Who knows from which side of the mountains any Guarani comes?'

That evening Mendoza said in a low voice, 'Gaspacho?'

'Yes?'

'Who pays us for the Guarani we bring back?'

After a long pause Gaspacho said, 'The Captain-General.'

'The Captain-General?'

'He is the head of all the planters. Hush now, I want to go to sleep.'

Early in the morning Gaspacho took Mendoza aside. 'You have no knife, I see.'

'No,' said Mendoza.

'You need one like this.' Gaspacho pulled a rondel dagger from its leather sheath.

Mendoza bent over it. 'Next time, perhaps.'

'No, now. Four reals.'

'The sheath is faulty.'

'I know.'

'Three reals.'

'Three, agreed.'

Gaspacho also sold him, for one real, a belt with which to sling the dagger across his chest. He felt a man now.

They reached a funnel where the river was broken by colossal square boulders, and the trees hung down. Here they got out and, leaving two conquistadores and six Guarani to keep watch over the canoes, set out on the climb.

'How far is the Portuguese territory, señor?' Mendoza asked.

'Over there.' Tiberio pointed to the distant hills shrouded in mist.

'You, boy,' said Victorio, 'can carry that.' He pointed to a jug of wine. 'Take care of it. It's very special.' Towards the end of a day of climbing, the bottle weighed like lead. But Mendoza was also carrying a dagger.

It took them a full month to scale the mountains. The Guarani carried the muskets, pots and bedrolls. At the end of each day, when everyone had settled down to sleep, Victorio would call Mendoza and demand a cup of wine or maté. This was something like tea or coffee made from the dried yerba maté plant; it made a stimulating brew. Mendoza would prepare the fire, mix a cup and take it to his master. Each morning he would find it by Victorio's bed, untouched. He would set his face hard, remembering how he had mixed it in the night. Then he would fold the bedding tightly and take it to the Guarani. Picking up the wine jar, he would commence his uphill journey.

'Do you like Victorio now?' asked Gaspacho.

Mendoza remained silent.

'Hey you, I'm talking to you.'

'I don't hear,' replied Mendoza.

'You are a prudent man.'

It was the first time he had been called a man. He was filled with a peculiar mixture of fear and exultation. He was fifteen.

Next day they came upon a trampled patch of earth with many prints of bare human feet. The conquistadores sat down and put on high boots, hide suits reaching almost to the ground, padded cotton armour and broad-brimmed hats.

'For the arrows,' Gaspacho explained.

Victorio was left in charge of the camp. He was excited, and set the Guarani to work building a high fence of thorn bushes in a circle to keep in the new *encomienda*.

Nothing happened during the first four days, but on the

evening of the fifth Tiberio and his party returned with four-teen Guarani, twelve men and two women. They were thrust inside the fence. They paced around it, came together to exchange a few words in a whisper and then separated again, sat down and would not speak. One of the Guarani servants gave them a pot of maize but was careful to avert his eyes.

Well pleased, the conquistadores drank. When it grew dark two of them pulled out the prettier of the two women. Tiberio took her with oaths and grunts, calling forth hissing groans and laughs for those waiting their turn. Mendoza went and hid in the undergrowth. When they shouted for him, he did not reply. The night sky had begun to flush by the time the woman rejoined the other captives. She hid in a corner of the enclosure. Two conquistadores stood guard over the prisoners and peace descended on the little camp. Mendoza came out of the jungle.

'Hey, that was good,' said one of the sentries, and yawned.

They went into the bush on three more expeditions, return-ing first with nine captives, then with five and finally with none. The last time they returned, one conquistador named Mandu had been pierced through the arm with a long, sharp arrow; it was broken off front and rear.

Mendoza asked Gaspacho in a hushed voice, 'Will he die?'

'Probably.'

'Do many fall like that?'

'Naturally.'

'It hurts him?'

And then Gaspacho, angered, called, 'Hey, Mandu, does it hurt?'

'Yes, like hell it hurts.'

'You see, it hurts.' Then the black man fell silent.

Tiberio sent Victorio and six other men to buy more slaves at the Portuguese town of Cruzeiro do Oeste, six days' journey away. They revelled in the trek like schoolboys.

Cruzeiro do Oeste itself was a little town in a fold in the mountains down among the trees. They lodged there at an inn, but Mendoza was sent to sleep among the horses. The next day Victorio bought a parasol and told the boy to carry it over him, to give the Portuguese the impression that he was an *hidalgo*. He inspected the slaves and then opened negotiations. It took all day to bargain for the twenty-five he wanted, seventeen men and eight women, all very young. When he had struck a bargain, he called for a bottle of wine, toasted his clients, and signed his full aristocratic name: Victorio Paramín Tijare López Lusavida y Jermano.

'Behold the Don of López,' said one of his men. Victorio laid down his pen and looked at him. Everything went very quiet.

'You are a servile pig, Allendras.'

'I am a servile pig?'

'Yes.'

Allendras looked at everybody, but nobody would look at him. 'Very well.'

'An abject pig.'

'No doubt.'

'No, no, you must of necessity say it.'

'If you say so.'

'Let me hear you say it.'

'I am a pig.'

'A servile pig.'

'A servile pig.'

'Now go. Take care I do not catch you in the evening.'

So Allendras left, and Victorio continued writing out his

name. The silence was broken by a little embarrassed conversation among the Portuguese.

When they were alone, Mendoza asked Gaspacho, 'What's a servile pig?'

'I don't know, but Allendras has left.'

'It was just a joke.'

'But taken *a mal*.'

'Should he have fought him?'

'Of course.'

'Victorio would have won?'

'Oh yes. He knows where to pick his quarrels. He would not have tried that on Tiberio.'

They stocked up with maize and mutton, loaded it on to the Guarani slaves and set off on their way back to the camp. The Guarani made slow work of it but stumbled along without a word, urged on by an occasional blow from a rope's end.

A fortnight had gone by before they saw Tiberio again. In the meantime Mandu, the man with the arrow wound, had died. It took the party another month to reach their boats and another five weeks to get back at last to Asunción.

Tiberio left them at the quayside, to return later in the evening dressed in new clothes. He had four men with him. They carried muskets and wore the Captain-General's badge on their sleeves. They had come to collect the slaves.

Tiberio pulled out a bag and paid the conquistadores off on the quayside. They said, 'Goodnight,' in turn and drifted off in twos and threes into the town.

When Victorio was paid, he said to Mendoza, 'Come.' The rest watched Mendoza labour his way up into town, laden with Victorio's baggage and parasol. Then they looked at Tiberio, but he pretended not to notice. His business finished, he too went off.

In the back court of his inn Victorio said, 'Here,' and threw Mendoza one dinero. The blood drained away beneath Mendoza's mahogany tan.

'You owe me five dineros, señor, for five months of work.'

'No, one dinero. You are a useful boy. I may have work for you again. *Adiós.*'

'I need the five dineros.'

'Now you – you make me angry.'

'See, you signed.' Mendoza produced his paper, but Victorio leaned across and took it.

'I see no paper.' He went in and shut the door.

Mendoza sought out Gaspacho, who said, 'But where is your paper?'

'Victorio has it.'

'Fool. You should have taken it to the officials tomorrow.'

'Will you not help me?'

'No. This is a blood-letting matter between men. Try Tiberio. You'll find him at Marcia's.'

Mendoza went to Marcia's. Tiberio emerged from an inner room.

'Do you remember, señor, a paper that Victorio signed for me?'

'Yes. Has he taken it?'

'Yes. Will you help me?'

'No help is possible.'

'Why not?'

'The paper was all. *Adiós.*'

Mendoza went down to the harbour and stared at the water. They all knew that Victorio had taken the paper and kept the money that was his by right, yet none of them would help him. It was a matter between the two of them. He looked down at the webbed image of the moon in the harbour waters, and then up at the peaceful sky, and said a prayer to the Blessed Virgin. Hiding his bedding near a pile of rubble, he took off his shoes, put on his dagger and went silently to Victorio's inn.

He spied Victorio alone, asleep in a bedraggled bed, and slipped in through an open window. Drawing his dagger from its sheath, he knelt by Victorio's bed. Then he placed the dagger against his enemy's neck and pressed gently. Victorio awoke with a start. The dagger went in further, and Victorio froze. 'What is that?' he asked in a soft voice.

'Me,' replied Mendoza.

Victorio laughed quietly. 'What do you want?'

'My five dineros.'

'Of course. I see you are a man to be reckoned with. I will get them for you.' He was half-way out of bed when, in wrath and panic, Mendoza struck. Reaching repeatedly for the dagger which he had torn out of Mendoza's hand, Victorio fell without making a sound.

Mendoza was dumbfounded. It had been so easy. The rest of the building was undisturbed. He must get the paper. No, the money, not the paper. The paper was of no use now. His enemy lay there without a sound. Blood had started seeping from the wound. Under the pillow he found a wallet with thirty-seven dineros in it. He would take just five. No, not five. He would take the lot. That was what a casual thief would have done. He took the money, slipped out of the window and walked back to the harbour.

Nothing had altered since he left the quayside. The reflection of the moon was just the same. He stared at the money. It was more than three years' payment, but if he kept it all he would be a thief, so, after counting out his five, he threw the remaining coins into the water and lay down to sleep. A few moments later he got up and took his dagger down to the water's edge to wash it. Then he again lay down to sleep. Five minutes later he got up once more, this time to wash himself thoroughly, standing naked in the still water of the harbour. When he lay down this time, he was feverish. Sleep would not come.

He was relieved when dawn broke, with Guarani, dock labourers and shipwrights arriving to start a new day. No one seemed to have heard about what had happened in the night. A passing labourer wished him good-day.

At ten o'clock, however, a group of people from the town came looking for him. They crowded round him: a constable, Tiberio and a bunch of sightseers. He should have had breakfast, he thought, as he stood up.

Tiberio asked, 'Have you heard what's happened to Victorio?'

'Victorio? No, señor, what?'

'Somebody killed him.'

'Last night,' added the constable.

'Did you have anything to do with it?' Tiberio continued.

'Me, señor? No.'

'Let us see your money,' the constable ordered.

Mendoza showed it to him. 'There are eight dineros here,' said the constable.

'Yes, señor, what of that?'

'Where did you get them?'

'In Spain.'

'Constable, Victorio had more than thirty dineros on him when he was killed,' Tiberio said.

The constable said, 'Now show me your knife.'

'My knife? Certainly.'

'This has recently been washed.'

26

'I always wash it at the end of every day.'

The constable thought this over. 'I see no reason to suppose this boy is guilty,' he declared.

'Neither do I,' said Tiberio.

'But señores,' Mendoza protested, 'he owed me five dineros. What shall I do?'

Said Tiberio, 'You can say goodbye to that,' and led them all back into town. There was a small smile on his lips.

'He knows,' thought Mendoza, looking after him. 'He knows, and I have gone up in his esteem. He is the confidant of the Captain-General. This is a strange world.' He shook his head. His mother too knew what he had done. What would it do to her love for him? He went to the Church of Santa Ana, in the shadows of the trees. It was blessedly cool within. There was a priest. Mendoza approached and asked to make a confession.

When he had heard Mendoza's confession, the priest wiped his forehead with a handkerchief and asked, 'Have you told me all?'

'Yes, father,' said Mendoza.

'What manner of man was it you killed?'

'Victorio, father.'

'Victorio!' thought the priest. 'It must have been a lucky blow! Good riddance to him!' Aloud he said, 'You have been engaged in an affair of honour. D'you know what that means?'

'Does it mean I am not guilty of murder, father?'

'In the eyes of the Heavenly Father you are guilty, but not in the eyes of men.'

'Thank you, father. Now, father, I have a worse sin to confess.'

'*Dios!*' said the priest to himself. 'What is it, my son?'

'I lied.'

'You did what?'

'Lied.'

The priest, upon reflection, decided that the penitent was not insane. 'I see,' he said. 'Well, do not lie again.'

'No, father.'

Imposing a lengthy penance, the priest dismissed Mendoza and watched him retreat the length of the nave, where he knelt to pray. His mother had been a saint, Mendoza thought, kneeling there in the church. That was why she had been able to live a life acceptable to Christ. Her soul was always ready for the transcendent vision. But she knew her son was not like that. She did not expect him to be a saint. She had only told him to be no more guilty than other men were. Well, he was guiltless in the eyes of men. The priest had said so. But he must be careful not to lie. Resolved in his mind, he started on the Hail Marys the priest had allotted him.

The priest parted the curtains at the end of the nave and left the church, thankful to be a priest.

When Mendoza came out, Gaspacho was waiting. He chuckled connivingly.

'My dagger, you see?'

'What do you mean?'

'You did it with my dagger.'

'I did what?'

'Killed Victorio.'

'Excuse me,' he said and walked away. He saw what his mother had meant when she said lying was the pathway to perdition.

Gaspacho caught up with him. 'Pardon. Somehow I thought that you had done it.'

'No.'

'I see now that I was mistaken. Come and have supper.'

'Tonight?'

'Yes, yes, tonight.'

'I thank you. Tonight then.' Turning towards the harbour, he thought, 'It is so easy.'

———————

That night at supper Gaspacho said, 'There's a new expedition in a fortnight. They need men.'

'I am only fifteen.'

'You are seventeen.'

'I am?'

'Aren't you?'

'I am seventeen.'

'You must get a sword.'

'I cannot afford one.'

'You can spend some of your thirty-seven dineros.'

'I haven't got thirty-seven dineros.'

'*Dios!* You can spend some of however much you have, then, on a sword.'

'How much?'

'About five reals. It is important. Listen, a man without a sword is like a *capón*.'

Gaspacho led Mendoza through the pitch-dark night to a high wall with a gate, on which he hammered. A man arrived with a candle. He recognized Gaspacho and took them to a low-ceilinged room where he lit more candles on a table. Through flickering shadows Mendoza saw rows of rapiers, muskets and pistols, and he felt his blood quicken.

Said Gaspacho softly, 'Aye, see.'

Now, Mendoza had been taught the evil of weapons by his mother. Moreover, he had not enough money to buy any of the swords. Looking past them, he saw a weapon with a thick, short blade.

'What's that?'

'A baselard,' said the swordsmith, 'for use on a horse.'

He drew it out of its scabbard. It was one and a half inches wide, two feet long and had a stabbing point. 'It was made a hundred years ago in Basle. A chopping blade.'

Mendoza took it and felt its solid weight. 'How much?'

'No, no,' laughed Gaspacho. 'You cannot fence with that.'

'It feels good in my hand.'

'No, listen, Mendoza, you mustn't take that.'

'You said I must have a sword. This is a sword.'

'But for use on a horse,' said the swordsmith.

'I understand. How much?'

'I do not know. Say, six reals.'

'You will regret it,' said Gaspacho. 'And how much for me?' he said to the swordsmith.

'For you, five reals.'

'Five reals is reasonable. But you will be discontented.'

The next day Gaspacho brought Mendoza to the new head of the conquistadores, Alejandro. 'This is a friend of mine.'

Alejandro asked how old he was.

'I don't know,' replied Gaspacho. 'How old are you?' he asked, turning to Mendoza.

'Seventeen.'

'I would have said as much. Seventeen,' he told Alejandro. Alejandro grunted and promised to pay him two dineros a month.

When Mendoza was outside again, he said, 'I lack the means to recompense you.'

'I will remind you of it. Now we must get your cotton armour.'

'I have no money for that.'

'There is no need for you to keep this up with me,' Gaspacho said, offended. 'The cotton armour will be useful.'

'Not this time. *Adiós*.'

He found a letter-writer in the market-place, a Jew, to whom he dictated the following letter to the Mother Superior in Cádiz.

> Reverend Holy Mother,
>
> I am sending you one half of the sum I owe you. Please accept it in the faith that more will come. I beg you to do this as Christ shall have mercy. I will be going away on a trading trip, and when I return I shall send you the rest. In four or five months. I implore you to have belief in this. For ever and ever, amen. I hope that Felipe is a satisfactory pupil. Teach him to read and write. If he is not good, beat him. And anything else you think necessary. I go to confession in the Church of Santa Ana here in Asunción. There are birds in the trees. I hope that you, sanctified Mother in God, are in good health. Amen. And give Felipe my brotherly love. I am your most obedient, true and pious servant in Christ,
>
> *Rodrigo Mendoza*

He went, without his sword and dagger, to a priest who was going to Cádiz. He gave him his money, explained who the recipient was, and thanked him.

'What makes you believe I will deliver it?' asked the Franciscan.

'You are a priest,' replied Mendoza.

The friar grimaced. 'Ah, would all priests were as you believe, my son.'

Five months later, when the Mother Superior received the letter and the money, she got down on her knees. Felipe was a high-spirited boy full of natural charm, and behold, he had a strong brother.

Mendoza went to a French fencing-master. Upon seeing the baselard, the master shook his head. 'That sword is not correct. Get another.'

'Here is my money.'

The master held out his hand for it, shrugged, and taught Mendoza to thrust and parry. When the evening came, Mendoza continued his thrust and parry outside in the open, and then went to sleep. He practised daily up against a tree until the time came to set off with Alejandro's conquistadores.

When they found the tracks of the Guarani in the ninth week, Mendoza was one of the party that Alejandro led in pursuit of them. On the second day they came across a fire still burning, and Alejandro went off with half the men. Four hours passed. Mendoza was half asleep when suddenly there was a bedlam of brown bodies tearing through the under-growth, and the forest was pierced with yells. A Guarani, his spear arm drawn back, appeared above Mendoza's head, only to plunge down upon a levelled sword. As the blade came out through his back, his face came very close to Mendoza's.

Gaspacho clapped Mendoza on the shoulder and said, 'Now pull out your sword.' He did so and watched while the man died, finding the sight even less disturbing than Victorio's blood had been.

'I am a killer,' Mendoza thought.

They thrust their captives into the thorn-bush enclosure, and darkness fell. Gaspacho drew Mendoza to one side. 'Some say you have; others say you have not. Have you?'

'With women?'

'Assuredly.'

'No.'

'It is easy, and pleasurable.'

'I will consider it.'

'No, do not consider it, do it.'

Mendoza went over to the Guarani captives and chose the youngest of the girls. He led her into a dark part of the jungle, looked round and then gazed at her nakedness. As he did so, he became excited and said, 'Lie down.' She, for her part, was relieved to find her ravisher so harmless. His penis stiffened, and he began to move it towards her crotch but could not find his way. 'Help me,' he said. Her hand came down. He came.

Liking him, she lay still under him for a while and his penis began to stiffen again. This time he thrust while she began to whine, and he came again.

Then she made him stand and, placing her lips round his penis, had begun to draw it in when all at once he heard the laughter of the others. Bellowing, he snatched his sword and hunted them, trembling with rage and shame, but they got away. Treading on a thorn, he was forced to sit down and take it out.

When he limped back to the girl, he found Gaspacho standing over her. The black man asked, 'Do you want her?'

Mendoza shook his head. He returned to the fire and wrapped a blanket around himself, crestfallen. All night he sat there, and all the while Gaspacho was astir upon the girl.

They went on two more missions and captured five more slaves, but after that nothing. So they set off for the Portuguese village of Bonito, a journey of seven days, to buy slaves. They bought forty to add to those they had captured, and transported the whole lot back to Asunción.

For this trip Mendoza received ten dineros. He returned to the letter-writer and sent this letter.

Reverend Holy Mother,
I have returned from the trading expedition. Here is the money which I owe you. I shall send you more when I have finished another trading enterprise, which is about to start. This will be under my first trade officer, Tiberio, who is the single most promising trader here. Be confident that I shall send the rest. The trading here is good. Thanks be to God. I hope very much, Holy Mother, to receive a letter from you, as your time permits. And also one from Felipe. I hope that all is well with my brother. Convey to him my kind regards. That is, if he deserves them. I have a sword, a baselard. I am your most obedient, true and pious servant in Christ,
Rodrigo Mendoza

The Jesuit missionary who took the letter gave Mendoza a long, severe look.

'Are you a conquistador?'

'Yes, father.'

'What you are doing is against the law.'

'I only do what Tiberio tells me to do, father.'

'It is against the law. Well, I will take it.' Six months later, when the Mother received Mendoza's letter, she said to the Jesuit, 'I did send him a letter. He has not received it. Is he well?'

'Mother, he is a conquistador.'

'I see; I shall write him about that, he does not understand. See, he sends me this money.'

'Blood money.'

'Thank you.' She rang her little bell to show the Jesuit out.

Mendoza went to the fencing-master once a day. He thought that because his weapon was not designed for killing men it was not evil, and he liked the solid weight of it in his hands.

The fencing-master was provoked by this new pupil, who had no respect for the rapier. He must not be allowed to cling on to that club of a sword. He demonstrated how the rapier could sweep aside the baselard.

'You see?' he said. 'You see? Again. You comprehend?'

'I see,' his pupil said, 'but I will stick to the baselard.'

The fencing-master struck a bargain with him. 'Listen, we will fence. If you can parry my attack, I will pay for all the fencing lessons you have had. But if you cannot, you will give up the baselard and adopt the rapier. Agreed, or are you afraid?'

They fought. Mendoza could not force his way through the glittering guard. The master smiled. Mendoza knew the one way was to rush it. Like a Roman executioner, he swung his face to one side, taking a short cut on the side of his neck, and then was at his opponent's throat with the point of his sword. They both froze, motionless. There was a moment's silence. The fencing-master stared. Then he said, 'Do not come here again.' He fetched the money. 'I will not teach a murderer.'

When Mendoza went to buy a musket and pistol, he took Gaspacho along to help. He also bought hide boots and cotton armour. Once he had put them all on, Gaspacho said, '*Madre de Dios!*'

'What?'

'You look like a real conquistador.'

Mendoza was sixteen when he embarked on his next expedition with Tiberio. He was seventeen when he returned.

There were two letters waiting for him. Gaspacho read them aloud for him as they sat in the square.

'"To our dearly beloved Rodrigo Mendoza, greetings. I did send you a letter in answer to your first one; I do not know where it can have gone. It came by the ship *Navidad* in May of last year – " The *Navidad* went down,' said Gaspacho.

'I see. Go on.'

'"Felipe is at the top of his group." Who is Felipe?'

'My brother.'

'I did not know you had one.'

'He is not like me. Read on.'

'"I send a letter to you written by him."'

'Read it.'

'"Dearest brother Rodrigo, I am well. I hope that you are well. This is the first letter that Sister Angela has permitted me to write. I hope you are pleased with it. I try hard with my lessons. Mother Julia will also say this, because she has promised. When can I come and stay with you? There are many ships sailing from Cádiz. There is a new game called 'Sabande'. I cannot explain it to you in this letter. It has a club and a ball and there is a wall. This letter comes to you from your most respectful brother, Felipe."'

'That letter is not a bad one,' Mendoza observed.

'Very good.'

'But maybe Sister Angela helped him.'

'I see that you are proud of your Felipe. Shall I continue?'

'Please. I truly think it is by him.'

'"I have a word of warning to you. It is about the slave-trade. I hear that you participate in this. It is against the law of Holy Church, and of the land also. Consider how you would feel yourself if you were the merchandise. Therefore, choose some other business."'

Gaspacho laughed, but Mendoza said soberly, 'Read that

again.' When Gaspacho had done so, he was silent. The rest of the Mother Superior's letter was concerned with holy practices. He went to the Church of Santa Ana and sought out the priest who had received his previous confession.

'Father, I earn my living as a slave-trader.'

'As an *encomienda* trader is what you mean.'

'We take them without their consent, father, and they often resist.'

Casting about in vain for help, the priest said, 'Well, that is wrong.'

'But we do it for the Captain-General.'

'You take them not as slaves but as *encomienda*.'

Mendoza peered at him. 'Father, shall I go and tell the Captain-General?'

The priest saw his quiet little benefice disappearing. 'The Captain-General would tell you that the trade was in *encomienda*.'

'You would absolve me of that?'

'Yes.'

'Even if I were already planning another expedition?'

The priest considered. 'If you were so foolish as to express it so –'

'How else should I express it, father?'

'No, then I would not.'

'Thank you, father.'

Mendoza knew that he must pay for his brother's education. Let the Mother say it was all one whether Felipe were a gentleman or a lighterman. She did not know. She had no experience of life. Thereafter, he ceased going to confessional and also to church, and no longer prayed to his mother.

He signed on for another expedition, this time at three dineros a month. When they had captured the first fifteen slaves, he said to Fernando, the leader, 'Why go to the Portuguese side? Why don't we push on till we come up with more in Spanish territory?'

'This way is easier.'

'Of course, but we would get more money the other way.'

. 'Go, if you will,' said Fernando with a shrug, 'and God go with you.' The others smiled. Mendoza stayed.

When he was nineteen he saw Palacio, who had just returned from Barcelona. He waited until nightfall and found Palacio chatting with a group of ladies and gentlemen in a lamplit yard. Mendoza went up to him and stood there until he was recognized and the conversation gradually ceased. The only sound was the flutter of the moths.

'Palacio, you recognize me?'

'But of course.'

'You owe me one dinero.'

Palacio said, 'Do I? Well then, so be it,' and he took a coin from his pocket.

'You have owed it to me for five years.'

'I see. What then?'

'Today that makes five thousand dineros.'

'Five thousand?'

'And I am here to collect them.'

'Go, while you still have time.'

'Palacio,' said Mendoza, recollecting the formality, 'you are a servile pig. It is I who say so.'

They went to a place by the river attended by a throng of people with lanterns, which were set up in the trees. A person who had appointed himself master of ceremonies said, 'Now, gentlemen, are you ready?'

'Ready,' assented Palacio.

'Commence then!'

Mendoza moved in directly and struck Palacio through the chest with his baselard. The dying man stared into Mendoza's face and fell against him. It was over. Mendoza wiped his blade.

A conquistador said, 'You were lucky.'

Mendoza turned round. 'Not luck.'

'Would you care to prove it?'

'No.'

'Luck.'

Another fight then, only this time his opponent's footsteps were sure and menacing. Mendoza was borne back. Then suddenly he turned his head to one side and thrust.

'My God,' gasped an elderly man.

Mendoza left the two prone bodies in the lamplight and walked away. A crowd of Asunción ladies and gentlemen, tradesmen and servants, poor whites, conquistadores and Guarani gazed after him.

Wrapping himself in his cloak that night, he thought first, 'I am a murderer.' And then, 'So be it.' And finally, 'That thrust with the baselard, it is good.' He settled himself and yawned and went to sleep. He slept as a man without hope.

'So,' said Tiberio, 'you are a fencing-master?'

'No. Is there another expedition?'

'Yes. Do you wish to come on it?'

'Yes.'

'I'm not sure about a fencing-master.' Tiberio glanced at the other conquistadores, who looked uneasy. 'Well then, come.'

Mendoza dictated another letter for the Mother Superior to the Jew.

Reverend Mother in God,

I read your last letter with attention. Thanks to your instruction, I am giving up the slave-trade and will enter the yerba maté trade instead. Thank Felipe for his letter. It is a great joy to me. Is there a hospice similar to yours in these parts? I mean in Montevideo, in Buenos Aires or in Asunción? I have asked the priests and they think not, but if there is, I could bring Felipe here. As usual I enclose the payment for his upkeep. This is a cruel place, particularly at night. I will send for him only if there is a quiet place like yours out here. I hope that you, Holy Mother, continue to enjoy good health. Your most obedient, true and pious servant in Christ,

Rodrigo Mendoza

He joined the little convoy of canoes under Tiberio, and they travelled up the river as usual, then left the canoes and walked. All the time he was aware of Tiberio's eyes following him.

'Look out! Here comes the fencing-master! On your guard!' Tiberio smiled, without revealing whether he said this in jest or not. He was an old man now, forty, and saw this new young man as a challenge. Mendoza and Gaspacho could see the others beginning to take sides. Finally, Mendoza approached Tiberio by the fire, in front of them all.

'Tiberio, you are the leader, I am just a conquistador.'

'Indeed. What else?' replied Tiberio, smoking his cigarillo.

'I am happy it is so.'

'Good, Mendoza, good. But how else could it be? I don't understand.'

'That is all.'

'Very well then, goodnight.'

When they went in pursuit of the Guarani, Mendoza was left to guard the camp. There was a sudden rushing through bushes and a trampling down of grass. Four braves came hurtling at him, yelling. He felled the first with his baselard and struck the second with his dagger, but the third dealt him a blow in the throat with his spear before Mendoza shot him with the pistol. He chased the fourth, for he was a huge fellow who would fetch a high price, and threw him down.

The conquistadores ran up, congratulating him. 'Well done, *hombre*, well done!'

That evening at the camp fire Tiberio called him over.

'Let me look at that throat. I will stitch it up for you.' He stitched up the raw wound with curious gentleness. 'Well done, *hombre*, well done.'

For the next few days Mendoza was left at the camp to recuperate, while the rest went hunting for more slaves. They caught only three. Tiberio, in an evil temper, went to the Portuguese town of Uguiriana to buy the rest, whom he drove back to the camp.

Gaspacho warned, 'Tiberio is in a funny mood, keep out of his way.'

Later that night Tiberio was drunk but did not show it. He called, 'Hey, Mendoza, it is time those stitches came out.'

'You can do it tomorrow.'

'No, now.'

After a pause Mendoza replied, 'Very well then – now.' He got up and went across to sit by him.

'Tiberio, wait till tomorrow,' Gaspacho said.

'Keep quiet, negro,' growled Tiberio. 'Mendoza, does this hurt?'

'A bit.'

There was silence all round as Tiberio nicked away with his knife. 'Now the last one.'

'*Gracias.*'

Tiberio jerked his knife and made a gash. A little runnel of blood started down Mendoza's throat. He got up silently and walked back to his place. Tiberio asked, 'Aren't you going to thank me?'

'No.'

'But you must thank me. Mustn't he?'

Nobody answered.

'I will thank you tomorrow,' responded Mendoza and pulled the blankets over his head.

In the morning he went over to Tiberio and woke him.

'I am ready to thank you now,' he said, 'for, do you see, last night I think you were drunk.'

Tiberio sat up rubbing his eyes and said, 'Not drunk. I did it on purpose.'

'I see. Then how shall we settle it?'

'I settle all things by the sword.' Tiberio threw off his blankets, but delayed pulling on a pair of shoes. 'I do not sleep shod,' he said. 'Do you?'

'Yes.'

'You have bad manners, then. That is bad manners.'

Tiberio got to his feet and made a little pass with his rapier, from which the conquistadores all backed away.

'Here?'

'Agreed.'

'That is good, you have – ' Without warning Tiberio lunged, forcing Mendoza to back off. Then he lunged again, and again Mendoza was forced to withdraw.

'What's the matter? Aren't you ready?' Tiberio asked.

'It is a pity that you – ' Mendoza felt a burning pain in his right cheek-bone as he smashed his short blade into Tiberio's chest, carrying him backwards until the point was buried in a tree. His victim looked at him, opening his mouth as if to say something, and then died standing upright.

A deep wound had uncovered Mendoza's cheek-bone. Gaspacho came and stitched it up.

'Listen,' he said, 'you could take command now.' Looking round, Mendoza saw that the others were waiting for him to tell them what to do.

He ordered four of them to bury Tiberio, and then said, 'Now we go.'

Back in Asunción nine weeks later, Mendoza left the others on the dockside and went to report to the Captain-General. He walked through the evening air to the quarter where the very best houses were. The Captain-General lived in an imposing official residence in an attractive square. Mendoza passed between two sentries lolling at the gateway, and found himself in the outer garden where Guarani servants dozed. Resolutely, he mounted a small flight of stairs underneath the portico, to fetch up before a Spanish sergeant sitting at a gilded table in the hall.

The sergeant looked at the ragged figure and demanded his business. Mendoza answered that he carried a message from Señor Tiberio. A secretary, coming to the head of the stairs, saw a conquistador who was very young and had an ugly wound on his face. Nevertheless, he beckoned to him, told him to wait and went to tell Don Cabeza.

Mendoza gazed around. He looked at the candlesticks and the Guarani servants squatting against one of the doors. Below where the sergeant was, a bright shaft of light came in from outside. Everything else was dim. This was where the ecclesi-astics and other diplomats held their consultations when they discussed Asunción's affairs.

A door was suddenly thrust open and Don Cabeza himself stood there, dressed in a loose cotton gown. He was fifty years old, fat and ungainly – particularly when, as now, he was without his wig – but still remarkably sure-footed on his short, thick legs. He was fourth-generation South American born. His great-grandfather had been a weaver and his grandfather an exporter of hides, but his father was an *hidalgo* interested in the ownership of *haciendas*. Now he, Don Cabeza, was at the centre of power in the Río de la Plata.

'Where is Tiberio?'

'I killed him, Excellency.'

'How?'

'He picked a quarrel. There are many who can testify to this, Excellency.'

Don Cabeza looked at this young conquistador. 'What's your name?'

'Rodrigo Mendoza, Excellency.'

'What about the *encomienda*?'

'I have them. Forty-eight.'

Cabeza called his secretary and instructed him to send six of the Spanish guards down to the harbour. Then he sat down. 'What made Tiberio pick a quarrel with you?'

'I do not know, Excellency.'

'Who has taken his place?'

'I have, Excellency.'

'How old are you?'

'Twenty-four, Excellency.'

'A liar,' thought Cabeza, 'but hard to see through.' He said,

'Very well, I will pay you what I would have paid to Tiberio, less Tiberio's share.'

'His share is mine now.'

'You did not organize the expedition.'

'Then who will get the leader's share?'

'Sharp,' thought Cabeza, 'and greedy.' He said, 'I will give it to you if you organize another expedition.'

'How much is the leader's share, Excellency?' There was a pause. 'I can ask the other leaders.'

Don Cabeza frowned. The boy was insolent. 'One dinero for each slave you bring in.'

'That is forty-eight dineros for the present lot, and the same for the next lot?'

'Correct.'

Mendoza left with his head spinning. That made nearly a hundred dineros; perhaps he would make two hundred for the year. He saw a way of raising it to three hundred or even four. Felipe was safe now. Nothing else mattered to him. Where else was he to place his burden of love?

He went to the most fashionable tailor in Asunción to order a suit. The cutters gave him sideways, supercilious smiles, but he returned a steady stare that made them cringe. The suit was black, the colour he had noticed the upper classes mostly wore, and he asked for it to be ready within five months.

Down at the quayside the conquistadores gathered about him and, standing with his back against a pile of sacks, he told them, 'Come with me and you will earn a third more than you did before.'

'Truly?'

'Truly.'

'But what must we do?'

'Follow me.'

'Where?'

'Who knows?'

'Into Portuguese territory?'

'Perhaps.'

'To commandeer slaves?'

'Not to buy them.'

'Things are all right the way they are.'

'Adiós.'

'I am with you,' said a young conquistador.

'And I,' said an old one.

It was the middle aged who hung back: they were too old to dream of windfalls and too young to feel the need of a lump sum.

The Spanish officials had no intention of inquiring where he meant to go. Officially they frowned on any incursion into Portuguese territory, but they were happy to pay good prices for *encomienda*, with no questions asked, once they were safely in Asunción.

Mendoza's conquistadores, therefore, were tolerated but not accepted. Cabeza watched them from a thoughtful distance. There was a fine profit to be made out of Mendoza, and officially he knew nothing about him. Meanwhile, sticking to Mendoza's side like a shadow, Gaspacho shook his head and smiled.

In three months they had captured as many Guarani as could be rounded up, but there were only six; they were getting scarce. Mendoza sent Gaspacho back to the river with one party and the captives, instructing him to wait with the boats.

Gaspacho said, 'Are you going west?'

'I will see what Guarani there are there.'

'Then you will assuredly trespass into Portuguese territory.'

'Is that so? Nobody knows the boundary.'

'Nobody, but it is there. God speed.' And Gaspacho left on the long trek back to the river.

Mendoza led his men west. After four weeks they encountered a tribe of Guarani who had seldom seen white men before, though they had heard of them. They fought tenaciously. Mendoza lost five men in a three-day battle, but he captured seventy-six Guarani before the rest suddenly disappeared. They had cost him no money.

Returning, he struck due south, back to the riverbed. One evening he came to the head of a rise and saw, in the far distance, a tongue of rose-coloured smoke rising a thousand feet into the blue air from the forest to the west.

'Look,' he said, 'look.'

'The falls of Iguaçú,' said an elderly conquistador.

'The falls of Iguaçú?' he repeated, looking at the distant column which was like an illuminated cloud. 'Have you ever been there?'

'I do not know of anyone who has.'

'There are Guarani there?'

'On this side of the falls, yes. On the far side, who can say?'

'I wish to see the falls of Iguaçú,' said Mendoza, looking under his hand at the distant jet of mist. 'There must be a fat profit to be made there.' And he stood looking at the tongue of spume while the night fell.

At last they reached the river and followed it down to their camp. They could not find Gaspacho or the boats, though they searched for them all the next day. At the end of the second day Mendoza sat on the banks of the river and realized what all the others had known the instant they arrived. He was still sitting there when darkness fell. He could trust no one. Two days later he and his men started off on rafts big enough to carry them and all their captives downriver to Asunción.

An old dockside worker who was smoking his pipe on the quayside told him, 'Gaspacho has left.'

'For where?'

'For Montevideo.'

'And the company with him?'

'Gone too.'

'They had some slaves?'

'Sold to Don Cabeza.'

Mendoza shrugged and turned to his men. '*Tiene cojones, este hombre*; I owed him that. It was he who equipped me for my first *encomienda* trek.'

'He has gone nonetheless,' grinned the old man.

'If you come across him, tell him I call it quits.'

He looked at the rafts loaded with Guarani and the conquistadores standing on the jetty. 'I go now to bargain with the Captain-General. There are seventy-six captives here and fourteen men; be sure they stay so.'

He went to the tailor's shop, washed himself from head to foot, pulled his hair back into a club and dressed himself in his new clothes. Then, a dark figure with a scar, he donned his dagger and sword and went to see Don Cabeza. He was admitted without difficulty, and Cabeza was impressed.

He said, 'Sit down, Mendoza.'

'Thank you, Excellency.'

'A glass of wine?'

'No, Excellency.'

'I have had Gaspacho through here with six slaves. Did you know that?'

'Yes. And he said of me?'

'He said that you were dead.'

'I am here.'

'Where have you been?'

'I have seventy-six for sale, Excellency.'

'Seventy-six?'

'Yes, Excellency.' Cabeza called for his secretary and gave orders for six of his soldiers to fetch the Indians, but Mendoza said, 'Send twelve, Excellency.'

'Twelve then.' When the secretary had gone, Cabeza said, 'Did you buy them?'

'Naturally, Excellency.'

'At what town?'

'I forget, Excellency.'

'Let me see them.'

'Of course, Excellency.'

'Will you take a glass of wine now?'

'No, Excellency.'

'I will.'

When the Guarani were herded into the back courtyard, Cabeza saw, delighted, that they were an outstanding lot.

'How many men did you lose?'

'Five. From disease, Excellency.'

'I shall pay you three-quarters of a dinero for each. Come along with me.'

When they returned to Cabeza's room, Mendoza said, 'Forty-eight for the last lot, and two dineros a head for this one.'

Cabeza turned on Mendoza and said furiously, 'Call me "Excellency".'

'That makes,' replied Mendoza, 'two hundred dineros.'

Cabeza struck the table. '*Cara de perro.* Call me "Excellency".'

'If you do not want them, I will take them elsewhere.'

Cabeza sat down at his chair, undid the collar of his shirt and drank his wine. He laughed shortly. 'Where do you come from?'

'Cádiz.'

'When do you go back?'

'I do not know.'

'Your next expedition will be for me.'

'It will be for the one who pays most.'

'I shall pay you the two hundred dineros for this lot.' He counted out the money. Mendoza re-counted it and dropped it into his coat pocket.

'My thanks to you, Excellency. I shall make my next expedition for you.' He left the room.

Cabeza sat and thought. Mendoza was taking all the risks, but then the conquistador was also a free agent. At first Cabeza was not altogether sure this arrangement pleased him, but then his grandfather came out in him and he decided that it did.

Letters from the Mother Superior and Felipe arrived for Mendoza and he sat down amongst the Jew's books to give them his full attention.

Dear Rodrigo Mendoza,

Praised be Jesus Christ, you are a good brother, and your brother Felipe is well. And to say truth, more than well – he is the chosen one of all the ladies in the town of Cádiz, and my dearly loved one. But he is now ten and must leave us. I was thinking of sending him to the Colegio de Loreto de Huérfanos, where the sons of the servants of the King are brought up, partially at the expense of the King, God befriend him. But now your letter has come and I have made inquiries. There is in Montevideo an orphanage funded by lay and church donations. It is run by the lay brotherhood. As well as teachers of languages and mathematics, they also engage special instructors for dancing, fencing and deportment. Or so I hear. Go and see them and let me know what you think. If you are satisfied with it, I shall send him out to you.

The rest of the letter was full of shrewd comments about his soul, from which Mendoza withdrew his attention and looked instead at the Jew's books. He would have nothing to do with his soul.

The letter of Felipe was full of his doings with the relatives of a classmate of his called Alfonso de Vicente. Mendoza had this read out to him three times.

He left by boat for Buenos Aires and then went to Montevideo and the orphanage of the Hospital of the Passion. The school had only twelve pupils, eight of whom had parents. Each boy paid thirty dineros a year to the Brotherhood of Refugio, which ran the school. The Brotherhood had fallen away from its original aims and now served the interests of the *hidalgos*. At first they regarded Mendoza doubtfully, but when he produced the thirty dineros their manner changed. He was not deceived by what he saw; he understood and approved. His letter to the Mother Superior was full of praise.

On the return trip, while waiting at Buenos Aires for a ship to Asunción, his eye was caught by the slavers riding at anchor across the water at Sacramento. He hired a boat and was rowed past the English, Dutch and French ships before landing there. The Portuguese standard flew above all. Two walks around the harbour told him that there was nothing there for him. The men gathered around the bollards were all slavers and pirates. Because of his scars, his sober suiting and the sword and dagger at his side, he was not molested. Before getting back into his boat, he spoke to a Spanish sailor and asked if he knew Gaspacho from Asunción.

'I know everything that happens here, señor,' said the Spanish sailor, taking off his hat. 'Gaspacho? He went off to the West Indies months ago, señor. In the *Esmeralda*.'

'A pity. Because now he cannot know how I regard everything as fair between us.'

'I see.'

'Say that, if you ever meet him.' Mendoza slipped a coin into the man's palm, telling him his name.

After three more expeditions he decided to rent a house. It was small but in the aristocratic quarter of Asunción. He also bought a small farm on the outskirts of the town.

On his return from the third expedition he found three letters from Montevideo waiting for him. One was from the Brotherhood to notify him that Felipe had been received under the care of a Franciscan priest, and the second was a stylish letter from Felipe himself, who had also enclosed a note from the Mother Superior in Cádiz. From the last of these he learned that Felipe was a good and charming boy, blessed in possessing so benevolent a brother, and that Mother Julia hoped she would hear from him soon. The word from the Brotherhood said that they allowed their charges to go home for three months each year or, if it so pleased him, Felipe could remain with them for that period at an extra charge. He dictated a short note saying that he would, of course, come to collect Felipe when the holidays started in three months' time. Felipe's own letter was full of amusing accounts of the new school and his longing to see his brother. Mendoza wrote the Mother Superior a formal letter of thanks and then dismissed her from his mind. She was sure of her place in Paradise.

When the three months were up, he went to Montevideo to fetch Felipe. The young boy, waiting in the courtyard of the school, saw a man approaching him, a man in his thirties. Surely his brother was only twenty-two? The man had a lined set face, with deep-sunk eyes and a scar. He was dressed in a linen suit of black and carried a sword and a dagger. Felipe, awestruck, was on his best behaviour instantly. The man gave him a long and searching stare but said nothing. Felipe smiled and said, 'Rodrigo?'

Suddenly the man embraced him passionately. Felipe wept. Proudly he showed him a letter from the Mother Superior in Cádiz. 'I will read it to you, for it is all about me,' he said.

Mendoza listened to the letter and then said, 'It appears you are not good at Latin. That is a pity, for Latin is what priests speak.'

'Some of them do,' said Felipe.

'No, all.'

'Some of them only pretend to.'

Mendoza looked at him. 'Is that true?'

'You didn't know?'

'No. That is very bad.'

'Why? You read no language, but you are not bad.'

Mendoza looked away. 'Listen to me. I live by the *encomienda* trade.'

'What is that?'

'Slave-trading.'

'But the Mother said you did not.'

'I lied to her.'

'Is it so bad then?'

'It is not a trade for *caballeros*.'

53

'I see.'

'I have told you this because it is a fact that you must know.'

'Do they not speak to you?'

'The *caballeros*?'

'Yes.'

'When it suits them.'

'Do they malign you?'

'No.'

'I understand.' He thought for a minute, then said, 'The Mother is far away from here.'

'Let me not hear you say so again. The Mother is innocent.'

Felipe wondered at his formidable brother. 'May I introduce you to my friends?'

'Who are they?' Mendoza asked.

'Martín, Joaquín and Sebastian. There,' Felipe said, pointing towards the house.

Mendoza looked up and saw a trio of Felipe's fellow-pupils on the third floor. 'Yes, of course,' he answered. Felipe signalled to them to come down.

'What are their parents?'

'Martín and Joaquín have no parents. They have inherited *haciendas*. Sebastian's father is a minister.'

'I see,' said Mendoza. 'Good,' he thought, 'very good.'

He shook hands with them while Felipe made the introductions. Mendoza then stood with his hands clasped behind his back. A stretch of silence in the closed courtyard followed, and Felipe said, 'I will go and fetch a porter to take my things, shall I?'

The four boys scampered up the upper flight of stairs.

'Hey, what a man your brother is!' Sebastian said.

'I think so,' said Felipe.

'*Tiene cojones*,' remarked Sebastian.

'Very much so,' said Joaquín.

'My father was much that kind of man,' said Martín.

'Yes? I am glad you like him,' said Felipe.

'Did you see his sword?' Sebastian asked.

'I think that has seen much use.'

Having arrived in Asunción, Felipe was taken to Mendoza's little house and invited to explore it. Mendoza waited while his brother went into every room – including the ones housing the three servants, who made bows, to which Felipe returned a friendly shake of his hand and a nod of the head. He saw the kitchens, wash-house, stables, the tiny outer courtyard. Mendoza waited without moving.

Felipe said, walking back, 'Brother, you have elevated your position in the world.'

'Thanks. Now let me see you make some use of it.'

'But how?'

'Haven't they taught you?'

Felipe blushed.

Every evening Mendoza took Felipe to the square. They sat and ordered drinks, the elder brother looking at his most forbidding. Felipe was full of respect for him. He noticed that Mendoza bowed to people and that they bowed back, but he had no other social intercourse.

Then, on the fourth day, a middle-aged man came over to them with a welcoming smile.

'Good evening, Señor Mendoza.'

'Good evening, Señor Quiroda. It is a most charming evening.'

'It is.'

'May I present my brother, Felipe.'

'Your brother. Good evening.'

Felipe was on his feet. 'Good evening, Señor Quiroda. It is a magnificent sunset, is it not?'

'It is, it is,' agreed the older man, laughing. 'Señor Mendoza, come across to our table. I must introduce your brother to my nephew.'

Mendoza glanced at the little family group on the opposite side of the square. They bowed. He shook his head. 'No, thank you, we will not inconvenience you and Señora Quiroda with our presence.'

'But I should like it. You see, our nephew has no companions.'

'I see. It is bad to be alone.'

'It is, it is.'

'Then, thank you.'

So they crossed the square and sat with the Quiroda family. Felipe charmed them all with his dry humour, good manners and stories of Cádiz. The next day Mendoza had a note from the Quirodas, expressing the hope that Felipe would be allowed to go round to their house.

Señor Quiroda came from Madrid. By trade he was a haberdasher, but he had prospered in Asunción. Moreover, he always knew how to take the next step up. In stages, it was easy. Felipe too went on a formal round of visits, first to the middle, then to the upper circles of Asunción society, and made acquaintances with becoming style.

One day he said to his brother, 'These invitations are always for me, never for you.'

'Invitations come also for me – this one from Señorita Vignola, for example.'

'But you never accept,' replied Felipe.

'No.'

'Because you trade in *encomienda*?'

'Perhaps.' Mendoza shrugged.

'Then I too shall not go.'

'That would be a pity.'

'Why?'

'It gives me pleasure.'

Felipe searched his face. 'So then, I shall go.'

Felipe touched everything that was tender in his brother's heart, for the boy was all Mendoza had ever found to love. Mendoza moved his younger brother both to pity and to hero worship, for Felipe was still a child.

The time came for Felipe to return to Montevideo and his schoolfriends. Mendoza came down to the harbour to see him off, watching his boat for as long as he could before it disappeared beyond a curve in the river.

On their last night together Felipe had said, 'The *enco-mienda* trade is a dangerous one.'

'No, no.'

'Yes. I have heard. If you fall, what shall I do?'

'I will try not to. If I do fall, then accept what God sends.'

———————

The next time Mendoza went on an expedition, however, he took four times as many conquistadores as usual and directed them from behind. He lost seven men, and one of the band made a sneering reference to his caution. In a fit of rage he challenged the man and killed him.

This time he returned to Asunción with 228 Guarani. Back in the city he shut his ears, but nobody dared to slight his honour. He was a man to be treated with the utmost politeness, one whom the townsfolk turned down alleyways to avoid if they saw him coming or, if it was too late for that, treated with punctilious civility.

He bought a larger farm and a bigger house for Felipe, whose vacations were the hinges upon which his years revolved. He taught him musketry, swordsmanship and riding, and watched his brother sweep all before him socially. By the time he was seventeen many ladies were in love with him, or claimed to be. He charmed them all with his dry wit and the way he had of connecting any subject personally to the people that he was with.

When Felipe turned eighteen, his brother said, 'Now is the time for you to go to Europe.'

'What – why?'

'To learn.'

'To learn what?'

'Whatever it is that young men learn in Europe.'

So he was sent with a Swiss tutor on a tour of London, Paris, Rome, Augsburg and Madrid. Mendoza saw them off at Buenos Aires. Felipe shed many tears, and stood by the rail until he could no longer distinguish his brother from the others in the crowd. Then he dried his eyes, smiled a melancholy smile at his tutor to ask forgiveness, climbed the mast-head and dreamed over the sea.

Mendoza watched the ship until it was out of sight and then turned back to his solitary existence.

On the edge of the jungle that lay behind the barrier of the Iguaçú falls, a tribe of Guarani were making their way to the bank of a river that fed into the main stream of the waterfall. Some were dressed in strips of cloth and others in animal skins. The flesh of the shaman who led them was painted in a pattern like the markings of some jungle creature. He was smoking a long cheroot and his face was creased in thought.

Behind him came the braves, followed by the women and children. They were all silent.

They carried a cross raised high, so that the lower branches of the trees that they passed struck at the face of Father Julien Dupleix, who was tied to it, naked, with ropes of twisted fibre. His face was expressionless, his eyes were closed, and he looked dead. On his head was a crown of jungle thorns.

The murmur of the river rose above the occasional whispers of the women and children. The trees thinned out, and soon they were standing on the bank. Together, with one upward swing, they flung the cross far out into the stream. It splashed, sank and then rose again. The children ran along the bank, screaming, as it began to float away, and then stopped to throw handfuls of mud after it as it disappeared into the distance.

It was not going fast as yet. A clump of water flowers caught it – irises, higher than a man, that leaned tenderly over the human burden. Then, turning, it found its way back into the current. A butterfly came to perch upon its end, opening and closing its delicate wings. Beneath benevolent trees the cross sailed on. It was going faster now. The water widened, and the trees drew back. Its motion was decided. There was only one way now. The main stream held it.

Even though the falls were still five miles away, the sky was already misted over with vapour rising from the rocks where the cataract crashed down, far below. On the banks the jungle leaves were drenched with fallen spray, and the roar of the water, muted but not obliterated by the distance, sounded a continuous undertone.

The cross gathered speed. Father Julien opened his eyes. He was not yet dead when, his face full of horror, he was carried over the edge. Somersaulting over and over, the cross rode down three hundred feet of tumbling water to be lost in the wet fog that rose from the churned surface at the bottom. Three hundred yards further on it reappeared, only to be snatched out of sight again by the frenzy of the current. At last, a mile further down, the river resumed a normal speed. Behind it the tower of spume still hung aloft above the falls.

Gazing from his perch above the quiet river, Father Sebastian Larrantozo noticed something lurching in the water and recognized its shape. He stood up, shading his eyes, and then scrambled down the sloping rock.

'It is a cross,' he said.

He and two other Jesuits pushed out their raft. The cross was floating with its burden hidden underneath, but when they reached it they saw the fibre. Sebastian managed to tilt the floating bulk of it and peered underneath. The expression on his face told the others what he had seen. He looked like what he had once been, a sergeant in the Royal Troop. They hitched the cross to the raft and poled back to the bank.

As soon as they got there, the other two waded out and dragged the cross on to dry land, where they turned it over. Sebastian cursed and cut the body free. He was about to lift it when Antonio stayed his hand and said, 'Let him lie there.'

They had a spade with them, and made a deep pit in the bank, in which they buried Julien, wrapped in Sebastian's habit. Sebastian said, 'Let us also set the cross here.' When the cross was upright, Antonio led them in the burial service. The next day they set out on their journey back to the Mission of San Miguel, poling into the quiet darkness of the forest.

They arrived, after a fortnight, to find a small crowd awaiting them; the Guarani always knew when someone was coming. Sebastian took Ibaye, a Guarani and deputy-chief of the mission, and said a few words to him. Ibaye went to the practice hall.

Father Gabriel O'Donnell, the Superior of the mission, was totally absorbed in a Guarani consort of viols when Ibaye quietly came and told him the news. He sat for several minutes in silence before dismissing the musicians. Then he went with Ibaye to his cell, where he found Sebastian waiting. Sebastian reported in a steady voice, watching to see how Gabriel would take it. For Julien had been one of the youngest and most amiable of brothers.

'Is he well buried?'

'Yes.'

Gabriel looked at the floor. 'I shall go and see him.'

Sebastian and Ibaye looked at one another, for Gabriel was ageing. Sebastian said, 'Why go? There is nothing to see.'

'Then I shall go and see nothing.'

Once they were both outside, Sebastian said to Ibaye, 'He will try to go where Julien went. He will try to pass the falls.'

'That is evident.'

'Will you try to dissuade him?'

'No, I will not.'

Ibaye ordered the great church bell to be tolled. It had been cast in Barcelona. Its knell sounded over the church square and the meeting house, and the rows of stone houses with pantiled roofs, and the workshops surrounded by moats, and over the fields and into the forests. Hearing the summons, the Guarani ceased their labours and looked at one another, lifting their hoes. Then quietly, unexcitedly, as one man they started to troop back.

Gabriel sat on his bed with his knees drawn up, confronting the fact that he had sent Julien to an awesome death. Then he shot to his feet and began striding up and down in his tiny cell, dogged by a thought that he could not shake off. He had been wrong to approach the Guarani above the falls; those who had objected had been right. If only he had listened to them, he would not have lost Julien.

Suddenly he stopped short. What would Julien himself say? Julien would urge him onwards, about that there could be no doubt. He was as sure as if he could hear the dead man speaking. He resumed his pacing. Come what may, the Guarani above the falls could not be abandoned to their ignorance. The work which Julien had undertaken must be finished. His sacrifice would not be wasted then. But what a death! He shuddered, and knew that he could not send another brother to face it.

He sat on his bed again and peered at one of the hard slivers of light that had slipped through the pantiled roof; he stared at it without realizing what it was, for his thoughts had taken him back to his childhood on the coast of Kerry.

A marvellous, overblown, strange, stormy place that had been, the tides racing to catch up with the boy and the girl he now remembered, and then ebbing out so slowly. And the hills that had seemed so high to him then, with the sheep and the bits of fields his father tended when he had finished his day's work for Mr Butler. Maureen O'Neill, that was the girl's name! He wondered what had become of her and of Seamus Kavanagh, the scared priest, forever looking over his shoulder for Protestants, and ducking into the little Catholic school he taught in the barn of Butler's homestead. It was Seamus who had picked him out to be a priest, all on account of his Latin.

One night the priest came to the draughty stone-built cottage and stood there in the light of a crackling fire, trying to persuade Gabriel's father and mother to let their son go for a priest. The whole family was there to hear it, his grandfather, his aunts, his nine brothers and sisters.

His grandfather, wise in the ways of this world, said, 'No, father, he shall stay here and learn to fish and look after the stupid sheep, which is what he was born to. Look you, he shall be a Catholic all his life, on that you have our promise. But a priest!' He shook his head. 'Look you, here's a question now I've never asked before, but, counting everything in now, how much do you get in a year?'

'It's not for the stipend the boy must be a priest, so I shan't be telling you what mine is.'

'Then let *me* tell *you*.' The old man leaned forward to look closely into the priest's face, which was even more worn and lined than his own. 'Eleven pounds,' he said.

Seamus had looked askance at this. 'Eleven pounds!' he scoffed. 'Why, even if you bate your own shilling I get plenty more than that.' He laughed, inviting the rest of the family to join him, but no one did.

'Eleven pounds is what I said and I stick to it,' the old man answered. 'And for the present year I shall bate that shilling you mention too. Where would I be getting a shilling, the way things are?'

'A penny a time you could put it by, if you had the wish,' the priest said sternly, 'but you have not.'

'The wish is it?' the old man asked. 'I've got the wish all right. We all have the wish, father – Pat Leary, the Hallorans, the O'Connors, the Fitzpatricks – all of us. We have the wish, but we haven't the shillings. I say eleven pounds. You're a good man, there's no denying it, and you'll see Heaven, that's sure, but don't take Gabriel, our boy, to be one like you.'

'I tell you, it's not eleven. Fourteen is what it is, and last year no less than that is what it came to.'

'Then I beg your pardon for underrating you, but I'd still like to know what good that sum does you, a man with the blades of his shoulders sticking out through his shirt and his skin as dead as paper. See here, Father Seamus, tonight you sup with us and tomorrow night you sup with the Mountjoys. We all take thought, you see, for your empty bowl, but that doesn't say we want this lad to join you in it.'

'He is a clever boy. Now, I'm not saying that he will, mind you, but what if he advances to be a bishop?'

'No, excuse me, father, but if it comes to bishops, now you raise the subject, let me say that if he came to be a bishop of the east there'd be great harm done to the lad, for he'd be little better than a Protestant. Here in the west, I grant you, bishops suffer with the faithful people, but of the many thousand priests there are in Ireland, father, how many get to be bishops, will you tell me that?'

'Not many, I grant you. What does Pegeen say?'

Gabriel's mother said, 'I say my father has said true, though God forgive him for saying that much to a priest. Leave the child be, Father Seamus, for the love of Christ.'

Gabriel's father, Michael, was whittling a lobster basket with his knife into the turf fire. So far he had not said a word. Seamus turned to him. 'Michael,' he asked, 'what's your opinion?'

Michael inquired, 'What does the big lad think himself?'

They all turned to Gabriel. He was an obedient son of Holy Church, but he did not know what to answer. To be sure, it was a fine thing to be chosen for a priest out of all the children in the school. But he knew the kind of life that Seamus lived, always looking over his shoulder in case somebody had given the word that would set the constable after him, for English law said the priests had no right to be there. He lived in the shadows, giving a wide berth to the Protestant gentry, doffing his headpiece swiftly if they happened to chance upon him. Of course his flock hailed Seamus as the bringer of the Mass and honoured him at births, deaths and marriages in their low cottages; but everybody also knew how he lived alone in his draughty cottage, never knowing where his next meal might be coming from. Gabriel said, 'I do not know, father.'

'Let us leave it there, then,' said Seamus. 'In a year's time I will ask again.'

'I suppose,' said his mother sorrowfully, 'that if the boy did go for the priesthood, it would be many years before we saw him.'

'He would go and study at the French academy. Then he'd come back to Ireland, and who knows but that he might be sent back here?'

'And he might not,' said Michael.

'He might not,' Seamus agreed. 'Do I smell a stew of onions and potatoes and mutton, can it be?'

'No, not mutton,' Michael answered with a wink.

So they all sat down at the board table, and after Michael said Grace they ate. It was obvious to Gabriel that the priest hadn't eaten mutton for several days.

When it was time for Seamus to go out into the starry darkness, he turned to Michael and said, 'Goodnight and God be with you.' Then, exercising that authority which all priests had, he said to Gabriel, 'Come with me to the end of the path.' Gabriel remembered how the starlight danced on the air above the hills and the sea, for it was the turn of the year into autumn. The priest was silent until they reached the place, switched by a cutting wind, where the moors began. His cottage lay beyond three hills. He stopped and said, 'It is a great honour I have done you this night, Gabriel. Do you know that?'

'Yes, father,' Gabriel said.

'A great honour,' the priest repeated and added, casting about for an explanation upon which the boy could pride himself, 'It is because you are good at Latin.'

'Yes, I know. My Latin is excellent,' Gabriel remembered saying. 'Is that all that is required to be a priest?'

Seamus had laughed. Gabriel now knew what he must have been thinking. 'No, not that only,' he had said with a sigh, 'though the Latin is a good beginning. What do you most like doing, Gabriel?'

'Playing my flute,' Gabriel answered, and he showed his companion the whistle that his father had bought at the local fair, which he always had by him, wrapped in a piece of cloth.

'Play,' Seamus invited, and Gabriel did not need to be invited twice. Even now he seemed to recall that, inspired by the silence of the night, he had played well. The notes had seemed precious to him, like pearls in the dark.

'Very good,' said Seamus when he had finished. 'Well, they can teach you the flute at the college, and many more things about music besides.'

He remembered thinking, 'Now that would be a thing, wouldn't it?' 'I suppose they can teach anything,' he answered, and returned to his cottage much impressed.

Seamus's offer to take him for a priest was known over the lands next day, and his mother got used to that special respect which was shown to the parents of a priest. Secretly she began to urge him to accept. But his father said that if God wanted him to be a priest, He would surely make it known to Gabriel. Already, however, the other children were treating him with the deference due to a boy who would be leaving the hills for the college across the sea.

He knew it all went to show what great power the Church had. If he went, he would become one of the Wild Geese, as they were called, the Catholics who could not bear to stay at home in slavery but flew instead to France. Sometimes their families paid for it, but only a hundred families or so could afford this. The rest went at the Church's expense. He would be one of them if he were to leave Ireland. There were times when, alone, playing his whistle over the sad land, he felt that he was already a marked man.

At the end of a year's time he asked his family what he was to say. 'No,' said his grandfather. His mother said, 'Yes.' His father's words had stayed with him ever since. 'Do as God counsels you.'

With this instruction, one evening he went off alone to a place where he could look over the sea. He played his whistle and, not knowing what might come of it, asked Christ directly, 'What should I do?'

It was the first of many such times. A tranquillity he had never known before descended upon him, and upon the cottages, the fields and the sea. 'Why,' Christ said to him very simply, 'do this.'

He went back down to his cottage, ducked under the humble lintel and said, 'Yes,' to the waiting priest.

The Jesuits took special note of the boy with the clear blue eyes, who had come from Kerry to the upper Loire in the heart of France; for, alone among the learners, while he said his prayers with a simple heart, unquestioningly, he reasoned subtly. Finding him enamoured of music, they asked him,

'Did you know that our founder, Saint Ignatius Loyola, was in love with music too?' and told him the story of the saint, a Spaniard. Although a dutiful Christian, he had at first devoted himself to courtliness and the disciplines of war. As a soldier he had performed many notable feats of arms, until at last, crippled by wounds received in a siege against the French, he had found himself at the gate of death. Then he had seen all things for certain, as a child might see them, and hung his sword and dagger by the statue of the Blessed Virgin Mary. From then on, going daily to Mass, he lived as a beggar, but followers came to him, attracted by his holiness. It had been for them that Saint Ignatius wrote the *Spiritual Exercises*, a book that Gabriel would be allowed to borrow when he had been at the school a little longer. That book would teach him how to be a soldier in Christ's keeping.

Then the saint took holy orders. At this point Gabriel was instructed to attend carefully. Observing how the saint had collected a large following, certain parties in the Holy City brought charges of heresy against him and he was imprisoned. May God pardon their foolish souls, and blessed be His Holiness Pope Paul III who clearly saw the charges were ridiculous! So when he was released, the founder added a vow of obedience to the Pope to his other vows, and the Vicar of Christ, seeing his servant's worth, commissioned him to found an order. That was how the Society of Jesus was founded, the Soldiers in Christ, among whom his present instructors were numbered. It was not for them in their humility to make a claim, but many certainly did say that in this present time of trouble the Order was the Church's trustiest shield – a factor for him to bear in mind as the time of his ordination approached.

As for music, they told him with a smile, certain people

called them the Operatic Society of Jesus. But in truth, as he must know himself, enthusiasm for music blended easily with a passion for Christ. There were many missionaries who made exquisite music. For instance, Brother Joseph taught the oboe and the flute. Lessons could be arranged for him. And one day he would read the autobiography of their blessed founder.

So, as he passed through the college, he learned to play the oboe and the organ like a master. As for his other studies, he found himself exactly in the middle of his class, and when he went on to the Jesuit College in Rome he was neither appalled nor puzzled by what he found there. He never sought out a courtesan to satisfy his lusts, even though one or two of the instructors were prepared to look the other way, thinking this a part of the mind a man ought to know about before he took his vows. When at last he became a member of the Order, his instructors found him to be a source of puzzlement, though they half admired him; for although there was no denying that he had understood everything he had been taught, and had a grasp of metaphysical fundamentals which nothing could now shake, he had somehow still emerged with the mind of a peasant.

Perhaps that was why the chief instructor in theology, a burly German with the blank eyes of a boiled fish, approached him privately the day after he entered the Order, and poured out an account of his doings with the girls who hung about the papal city. The German went down on his knees to confess, and when he had finished squinted up at the young man with a laugh, waiting for absolution. Gabriel said, 'What is tormenting your soul has nothing to do with any of that. All that matters very little. Your torment is that the Head of our Order did not consult you when he finalized the conclusions he is putting to the Pope. I suggest you pray he will not need the assistance of your sophistry. Shall I pronounce the absolution now?' The German was astounded. Then he gave a little smile, and finally accepted absolution with a roar of laughter. That night he slept better than usual.

Gabriel returned to Ireland and saw his family. His grandfather was already dead, and Father Seamus looked very near his end. Although none of them knew it, this was the last time he would see any of them. His father, mother, brothers and sisters joined with all the neighbours to persuade him to address them in French and Italian, and they were duly impressed; but he could see, despite their admiration for his learning, that they were anxious on his account. They thought of him as a helpless innocent.

'You mustn't worry about me,' he tried to reassure his mother. 'I am no longer a child.' He told her this just as he was about to set out for Tipperary, where he was being sent to assist a priest. She watched him as he walked farther and farther away from the cottage, even after he waved to her from the turning.

The priest he was to assist in Tipperary was even closer to death than Father Seamus. After Gabriel watched at his bedside for a month, the priest closed his eyes. In the grounds of a chapel that was hardly more than a cottage by a lake, he buried him with proper ceremony in the presence of thousands of mourners. Before he died, the old priest had tried to tell him how things were in the parish, but he had only been able to say, 'Terrible, my son, and pitiful. I will introduce you to John O'Burke, and he, God save his soul, will tell you more of it than I, so close to death as I am, can do. Why have I lived? I don't see why, no, I don't, I don't.' He turned over and all that day stared at the limestone wall in which were wedged segments of gorse roots, fretted even here by the wind blowing in.

John O'Burke had introduced himself while the old priest was still alive. After the funeral he summoned Gabriel to his big, dank house, surrounded by his dwindling estates and backing on to the lake. A couple of spires of smoke were all that emerged from its crowd of chimneys; these were from the only two hearths that remained alive: one in the kitchen where his entire hangdog household spent the day, and one from the hallway where he lived himself. It was over that fire that he had hung the sword he was no longer allowed to wear like the gentleman he was. A big-made man, as old as Gabriel's father, he sat by the fireplace handing out instructions and advice to the peasants who still came to him when they were in trouble.

'I am not the local landlord, you must understand. That's Mr Edwardes, JP, a Protestant. He owns more than half this county, and is a Member of the Dublin Parliament as well, although, do you see, he lives in London, and that despite the fact he is now the owner of Crowell Castle that is here by and has belonged to the O'Burkes for as long as living memory. Now it belongs to the JP, MP, and so will this house too belong to him when I am dead, isn't that so, Charles?' He turned to a slim young man who had been fondling the dogs at the fireside, but now straightened himself and approached Gabriel to shake his hand with a friendly smile.

'So it will, father, the more's the pity. Charles O'Burke is the name. What I keep explaining to my father is it doesn't matter who the property belongs to.'

'It doesn't matter?'

'No, in good faith, it doesn't.' He pointed a finger at his senior. 'I will not even try to claim my inheritance when he is gone. If you want me then, seek me among the Wild Geese. I'll be joining the flight.' He struck a pose and smiled.

'The fellow is in love with those lunatics over there in France,' the old man said proudly and glowed with warmth at his son.

The parishioners of Durraine in County Kerry were only destitute, whereas those of Mamegoff near Tipperary were starving. The law was in the hands of Mr Edwardes, the local Justice of the Peace, with the exception of serious cases, which went to Mr Martin and Mr Howarth who, acting jointly, were empowered to punish serious breaches of the law with long terms of imprisonment. Although nine-tenths of the peasantry were Catholic, Catholic gentlemen could not become Justices of the Peace, nor could they sit in Parliament. A Catholic was not even permitted to purchase a piece of land, no matter how long he had farmed it, if a Protestant also happened to want it. If a Catholic presumed to buy a horse, it must be worth less than five pounds. Catholics could neither vote, nor be schoolmasters, nor hold office under the Crown, nor could they marry Protestants. Acts of the Dublin Parliament became law only after being authenticated by the Parliament at Westminster. On the other hand, any act passed in Westminster *ipso facto* became the law of Ireland. In any case most members of the Dublin Parliament were nominees of English aristocrats. Mamegoff, for example, was represented in Dublin by Mr Edwardes as a result of a wager with the Earl of Berkshire, whom nobody in Mamegoff had ever seen.

The laws were one thing, their enforcement was another. In Mamegoff the constable, a Protestant surrounded by Catholics, was happy to let sleeping dogs lie. The JPs too were an idle lot, with little interest in persecution as an official duty. Persecution as a source of profit, however, was another matter. They were intent on converting arable land into pasture, and this meant turning their tenants off of the lands. The anti-Catholic laws gave them a way of doing this. When a Protestant landowner had a mind to turn his estate over to pasture, he had only to enforce the law with energy to squeeze his tenants on to scraps of land not big enough to feed a goat. Some were dispossessed entirely, and left to wander homeless over the hills. The peasants did not take this oppression lying down, of course. Troops were brought in, and then the law began to lay about it with a vengeance.

When Gabriel arrived in Mamegoff he was soon recognized as a priest who knew that the fruits of harvest did not last all year and that there were times when a hard-working man and his family had to live on gorse. He never looked to a parishioner for a bite to eat, and if he was offered one he was not embarrassingly grateful either. Late and early he was to be seen on his way over the moors with a hunk of bread, and maybe more, to some sick cottage. If he chanced to cross the path of another man who perhaps was out to deal with Mr Edwardes's sheep, he averted his eyes.

Not everyone in the locality was poor, however. There were some who lived comfortably in stone-built mansions. But these families – the Martins, the Howarths and the Greensides – although neighbours, were Protestants and not in Gabriel's cure. Nevertheless, when Christmas approached he did not scruple to warn them that their mansions were built on foundations of sand, because their brothers and sisters were starving around them in hovels. He also informed them that their silks and velvets had been torn from backs which they could catch sight of by looking out of their fine windows or into their own servants' quarters. Nor was he satisfied with just saying his say. He stood fasting in the cold where all could see him, and refused to talk any more when they invited him to eat with them and discuss the matter further. 'I have nothing more to say,' he declared.

In the end Mr Cox, the rector of the Established Church of Ireland, visited each of these mansions in turn, and as a result the Martins, the Howarths and the Greensides dipped cautiously into their pockets and a not inconsiderable sum was applied to the cottagers' needs. The donors felt some self-satisfaction when it was over and done with, and Mr Cox thanked and congratulated them in an appropriately gratifying way. Gabriel, however, had received their charity ungraciously, they all agreed. All he had said was, 'Well, I shall go now and do what I can with this, which is less than justice would bestow on them.' He was not the only Jesuit in Ireland at that time to make levelling remarks, a fact which contributed not a little to the Order's sinister reputation with the establishment.

Yet Mr Cox, although he lived in a fine brick rectory which was almost as grand as Mr Howarth's mansion near by, respected Gabriel greatly and enjoyed nothing more than to walk along with him discussing questions of theology. In the end, however, he too was disappointed. The day came when Gabriel said, 'I have had enough of this talking. I am no good at arguing and I don't want to be. I believe the Blessed Virgin was seen ascending into Heaven because I have the Pope's account of it. I should be glad if you could believe it too, Mr Cox, but you inform me you cannot and I accept your word, so there's an end of it. In conclusion I have to say to you that, as a priest cannot live with women, then either your wife really is your wife – which I think is the case – and therefore you are not a priest at all; or else she is not your wife, in which case you must be a bad priest.' And he said all this with the glowering expression that sometimes made him an oppressive companion; but there were other times when, although he never obliged a gathering with a jig, the lilt of his oboe lightened a gloom that seemed to have settled on Mamegoff for ever.

John O'Burke was well pleased with the new priest, but cautioned him to keep his head down. 'For you know yourself, the law says you've no right to be in Ireland. Bide more still. Let the Protestants be, at least.' But when any wrong came to his notice, Gabriel could not let anyone who had power to right it rest easy, and the sight of him trudging up to their doorways became so wearisome to the Martins, the Howarths and the Greensides that the time came when they informed their servants (who were Catholics) that they were no longer at home to the priest. When John O'Burke died, the bishop who came to bury him, in addition to the comforting words he bestowed on the hundreds of peasants who had turned out to pay their last respects to their protector, also had a few sage words for Gabriel in private. 'A light rein,' he said. 'That's my advice to you, a light rein.' Then he drove away in his own horse and carriage.

A week later Gabriel went to pay his respects to the new O'Burke and to commiserate with him, remembering what the dead man had said about the law affecting inheritance by Catholics, on the loss of the family house. It was an uncomfortable interview. Young Charles O'Burke seemed to brush his remarks aside.

Two months later, however, he was passing the rectory when Mr Cox came dashing out to invite him in. To his surprise he found Charles there, sitting in awkward silence in the rector's study.

Cox said, 'The time has come for you to know that Mr O'Burke has decided to become a member of the Church . . .'

'Look,' said Charles, 'sit down. I do wish you would sit down, father.' He smiled charmingly. 'Well, anyway, it's true. Mr Cox and I have been having long talks.'

'I have cleared up certain points for him,' Cox put in.

'You, Mr Cox, cannot clear up anything. O'Burke, is this true?'

'I've already told you. Next Sunday I will receive the Mass from Mr Cox.'

'Call it communion,' said Cox with a nervous laugh. 'Communion is what we call it.' He turned to Gabriel. 'I thought it best to tell you in advance.'

'I've given it a lot of thought, you know,' Charles assured him. 'Theology is not one-sided.'

Gabriel's answer was an impatient gesture. 'You never saw fit to discuss your doubts with me. Why not?'

'I thought it best to wrestle with them alone.'

'Quite so,' murmured Cox.

Gabriel rose to his feet, white-faced. 'This has nothing to do with doubts,' he said. 'What has happened is that you have turned your back on Christ entirely. In your present opinion, being true to your Saviour matters less than being a country gentleman, and no doubt a Justice of the Peace into the bargain. You haven't changed your faith, my lad, you've decided you can do without it. Well, you don't feel the need of it now, maybe, but the time will come when you do feel the need of it, believe me.'

'You see?' said Charles turning to his new guide. 'I told you.'

'Can't you at least wish him well in his new faith?'

'What nonsense is that for a priest to be saying?'

'Well, Charles, we priests are as weak as other men,' Cox pointed out smoothly. 'May God forgive us!'

'Amen!' quoth Charles.

Cried Gabriel, 'You disgust me, both of you.' He put on his cap and strode out.

Many of Charles's dependants peered through the church windows to see him take the Protestants' bread and wine. When they dropped down from the sills, they knew that they had lost their last protection against the full force of the law. As Gabriel had foreseen, the debonair young man was welcomed into the ranks of the local gentry, and it did not take him long to become a JP. His manner was so easy and obliging when he was with them. To his house-servants and tenants he was a different man. Most of them had known him since he was a baby, but now he could no longer be on intimate terms with them; ashamed of his betrayal, he turned against them. In the space of a year he became a rabid persecutor of Catholics. His new friends, the gentlemen of the Protestant ascendancy, confined their excesses to gambling and the hunting field. They had too much confidence in themselves to run into denominational excess. Secretly smiling at the zeal of the recent convert, they advised him to take it easy, but he would not listen.

On his own estate – securely his now – sheep were soon grazing where his father's Catholic kinsmen had tilled the soil. He did not go so far as to evict his tenants, allowing them to remain in their cottages, but he made no provision for their subsistence. After they had scraped a living like this for two years, at the start of the next winter Gabriel led a ragged collection of men, women and children up to the hou... Hearing they were there, Charles came to the door back... by three outsiders, strangers to the place, whom he had ta...

on and armed with guns. He asked the peasants what they wanted.

Gabriel answered, 'See!' Then he turned to his followers. 'Kneel,' he told them.

The women got down on their knees and so did the children. The men did not.

Charles O'Burke was infuriated. 'It's no use!' he shouted. 'Your priest has misled you. You'll get nothing from me. Be off, before I tell my men to shoot.'

Gabriel replied, gently, 'When they told me they were starving, I counselled them to come to you and ask for bread. I cannot believe I was misleading them in that.'

'Bread!' one woman repeated.

'Bread!' echoed another.

'Bread, bread, bread!' the entire crowd began to chant in unison. 'Bread, bread, bread!'

Trembling, Charles signalled to his men to go back inside and slammed the door. At that time the housekeeper who had served his father still served Charles O'Burke. Hearing the cry outside, she came up to him and told him that by the mercy of God there was a full batch of loaves all ready for the oven. He stared at her for half a minute and then told ͡er to go ahead. 'You're a good woman,' he added, which ͡couraged her to make some broth while the loaves were ͡ng.

͡side at the doorway the men surged round Gabriel. ͡given him his chance,' growled one of them, 'and ͡n what he thinks of it. Now it's our turn. Come on, ͡'s only three of them!' He had brought a cudgel ͡ich he now flourished. The younger men cheered. ͡looked pensive. The speaker turned to Gabriel. ͡ealed, and he did not smile to use the word to someone young enough to be his son. 'What do you say? If we're going to do anything, we've got to attack, and we want you to lead.'

'If you do want to attack, then yes, I will lead if you wish it. We've seen they have guns. Before we break in, quite a few of us will be wounded or dead, you realize that don't you? But when the rest of us get inside, what happens then? Have you thought of that?'

'We kill them,' a younger man answered in a low voice.

'Very well. And then what?'

'You tell us,' answered a third voice, an old woman's this time.

'After that it won't make much difference what we do. We could wait here for the soldiers to take us all together, or go back to our homes for them to arrest us one by one, or we might scatter for them to hunt us in the open.'

The young man who had spoken of killing said to him, bitterly, 'I know your sort, Father Gabriel. So far and no further, that's the way of it with men of your cloth. You see,' he remarked to the others. 'Already he's got us talking instead of doing.' And there were sounds of agreement.

At this stage, however, the servants of the house came out to set up the long trestle tables that had not been seen since John O'Burke had died, and told them that they had softened the young master's heart. Maybe he had changed his mind about being a Protestant. Smiling all over their faces, they said that there would be bread for everyone in a couple of hours and a bowl of good broth to go with it. So the whole crowd sat down – the men too, this time – and waited. Some women went back to the village to collect any children who had been left behind.

The men told one another what a good thing it was the

priest had held them up with his talking. After a time Charles O'Burke came out again and confessed he was most impressed by their orderly behaviour. If they had grievances, he said, he was prepared to hear them, and invited them to select six spokesmen to come and see him after their meal, to which they were most welcome. The spokesmen were chosen, with Gabriel as their leader, and, after noting their names, their host retired into the house to await developments.

For what they did not know was that he had secretly despatched one of his new men to Tipperary to fetch the military. The dragoons appeared over the hill on their horses before the feast had begun, and at the sight of their drawn sabres everyone scattered. There was no escape for the six men whose names Charles O'Burke had noted down, however, and he took special care to tell the sergeant not to forget 'the Catholic priest', as he had now for some time been referring to his father's old friend.

Only one outcome was possible. Five of the six 'ring-leaders' were sentenced to ten years' imprisonment. Gabriel was to be imprisoned for life by a regretful judge who had never quite succeeded in reconciling himself to those occasional cases where justice required the ill treatment of just men. It was obvious, however, that as long as this impressive young priest was loose in Ireland he would be a source of unrest. He belonged to an Ireland that was dead and buried, or very soon would be.

Out of sight in the squalid, gloomy and disease-ridden prison of Glenmarie, Gabriel was soon forgotten by everybody except Charles O'Burke, who never tired of regaling bored guests with the story of how he had foiled the Jesuit's plot to raise a rebellion. As for the prison itself, it was in a state of utter neglect and nobody capable of doing anything to improve it ever came near it. It was left entirely at the mercy of a gaoler whose sole interest in its inmates was the perquisites he could extract from them. In other words his solicitude – for which he charged heavily – was confined to prisoners who could pay extra for better board and lodging. Debtors were the object of his peculiar care. Catholics, footpads and murderers fared badly. Atrociously housed and fed, in cells which were murky by day and pitch-dark at night – for how could they pay for candles when they could not even afford a blanket? – the only money he was able to make out of them came from the tips donated by sight-seeing ladies and gentlemen.

When Gabriel's funds were exhausted, his immediate reaction was one of relief. Now that his money was finished, he could no longer buy food or blankets for the needier prisoners as he had been doing, but it was nonetheless a blessing to be at one with them all alike, at the same level, in the presence of their common Saviour.

The actual experience of this lowly condition, however, affected him like a stunning blow. One of the most shocking discoveries he had made so far was that the gashes and bruises he found on the stinking, half-naked bodies and tried to salve had not all been inflicted by the warders. Some were the handiwork of their fellow-sufferers. The realization that humanity could sink to such degradation shook his belief in the possibility of redemption.

He had never shirked the duty of rebuke, however, and whenever inhumanity, whether committed by warder or prisoner, presented an occasion for it he did not fail to administer it as liberally as he administered food and medicine for as long as he could buy them. When his funds were exhausted, he saw no reason to discontinue these admonitions. He soon learned there was a reason of a kind. When it became clear that no more payments were to be expected from him, the gaoler ignored him. This, perhaps, was only to be expected. He did not expect anything from him, but he regarded the warders differently. However slight the heed they paid to it, they had at least listened to his reproof, and he had taken this as a sign of respect for his priestly calling. He was soon to learn differently. As soon as it became known that he was penniless, the next time he remonstrated with a warder he was knocked down, the other two were called, and he was kicked and beaten senseless. The last perception he registered before he became unconscious was the sight of the faces of a crowd of fellow-prisoners – men, women and children – that had gathered to watch the unusual sport of thrashing a priest with lively interest.

His initial reaction to this was to keep his mouth shut. He began to look in another direction when a beating was being administered, and in general to keep his face to the wall. At first he had tried at least to offer the victims his assistance when their persecutors had gone. To his chagrin, however, he discovered that such ministrations were not welcome. On the contrary, the great satisfaction he now gave the other prisoners, no less than the warders, was an opportunity to vent their hatred. The priesthood, in their experience, was in league with the rich and comfortable and complacent. They knew of no cause to love or even to respect it.

These were the blackest days he ever knew. Gradually he discontinued the practice of prayer. He put his Bible aside somewhere; when he looked for it, he found that it had disappeared. He did not care. What mattered was making sure that he got his fair share of the soup. Then one night he cried out in his sleep, protesting that there was no justice, and seemed to hear the mocking laughter of the Creator he used to worship, and awoke with his cheeks wet with tears. There came a night when he had a dream of Christ. Christ spoke to him, and asked, 'What ails you? Has what is good ceased to be good, just because you suffer? What I promised you at the beginning is still true. You are in trouble, that is true, but nothing has altered. I am still the same, and always will be.' Gabriel was surprised and delighted. 'I had forgotten!' he exclaimed, and awoke laughing. Then he fell asleep a second time and slept as he had never slept in that place before.

Next morning he found that his dream remained with him. Later he tried to intervene with the warders in defence of a very old and frail prisoner, and the warders again dragged him into a corner and beat him, and a crowd of prisoners gathered to watch as before. He was becoming one of them, they thought, but something told them that it was not so. Later in the day the children made friends with him. Their mothers, though they still jeered at him, addressed him as 'father' once again. Some of the men came and sat near him, and when they found he was no longer disposed to find fault with them, they began to talk freely. He was at one with them. It was they who asked him to offer a prayer.

One day the gaoler himself came and kicked him where he lay. Gabriel opened his eyes and said, 'Tell me if you want me to do something, but why kick me? I am not a stone, neither is any creature of flesh and blood a stone.'

The gaoler made a show of bafflement. 'This one's gone mad now,' he remarked, and walked away. After that incident, however, it was noticeable that all the prisoners were treated more leniently when Gabriel was by, and Gabriel himself was never beaten again.

Meanwhile Charles O'Burke was putting on weight and his handsome face was growing heavy with drink. His hospitality had become notorious, and his oft-told tale of how he had foiled a Jesuit's plot became a standing joke. One day, in the course of a shooting party, the guest standing beside him waiting for the next flight of pheasants inquired, 'How is he these days?'

The question came out of the blue, but Charles replied, 'How should I know? He's in Glenmarie gaol.'

'I bet fifty guineas he doesn't exist and never did,' another guest offered. 'Why not show us the creature, if you want us to believe in him?'

'My faith,' said Charles, 'but I will at that.'

The gaoler made almost as much from sight-seeing visitors as he did from his charges. Two coach-loads of guests arrived two mornings later, chattering, to fall silent as soon as they entered at the sight and stench of the half-naked wretches on display.

'It may be pestilential,' a lady said through her handkerchief. 'We mustn't stay too long. Which one is the Jesuit?'

'Here I am,' said Gabriel. He was squatting in a corner with a child in his arms. They all stared at him, and then at Charles, for Gabriel's gaze was fixed on the man who had put him where he was, not malevolently but with serious attention, as if he were confirming certain truths.

Charles made a valiant effort to return this scrutiny. Then, gasping, he turned round and rushed out. His guests were more than ready to follow him. Undeniably, the jaunt had been a failure, best quickly forgotten. Charles had enjoyed it least of all. In answer to a question from the lady, he replied that he'd be damned if he lifted a finger to get the traitor out. He was where he belonged.

In many a night thereafter Charles's dreams were haunted by a pair of unusually clear, light-blue eyes that followed him in judgement everywhere he went. Little more than twelve months later Gabriel was released from prison in response to a statement deposed by Charles O'Burke, JP, to the effect that the said Jesuit had seen the error of his ways, and recommending accordingly that upon giving an undertaking to leave Ireland and never return, he should be released. The said Jesuit was unwilling to give such an undertaking; but, upon the deposit of such an undertaking by a bishop on his behalf, he was released nevertheless. This same bishop drove in his coach to collect him from the gaol and, although the day was a raw one, found it necessary to open the windows when his passenger got in.

So it came about that Gabriel found himself back at the Jesuit college in Rome. The German teacher of theology found his old pupil – and, as he reminded him, confessor – had turned into just the intimidating figure he had expected. He had brought along with him a present of a dozen bottles of red wine, and was delighted when his host immediately opened one of them.

'That was the truth you handed out to me that time,' the German said. 'Do you remember?'

'Yes, I do. Does he do you the honour of consulting you now?'

'All the time. It is very boring.' He opened the second bottle himself. 'And where are we going to send you now, do you suppose?'

'Wherever I am wanted.'

'That could be anywhere. It will be the father I secretly call "Calvin" who will make the decision. Shall I narrow it down for you? India, the Congo or South America. How do they strike you? I mean, supposing we were talking about someone else, not about you?'

'It would seem fitting.'

'Then let us hope it fits.' He raised his glass.

Eight months later, after braving stormy seas and pirates, Gabriel had come to rest in the Mission of San Miguel, which was the farthest into the interior of them all. He was regarded there as a model priest. His regard for order and discipline was meticulous and unremitting. So was his love for the Guarani who lived on the mission lands, whose language he quickly mastered. Four years later, when he became Superior of the mission, nobody thought of questioning the appointment. No more did he. As far as he was concerned, it was simply a question of carrying on the work they all believed in. That the others thought of him personally as a leader was a notion that never crossed his mind, but it was so. Even his bouts of temper were welcome to his subordinates. They loved him too much to wish him to be perfect, although they believed he walked with Christ.

This last was true. Gabriel argued, expostulated and pleaded with his Saviour all day and every day. In this he found nothing notable, because he believed that every Christian did the same. Now, alone in his hut, he laid before his divine confidant the question of Julien's martyrdom.

When evening fell, Ibaye knocked at the door to tell Gabriel all was ready for the Mass. He invited the Guarani father into his cell and asked him to make himself comfortable while he robed himself. Robes he personally thought an encumbrance, but as they were prescribed he kept his carefully laundered and pressed. When he emerged, robed, with his grey hair flying and his mouth set in a straight line, he looked the picture of priesthood. No words were spoken. He immediately set off behind the train of Guarani altar boys and two priests in the direction of the mission church.

As he went along, every Guarani he passed knelt and those who were near enough reached out to kiss his hand. At first, scenting idolatry, he had requested them not to do this, but he had submitted in the end. Reaching his goal, he passed through the church's wide double doors into its candlelit interior. The organ burst into harmony with guitars, violins and flutes, and the choir began a deep plainsong.

'Brother Julien,' he thought, 'we mourn for you. Pray for us sinners.' Yet, looking over the crowded congregation of Guarani, though he knew them so well, he wondered whether they were not mourning some different loss from his. He raised his eyes and looked, as he so often had, at the strange winged beast, half angel and half threatening hooded bird, that a Guarani had carved.

The psalm soared out from the church into the night. When silence had fallen, Gabriel said, 'Almighty and most Merciful Father, we commend to Your special care the soul of our brother Julien who, we doubt not, will make intercession for Your ignorant children, the Guarani of the Upper Paraná.'

In the morning thousands of Guarani stood silent on the bank of the river while Gabriel and three other Jesuits cast off their two canoes. After they had vanished, the Guarani returned to their labours. Many were sure that they would never see him again.

———

It was two weeks' journey, part by canoe, part overland and finally by raft. At last they neared the falls of Iguaçú and heard their thunder. Rounding a bend in the river, they saw the gaunt, lonely cross. Gabriel raised his eyes to the top of the falls and could see the smoking spray that mounted from below.

They ran their craft up on the beach and surrounded the cross with flowers from the jungle and the backwaters. Gabriel would have it so. They then conducted a lengthy service. After that they built a fire, ate their meal and fell asleep. The air about them shook ceaselessly from the falls.

That same evening, five miles above the falls, Julien's killers were starting to feast and get drunk round a blazing fire. The women had spat maté seeds into a murky mixture of brown liquid in a hollow log and now this was tested. The shaman rolled his eyes, smote his stomach and pronounced it ready. He brought some to half a dozen mature warriors and they confirmed his judgement. He then turned to the rest of the tribe and told them to begin.

Two hours later they were all happily drunk. Men, women and children ate the flesh of deer, and the grease ran down their flesh. A father offered his cup to a sticky-faced five-year-old, who drank thirstily. An old man and an old woman with humourless faces exchanged time-honoured tribal witticisms to howls of laughter. A young buck leaped to his feet and pranced straddle-legged before a line of seated girls, brandishing the treat he had to offer. A girl looked straight into his eyes invitingly, and he flung her down as half the tribe got up to watch. The oldest and the youngest, however, just went on eating and drinking.

By the time first light of the morning filtered through the dense foliage, they had all fallen asleep. By early afternoon they were all awake. They had vanished by nightfall.

Camping below the falls, Gabriel sat with his companions by the fire. He said, 'I shall be the next to go up there. It must be me.'

Said Antonio, 'Father Gabriel, you are old. Let one of us do it.'

'No. It was I who sent Julien.'

'So let us all go, then,' Sebastian said.

'Yes,' said Gabriel sarcastically, 'and let us also take a troop of conquistadores and a train of artillery. They will take us for slave-traders if we come upon them all together.'

'At the head of the falls, that is, supposing that you get there, what will you do?' asked Antonio.

'I shall pray.'

'I mean, what will you offer them?'

'Music.'

'Music!' Sebastian threw up his hands.

'You don't believe in music, Sebastian?'

'It leaves me indifferent.'

'I speak of more tractable people, the Guarani. You know what Minoria said: "Give me an orchestra and I will conquer South America." I shall try it.'

'Splendid! So when you reach the head of the falls, you will play them something.'

'The slave-traders brought them firearms.' Gabriel took an oboe out of his roll and extracted it from its sleeve of wool. 'We bring them music.' He fitted the reed into the oboe.

'They are not ready,' stated Fernando.

Gabriel stopped fitting the reed and asked, 'Oh? And how do you know that?'

'It is no good trying to reason with you,' Sebastian complained. 'The death of Julien was the will of God, but you yourself assume responsibility for it.'

'Ah yes. Yes, perhaps I do,' said Gabriel. 'I shall think about that.'

'You can't reverse an argument by pretending to accept it,' Sebastian told him.

Gabriel answered with a smile. 'It seemed a logical thing to do.' Lifting the oboe to his mouth, he played a simple melody against the background of the falls.

The next morning the others said, 'God be with you,' but Sebastian accompanied Gabriel to the foot of the falls. When they arrived there, the ceaseless thunder of the water made it impossible for them to speak to each other. They could only embrace. Gabriel smiled a smile of pure benevolence. Sebastian scowled. Back at the camp he climbed on to his rock and refused to speak to anyone.

Meanwhile Gabriel had found a left-handed fissure and was following it uphill. The sides grew together and the trees closed in. Then it petered out against the face of the matted cliff. He was forced to turn round and go back to the start. This time he found a narrow aperture to the right which brought him through a narrow chimney to the edge of the falling cliff of water.

'Christ, tell me why it is I who am doing this,' said Gabriel, appalled.

He struck off left again through the dripping leaves. When the time came, he leaned himself back and said vespers in a loud voice that was derided by the surrounding din. Then he went on.

It was dusk when he emerged from the undergrowth that covered the head of the falls, and knew he had succeeded. Awestruck like Adam, he stood and gazed at the landslide of water as it vanished over the edge. While he stood there, the sky above became night and was pierced by stars, but he continued upriver in the darkness. The noise of the falls came more gently, and the river too was growing less disturbed. A moon came up, glinting through the foliage. He struck inland. A dead branch cracked.

In the camp below where the others waited, Sebastian lay motionless, looking up at the moon.

Antonio asked, 'Do you think he's found them?'

'I don't know.'

'He may never find them.'

'True.'

'What will he do if – '

'I don't know!' Sebastian shouted.

At that same moment Gabriel was bending to examine the smouldering remains of a fire. How long since it had been burning? He could not tell. The forest was all around him; the falls were far away. He straightened up and asked Christ a question: 'Did you, in the Garden of Gethsemane, feel the onset of death as clearly as I do here? If so, You were a man. If not, You were a God. What help can You give me?'

He sat down and took out the oboe, with the reed. Sweat poured down his face, and he looked again at the opaque forest. He raised the oboe to his lips, cleared his throat and began to play. It was a favourite of his, an oboe sonata by Handel.

In the forest a pair of monkeys, catching the tremulous notes on the night air, stopped combing each other's hair and listened.

A score of blue and purple birds, half asleep, raised their suddenly alert heads at what they heard.

A hog came to the opening of its burrow with four little ones and, with the bright moon reflecting in their eyes, they attended.

A jaguar, prowling stealthily over the rocks, paused and drew back its mouth into a silent snarl.

Gabriel caught sight of a brave's face peering at him steadily from the undergrowth and stopped playing. Their eyes met and they caught each other's fleeting message of fear. The savage's face withdrew and Gabriel hastily resumed his playing. The brave reappeared. Gabriel's scalp rose when he realized there was now a second brave standing just behind him, so close that he could smell him. A third came a little way out of the brushwood about forty yards away, cocked his head sideways and peered slantwise at Gabriel. The first savage now pushed out of the undergrowth and stood about twenty feet away with his spear held high, but, seeing the musician was unarmed and went on making music, he drew closer and squatted down upon his heels. Now more emerged from the jungle. They all stood round bemused and began to discuss him in undertones.

'It does not come from his mouth.'

'No, it comes from that whistle.'

'It is pleasing.'

'Yes. It is like the first call of the birds.'

'Like the first call, yes. It is new.'

'Like the first breath of the morning breeze.'

'Yes.'

The figure of the shaman entered the glade in a rush. He yelled, 'Fools. Can't you see? Behold.' And he dashed up to Gabriel, seized the oboe and broke it upon his knee.

At first no one spoke. Then one of the first-comers said, 'You have broken the whistle that made it.'

'Yes, the whistle, not the man who blew it,' said the shaman.

'Now mend it.'

'I do not know how.'

The brave nodded, took the broken halves of the oboe from the shaman's hand and offered them to Gabriel.

'You mend it.'

Gabriel took them, but it was smashed beyond repair. 'I cannot do it here. Perhaps at your village I might do better.'

The brave looked wary. 'You speak our language?'

'Yes.'

'Kill him,' said the shaman. 'Throw him in the river.'

'Yes,' many agreed. 'Kill him.'

'Eat him,' urged the shaman.

A brave with white hair asked the one who had spoken first, 'What do you say?'

'Let us see if he can mend the whistle.'

'If he cannot mend it, we can still throw him in the river,' the white-haired brave pointed out to the shaman. 'There is plenty of time to decide.'

'Yes. Later we can decide,' the majority agreed.

The warrior who had spoken first held out his hand to Gabriel and led him along the narrow stream. The rest of the braves followed while the shaman fulminated to himself. Gabriel turned his attention to the man who had him by the hand; his grip was amicable. So, as they walked, Gabriel said, 'My name is Gabriel.'

The brave looked at him hard, then said, 'Mine is Hacugh.'

'You are the chief?'

'We are not at war.'

'You make the decisions?'

'That one,' he pointed to the shaman, 'is the wise man.'

'Is he wise?'

'Yes. Very wise.'

'Kill him,' the shaman said. 'Do not listen to him.'

They arrived at the village, which consisted of three huge huts whose papaya-leaf thatches brushed the ground. A fire was burning. There was a stream for water. Watching their arrival gravely were the women and children.

Hacugh said to Gabriel, 'Now, you sleep.'

With all the tribe as spectators he said his prayers and, rolling over, pretended to sleep.

In the morning he was given a thick gruel and then brought before the entire tribe. In front sat the women with children in their laps, while behind them the braves remained standing. He asked for a clean white sheet of cloth on which to lay the two halves of his oboe. He screwed up his eyes and pretended to examine the two halves of the instrument very closely. Then he said, 'What is the name of your shaman?'

'Tanretopra. Why?'

'He is a man of great potency.'

'Why?'

'He has destroyed the whistle.'

'You cannot mend it?'

'I fear not.'

'Kill him, kill him,' sand Tanretopra.

A woman who had been watching Gabriel closely disappeared into her hut and returned with a sheaf of fine reeds. He bound the oboe with reeds, blew on the reed and was rewarded with a hoot. He heard the whole tribe suck in its breath with satisfaction and then break into a murmur. He operated the keys, and the oboe uttered a series of groans and then one high, magically lovely note. They laughed at it and then were quiet.

Gabriel, thinking hard, said, 'Perhaps, given time, I can mend it.'

'How much time?' queried Hacugh.

'That is in the hands,' a pause for breath, 'of Jesus Christ.'

Hacugh looked at his tribesmen and then said, 'We have heard of him.'

'Of course, Julien told you of Him before you cast him into the river.'

The shaman said, 'Now we will cast you there.'

Gabriel said steadily, and his steadiness impressed them, 'That will be as Christ wills.'

The woman who had fetched the reeds said, 'What more would you say of him?'

Gabriel told them that Jesus Christ offered the greatest of friendships. For example, He guided His friends through the dark places and across the open spaces of life, and at their death He opened His Kingdom to them, where they lived for ever.

The brave with white hair asked, 'Does he do this for you?'

Gabriel thought for a minute. Then he laughed softly, 'He does.'

'Why do you laugh?'

'I have never been asked that before. But it is true, He does.'

'This Jesus Christ must be a warrior of gigantic size.'

'He was born a baby.'

'A baby?' the woman asked.

'Born of woman. Look,' he said and brought from his pocket a cheap picture of the infant Christ sitting upright in Mary's sentimental arms.

'He looks unforgiving,' she said, peering at him.

'That is the fault of the painter,' he explained. 'Have you ever seen a child look unforgiving?'

'Many times,' she answered.

What a convert she would be! 'Yes, you are right. Perhaps he looks like that because he has just seen the Devil.'

'The Devil is one of our gods,' Hacugh said.

'Are you sure he really is the Devil?'

'Kill him, kill him, there is still just time,' urged the shaman.

'What harm do I do to you?' asked Gabriel.

'I do not know. Therefore I say, "Kill him".'

'I do not think that you will kill me, but if you do you will find me ready. Look at the Christ child. Is that a God who harms people?'

The woman passed the crude picture round, each group studying it carefully, women, men and children.

The woman looked at him. 'It would be nice if he was ruler of the world,' she said.

'He is.'

'Then he will help you to mend your whistle,' argued Hacugh.

'Of course,' Gabriel agreed, 'but it will take time.'

As the days went by, he came to marvel at their silent passage through the jungle, the accuracy with which they hurled their spears and the power of their humming bows. Gratified, he watched the women returning with wild vegetables for the tribe and observed their benevolence with the babies.

He also brooded on their polygamy, their drunkenness and their sloth. When they had culled and caught all they needed for a single day, they were content to sit and talk, or sleep.

The Guarani discovered him in the forest when he thought he was unobserved, praying and communicating with Christ, and this impressed them greatly.

Tanretopra detested Gabriel from his heart. Each night he would come to him and say, with a kick of his foot towards the oboe, 'It is mended yet?'

Gabriel replied, 'Not yet.' The shaman would laugh and each day turn with increasing mockery to the others who were watching and then walk off.

At length Gabriel took his courage in both hands and said, 'Christ does not want me to mend it here.'

The shaman said triumphantly, 'Did I not say so? He is a false prophet.'

'Not so. For instance, I could mend it at my mission.'

Tanretopra leaped to his feet. 'Did I not tell you? Behold, he wants to take you back with him to his mission. Now, while there is yet time, kill him!'

'Aye,' said a very old man, 'kill him!'

'Kill him!' said others, rising together to their feet. 'Kill him!'

Gabriel asked, 'What have I done to hurt you? Tell me.'

'That is true. He has done nothing,' Hacugh said.

'Listen to me very carefully and think of what I say. I have three brothers waiting for me at the bottom of the falls. They can take the oboe back to the mission and get it mended, and then return with two others who can also make music on their instruments. We shall all play for you.'

Hacugh said, 'I would like to hear the oboe and the other instruments.'

'Thereafter, if we so desire, we can cast them all in the river. Tanretopra, we thank you for your counsel, but now we have heard you. Be silent, if it please you,' said the white-haired brave. And most of the tribe agreed.

Then they piled into their canoes, men, women and children, and made for the head of the falls. Squinting over the river at the forest below the cannonade of water, Gabriel said, 'I cannot see them.'

'Could you see them from there?' Hacugh asked, pointing to an islet at the very edge of the falls.

'Yes,' said Gabriel, 'but that is impossible.'

'No, no, that is easy.'

They put out to the islet in the canoes, with Gabriel marvelling at the gentleness of the current just before the final drop. He clapped his hands, crying, 'Marvellous, marvellous!' Once there, they built a fire and fed it with wet grasses, so that black smoke poured out.

Within ten minutes Sebastian down below had seen it, and within an hour he was standing immediately below them, tiny, looking up towards them. Gabriel signalled joyfully for him to come up, and he disappeared into the forest.

'See, he is coming up,' said Gabriel, and then they paddled back to the bank to wait.

From four miles away Mendoza also saw the billowing smoke. He was working his way upstream on a raft with five conquistadores. He called a halt and they paddled slowly to one side of the river. After watching for a while, he decided that it was a Guarani fire, but could not guess its significance. All that he and the Spanish settlers knew about the unexplored territory above the falls was that it was inhabited by Guarani. He did not know of Father Gabriel's mission, just as the Jesuits at San Miguel knew nothing of Mendoza's raid, for he had stolen past them in the night. Each party deemed itself to be the first thrust from the old world into the new one beyond the falls.

The Captain-General had given him the nod. Cabeza's plan was to extend his territory at the expense of the Portuguese, but none of that concerned Mendoza. Ever since he had first seen them, far off, from below in the forest, the falls had seemed to him the gateway to El Dorado.

He ordered his conquistadores to remain silent, and they set out again on their slow passage upriver.

Meanwhile Sebastian had reached the head of the falls. Filthy from his climb, he embraced Gabriel. Then he took in the wild Guarani and asked in a low voice, 'Holy God! You are all right?'

'I have been all right. I do not know whether the two of us shall be.'

'What am I to do?'

'Just wait.'

'Can you mend this?' Hacugh asked, displaying the two halves of the oboe.

'Tell him yes,' said Gabriel.

'Yes.'

'Where?'

'At the mission,' said Gabriel.

'The mission.'

Said Gabriel, 'Let him take away the oboe and bring it back made good.'

'And if he does not come back?' asked the shaman.

Hacugh said, 'Then we shall crucify this one.'

'And what if he returns with slave-traders?' the shaman asked.

'I am the enemy of all slave-traders,' Sebastian said.

'Ha, hear him,' mocked Tanretopra. 'Who believes what he says?'

'If they come,' said Hacugh, 'they will come. I do not think they will come quicker because of that one.'

The shaman made a last appeal. 'Come! Let us cast them both into the river and be done with them.'

Hacugh said, 'I have given my word. Who agrees with me?' Some said one thing and some another.

Gabriel said to Sebastian, whose huge figure dominated the whole assembly, 'Shrink! Make yourself small.'

The argument went on into the evening. 'I think we have won, saints be praised.'

'Amen.'

Hacugh announced, 'He can go with the whistle and you shall stay.'

Sebastian said, 'It will take four weeks.'

'Four weeks.'

'Perhaps even five.'

'Five weeks. Then we shall kill him.'

Gabriel gave Sebastian these orders: 'You and the others go back to the mission and get this instrument repaired. This very one, mark you, and no other.'

'That may take time.'

'Five weeks. Then bring it back with you. Bring also Mateo and Pedrería with their instruments. No one else.'

'I understand.'

'Do you believe now, Sebastian, that music does work miracles with these people? They are passing spiritual, you see.'

'Father, you are profoundly mad and holy.'

Then Sebastian climbed back down the overhanging cliffs, bearing with him the two halves of the fissured oboe, and explained the situation to the others. They struck camp and made their way downstream with all speed, while Gabriel went back upriver with the tribe.

In hiding, Mendoza and his conquistadores watched the Jesuits pack up and go. When Sebastian floated past, Mendoza's raft was hidden in a backwater. After they had gone, he looked up at the falls.

He said, 'There may be more of them up there.'

'We have the Captain-General's permission,' said one of his men.

Mendoza said, 'We have Cabeza's permission to bring back

what we find beyond those cliffs. But he'll deny it if we tangle
with the Jesuits.'

'They are big cliffs.'

'What?'

'Big.'

'Yes, big.'

When they arrived at the top, the tranquillity which closed
around them as the night fell made him uneasy.

The next day they set off as usual into the jungle. In the middle
of the day they came upon the prints of many bare feet on the
ground. Mendoza's half-breed looked at them and whispered,
'They are near.' They cocked their muskets and pistols quietly,
and pressed on cautiously through the undergrowth among the
massive trees, until suddenly they were there.

Hacugh was standing in a glade. He stood up and raised a hand
for silence. There was a moment of stillness, and then Mendoza
fired his pistol and his conquistadores rushed in. The Guarani
hurled their spears and then made off, haring through the thick
tangle of creepers, leaving the conquistadores with five taken and
two fallen, one dead and the other with a long, grazing wound.

Suddenly a spear flashed by Mendoza and stuck, quivering,
in a tree. The thrower was invisible, but Mendoza went
charging into the undergrowth in the direction from which it
had come. He was rewarded only by the sound of footsteps
rapidly growing fainter. Then silence fell.

He stopped, crouched, went forward, and stopped again.
Straining his ears, he could hear only the steady drone of
insects. Then came the whizz of an arrow. It lodged, vibrating,
close to him. The voice of Gabriel cried, 'Stop!' He emerged,
accompanied by Hacugh, and came within fifteen feet of where
Mendoza was now crouching under cover. 'You in there,' he
said.

Mendoza, whose eyes never left Hacugh, said, 'Yes, father.'

'I can get a score of these men here.'

'I have a musket and a pistol, father.'

'How many have you captured?'

'I do not know, father.'

'Let them go.'

'No, father.'

'Do you think it makes a difference to me whether you "father" me?' He thrust his way through to Mendoza's hiding place but found no one there.

'Let the braves go,' he cried. And then, in a strident voice said, 'Tell Don Cabeza you have found me here. Tell him these people are outside his authority. Tell him we will make Christians of these people.' Then, turning to Hacugh, he warned, 'Do not go after them, they have muskets and will shoot you down.'

Hacugh said, 'We would have done better to heed the shaman.'

When they were back in the village, the shaman said in deep tones, 'Did I not tell you? After the men of Jesus, the slave-takers.'

Gabriel said in agreement, 'What you have said has been made good. So kill me.'

'What do you counsel, oh shaman?' asked Hacugh. 'Is this a bad man?'

Tanretopra drew close to his alien rival and studied him searchingly. At length he moved his head slowly from side to side and said, 'No. It is a good man. Nevertheless, I have told you what to do with him.' He went into the forest.

Gabriel lived, and stayed. Before long Sebastian, Mateo and Pedrería joined him. On the still, sun-soaked, butterfly-laden air, they made the music of Handel and Tallis and Scarlatti, and thereby won the hearts of the Guarani, although not as yet the minds.

When Mendoza showed Cabeza the five braves he had captured, the Captain-General said, 'They are superb, first class.'

'Yes. For outside work, Excellency.'

'Of course. Are there many of them there?'

'I do not know. The priests are also on the ground, Excellency.'

Cabeza stared. 'What?'

'They have a place above the falls.'

'*Me cago en Dios.* How many?'

'I saw only one.'

'*La puta madre.*' He took a turn up and down the room and then came to a stop. 'Tell me, how soon can you lead another expedition up there?'

'In two months' time, Excellency.'

'No, in one month.'

'In two months. It needs careful handling, Excellency. For one thing, I shall have to give a wide berth to the land occupied by the Jesuits.'

'Well do it, do it, do it.'

However, in less than six weeks Don Cabeza received a formal visit from Father Ribero, the Provincial Superior of the Jesuits in the Río de la Plata. Ribero was a subtle politician who despised Cabeza, although naturally this did not prevent him from flattering him. For his part, Cabeza was not deceived by the flattery and deeply resented the Jesuit's contempt. Nevertheless, he too smiled as he asked his visitor to sit and, indicating the heavy leather file the Jesuit laid on the table, said, '*Oh Dios*, is this a formal visit?'

'Alas, it is.'

'Can it wait until I get you a glass of wine?'

'Is it the same as the cask you sent us last Easter?'

'Is it?' Cabeza asked the secretary.

'It can be made so,' said the secretary, also smiling. He bowed himself out, and his soft footsteps echoed on the flagged floor outside. The cheeping of birds in the carved rafters was clearly audible. Ribero glanced up at them, looked down and said, 'I have heard from Father Gabriel.'

'A good man.' A servant entered with the wine.

'He sent a message by a brother Sebastian.'

'Oh yes?'

'From above the falls.'

Cabeza mimed astonishment. 'Above the falls?'

'Yes.' He stroked the cover of the file.

'Well, this is interesting. Tell me, what did he find there?'

'The Guarani.'

'Ah. And they were – '

'Wild. Unfortunately, other people have been there too.'

'Other people?'

'Rodrigo Mendoza. He went there after slaves.'

'Slaves?' Cabeza frowned and formed his fingers into a steeple and examined it carefully. 'There are no slaves in the Río de la Plata. You know that, father.'

'*Encomienda.*'

He unsteepled his fingers and smiled. 'Ah, that is different.'

'Father Gabriel's letter says they have been taken by force.'

'By force. I see. He says this against Rodrigo Mendoza?'

'Yes.'

'Father, that is a serious charge.'

Ribero's sandalled foot started tapping on the floor. 'I should like to see Mendoza, now.'

Cabeza looked at the careworn, subtle face of his antagonist and congratulated himself on having such a ready liar as Mendoza at his service. 'Certainly. I shall make inquiries when he is expected in the city.'

'I saw him on my way here.'

Cabeza despatched a servant. While they waited, they remarked on the birds in the rafters, the maté yield, the sugar-cane crop, the steady influx of new citizens to Asunción.

Mendoza knocked at the door and came in. Cabeza put on a threatening face. 'Attend you to Father Ribero.'

'Father?'

'You have been above the falls.'

'Yes, Father Provincial.'

Cabeza protested, 'You did not tell me that.'

'I wasn't asked, Excellency.'

'True.'

Ribero said, 'You returned with five slaves.'

'*Encomienda,* Father Provincial.'

'They volunteered?'

'How else?'

'Where did you get rid of them?'

'To a sugar planter.'

'What was his name?'

'I forget, Father Provincial.'

'You forget?'

'Yes, father.'

Cabeza was studying the birds in the rafters. 'Do you see that one?' He pointed. 'That one is the boss.'

'It makes the most noise,' replied Ribero, and then continued speaking with Mendoza. 'You spoke to Father Gabriel.'

'Yes. Excuse me, but I think he is too old to be up there, Father Ribero.'

'He can take care of himself. You told him you would take your Guarani to Don Cabeza.'

'What?' said Cabeza.

'No, that is a mistake,' said Mendoza. 'It was not I who spoke of the Captain-General. Father Gabriel did.'

This was correct. Ribero pulled angrily at his chin.

'Well, Mendoza, you will not go up there again.'

Cabeza shot him a wary look. 'I do not understand, Father Ribero.'

Ribero reached for his spectacles and, opening the leather file, produced a folded document which he straightened carefully, for it was old.

'I have here the granting of the mission to my Order. By His Catholic Majesty, Philip III, whom God preserves.'

'Amen,' said Cabeza, taking it from him. He studied it for a minute or two and then, his breath coming quickly and his finger loosening his collar, he coughed.

'Good,' thought Ribero. 'Good.' He went on, 'His Catholic Majesty – '

'Whom the saints preserve, assigns the land above the falls to you.'

'Yes.'

'But that land was unoccupied then.'

'Nevertheless, the rights are clear.'

'To all the lands from the falls up to the Portuguese border of the territory?'

'As you see.'

'Whereabouts do you place that?'

'Who knows? But it is all contained within the grant of land. Is it not?'

'Yes.' Cabeza got to his feet and made a short tour of the room; he came to a halt and stood threateningly over the seated Ribero. 'I must warn you, I will have that altered.'

Father Ribero made a gesture with his open hands. 'Possibly. But I think that may take rather a long time to do.' Then he said inflexibly, looking at Mendoza, 'Meanwhile, that land is denied to you and to anyone else like you. It is denied to all members of the government who do not have permission from myself. Captain-General, will you repeat that to him?'

'You heard that?'

'Yes, Excellency.'

'Obey.'

'Admirable,' said Ribero, with a look of enjoyment on his face. 'That is all I came to say.' He folded up the document, and while he was doing so the belfries began to chime in the city. On the way out he turned his attention to the rafters again. 'Oh look, Don Cabeza. They have chased the fat bird through the window.'

When the door was shut, Mendoza asked Don Cabeza, 'Do I take that at face value?'

Shouting, Cabeza answered, 'You heard him, didn't you?' There was a pause. He felt Mendoza's eyes upon him. 'Yes, yes, it must be taken at face value.'

Mendoza went back to his shady house and took some cheese and wine. He lifted his feet on to the shiny table, crossed one over the other and clasped his hands behind his head. He was smiling.

Carlota María Herminda Teodosia Antonia de la Cadena

de Villasante had been born to the Conde de Villasante twenty-three years ago. She was the only child of the Conde and his lacklustre wife. It was owing to the drab Condesa that they were rich in blood that could be traced back to Fernando and from there back to Otto. It was owing to the formidable Conde that they were rich in virtue, for he was a stern son of the Church, an honest overlord and a fair-minded husband and father. Carlota was raised in the gloom of their castle in Córdoba, famous for the strict piety of its rule. However, the Conde was poor, so to the shadow of piety was added the forbidding darkness of heavy debt.

Carlota was a source of joy to both her parents. Her infectious laugh resounded through the ancient vaults of her home, calling forth a sober smile on her father's face and the remains of a smile on the face of her mother, which made one see how attractive she had been.

When she was fourteen, her father died from a furious riding fall that had occurred while hawking. Her mother was stricken. The castle became a house of permanent mourning, not to be disturbed by the faintest sound.

She sank into an unsettled torpor, drifting through the lofty stone corridors of her home, until her mother's old Jesuit confessor realized that he hadn't heard her laughter for many months. He went to the Condesa and spoke to her wisely and sensibly, using words which he had gleaned from the yellow shelves of the seminaries where he had been educated, recognizing their wisdom without fully understanding what they meant.

Her mother sighed and agreed, and took her to the court of Madrid, where they were made welcome because of that line extending back to Otto.

She was taken up by the Queen as a young *dama*, and saw

a great deal that it was not good for her to see. She was extolled as the model of a Spanish lady. However, the blood of her father, the Conde, was warm in her, and when the young sparks of Madrid watched her slight figure emerging from the confessor's box, to be borne away by her mother, she cast them a look out of downcast eyes which set their pulses thudding.

When she was nineteen, her mother was afflicted by a swelling disease that left her dead, looking like a monstrous, rubicund doll; packed in an enormous coffin, she lay in the cathedral for three days and then began to stink. Carlota, kneeling there, knew that she must henceforth take care of herself. There was now no one who would anticipate the awkward passages and make them smooth for her. This realization left her with the resolution that she had lacked before.

When Carlota's period of mourning was over, the Conde Marcos Haro y Monteresa informed the ancient Jesuit of his desire to marry her, and this trusted adviser, seeing an easy way out of his responsibilities, earnestly advised her to accept the offer. The Conde was of good repute and the overlord of a great estate. She refused, however. She objected to something light-minded and skittish that she found in him. In reply, the Jesuit reminded her that the castle was all she had.

Carlota said, 'Very well. How much is it worth?'

Hardening himself, he told her, 'Three times as much as a large farm.'

'As little as that?' she said, astonished.

'Yes. Think again about the Conde.'

'There can be no question of my marrying him, father. Make what excuses you think fit.' She ushered him out, kissing

109

him to stop the flood of empty words which was beginning to pour from his mouth. Then she drew the tiny curtains that were high up on the lofty wall and slowly sat down on the bed. Why had no one told her this before? She lay flat and wept with helplessness.

When Carlota emerged three days later, she was dazzling. Her shining black hair was wrapped round her head in a French coiffure. Her manner was adroitly poised between gaiety and gravity. She was the talk of the court. On her instructions the castle was rented to the bastard son of a local duke, and the elderly Jesuit was sent to spend the remaining years of his life elsewhere.

A letter came from a second cousin, Blasco, in Asunción, containing a few conventional words about her mother's death. He was an official and promised, in the course of the letter, to call on her when he came to Madrid. In reply, instead of thanks he received a carefully worded letter asking if she could come and stay with him in Asunción, where, of course, she would pay for her keep.

Her cousin thought, 'She is overspent,' and went to consult his wife, who swooned at the prospect of having the Condesa as a guest. With one step she would advance to the front ranks of their little society, let her father be an exporter of hides or not. She begged her husband to say yes. He, with a glance at the cobwebs which the Guarani always left on the dull white ceiling, did so.

When she received his letter, she was filled with elation. This would show the court that she could manage her own life, her own way.

The King waxed enthusiastic about her going to Asunción. She would serve as a bond between the old world and the new. He gave her a gold-bound Bible. Granting her leave, the

Queen stroked her head, smiled secretly, and arranged a special assembly for her. Carlota made a series of little farewells and finally drove out of Madrid, with a gathering of well-wishers waving hats and hands. Then her existence was forgotten. But she blazed into view in Asunción like a comet.

She took a long time preparing her appearance before Blasco, his wife and other hangers-on came down to the waterfront to welcome her.

'My God,' her cousin exclaimed when he caught sight of the slight figure with the olive skin and coiled black hair. He turned to a Guarani servant and said, 'Go quickly to the house and fetch a parasol.'

Blasco was a proper-looking man of forty, tall and straight, with a tiny beard. She stepped ashore in sombre black and gave him her hand, which he took with admiration, bending formally to kiss it. His wife, Bernadette, looked like what she was – a trader's daughter – but by adopting a note of humour in his introductions he pleaded with his cousin not to mock her. Bernadette gave a curtsy, looking upwards through huge solemn eyes, and Carlota rewarded her with a languid half-smile.

Sheltering beneath the parasol, she was then introduced to all the citizenry who somehow happened to be there. They were either would-be gentlemen in government service or, still more distressingly, mere tradesmen. Blasco ushered her into a barouche and they set off down the narrow, shade-dappled streets. The road drew out into a square with a fountain, but it was unpaved, raw red earth. Then the carriage swung round and stopped outside a presentable-looking town house. She recognized the pride of ownership in the look Bernadette darted at her, so she said, 'Cousin, I must felicitate you upon your residence.'

'Do you like it? It was my father's.'

'Come,' said Blasco.

'He died last year.'

'Come,' Blasco repeated.

'He died of a befuddlement of the heart. What was it, excuse me, that took your blessed mother?'

'I don't know.'

'This way,' said Blasco, 'come.'

'Nobody knows.'

'I am sorry.'

They went past half a dozen servants, two of them Spanish, to a suite of rooms upstairs. Carlota went to the window and saw across the square a palatial house with a listless flag dangling over it.

'That's the Captain-General's residence,' said Bernadette. 'Next to him lives the Colonel of the Guard; and next to him is Hernández Zunquiza; on the other side is – '

Blasco interrupted, saying, 'You will have plenty of opportunity to show the Condesa what elegant neighbours we have after she has taken a rest.'

'I am sorry,' said Bernadette, flushing. 'I do not know how to behave.' This drew from Carlota such a ravishing and wholly spontaneous smile that she had the satisfaction of seeing her hostess fall head over heels in love with her.

She went to the balcony window, and it was not until later that she realized how she had dropped her voice under the rustling of the palms and the gentle splashing of the water from the fountain to ask, 'Who is that?'

A man dressed in black, with black hair pulled back from a scarred face, was looking up at her. Blasco said, 'Where? Oh him! That's Mendoza. You won't be troubled by him.'

The man, as if he had heard, turned and went across the square to disappear down one of the shadowy side streets.

Mendoza had taken note of Carlota when she first set foot on shore. He had never seen anything like that Madrid beauty. In the evening he visited the mulatto women who plied their trade along the waterfront, but for the first time they failed to ease his desire.

Carlota was automatically invited to Cabeza's residence, to be diverted by his uneasy mixture of caution, pomp and parsimony. Nevertheless, she also noted the rough manner with which he rode over any obstruction that presented itself. He was a man to treat with care, if not respect. He gave a ball in her honour, and through Bernadette she met all the ladies of the city there. They were illiterate. The men, for their part, were more vainglorious than those she had known at Madrid. Each man invested his honour in his sister; each strove to sully another man's honour. Yet they were only farmers.

Suddenly she saw Mendoza sitting alone at a table. His eyes, still fixed on her, conveyed a glint of something sinister.

As they walked back home across the square, Carlota said to Bernadatte, 'Mendoza. There is something terrible about that man.'

'He is a conquistador. Did you not notice how no one spoke to him all evening?'

'But the *hidalgos* bowed in his direction.'

'He is Don Cabeza's agent.'

'For doing what?'

'He is a slave-trader. Goodnight, Carlota.'

Next week a bull-running was organized, and Mendoza came upon her walking the other way with a Guarani servant.

He gave no hint of having seen her. It was she who stopped and said, 'I don't believe we have been introduced.'

'Rodrigo Mendoza.'

'My God,' she thought, 'he is formidable. Just like my father!' 'I am the Condesa Carlota de la Cadena de Villasante. I have come to watch the bulls.'

'You can either watch them from up there,' he said, indicating a bank of seats where all the ladies and gentlemen of the city sat in state beneath an awning, 'or from here.' He pointed to an evil-smelling crowd pressed in together close to the bulls. As she followed his pointing finger, a bull tossed its head with a flourish of its threatening horns. Its eyes seemed to signal danger.

'That's where I want to go.'

The arrival of this incongruous pair caused a stir in the crowd. They nudged one another and grimaced as the couple made their way to the front. Carlota noticed how quickly a path was cleared for them. The arrival of the 'Duchess from Madrid' spurred the young men to fresh feats of athleticism and swordsmanship. She clapped and cried, 'Well done, *muchacho*,' the common people taking up the applause until there was just one massively horned bull left. Nobody cared to enter the ring with this one. He had already wounded a *muchacho*.

Carlota said, 'Ah, that is a bull.'

Doffing his topcoat, Mendoza drew his sword and stepped out. There was a general whisper. Never before had they seen him share in any festival. Then there was silence, a murmur, a cry and a sucking in of the breath as he drew the bull towards that notorious short sword of his and despatched it practically at Carlota's feet. The shout which greeted his success echoed to the edges of the city.

He cut off the ears and handed them to her. Then he stared

around at the rabble. A sudden silence fell, during which he collected his coat, bowed stiffly and left.

Of course Blasco was given the news in no time. That evening he cautiously tried to hint his disapproval and was snubbed.

Soon after this, there was a *fête champêtre* at the house of the Colonel of the Guard. Carlota saw Mendoza standing in the shade beneath some pillars, and he bowed stiffly to her once again. Then he turned away. She sent a servant over to him. As she watched him approach over the flagged pavement, she noticed how all around the conversation redoubled, while everybody spied on her out of the corners of their eyes.

He said, with a swift glance round, 'Listen, Condesa, this time there is no sport for the canaille.'

'I go riding with my friends tomorrow.'

'Indeed?'

Heavens, he made her do everything! 'Will you not join us?'

'If your cousin desires it.'

'I desire it.'

'Then I will come.'

Next morning she called him up to the head of the file and saw that his seat on a horse was expert. When the riding was over, she invited him to be one of a number of guests who were to breakfast at Bernadette's. Here, he was asked conventional questions about himself, about his farm, his dogs, his opinion of the strange things that were coming out of Europe. Around him, meanwhile, whispers were devoted to him and the Condesa. As soon as two ladies made their departure, he rose to follow them, but Carlota whispered, 'Please stay. For my sake.' So he returned to his stiff chair. He remained there, stone-hard with tension, till all the guests had gone and only Carlota remained.

'Asunción bores me,' she told him.

He glanced swiftly around the spacious room, now empty save for the Guarani servants slumbering by the door, before replying, 'I'm sorry.'

'There's nothing here.'

'There are one or two things worth seeing.'

'Is that so?'

She watched his drooping eyes rise slowly to meet hers. 'On Sunday there is a wild-boar hunt that señoritas go to – if they have a mind to it, that is.'

'I would have, if some gentleman were to be kind enough to take me.'

'Ask Señor Blasco.'

'He is too busy with his documents and bonds. Won't you be going?'

'I never go.'

'A pity. I would have liked it.'

He inclined his head. 'If Señor Blasco approves, I shall accompany you.'

'Blasco!'

He inclined his head gravely.

Bernadette came bustling back and, finding her fashionable guest alone with such a disagreeable companion, seated herself with a look of deep apology in Carlota's direction. At Mendoza she did not so much as glance. Then Blasco returned from seeing off the Captain-General. There was alarm in his eyes at finding the slave-trader there, which prompted Mendoza to take his leave immediately.

The following morning Mendoza went to the premises of the Jewish letter-writer, where he was at once ushered discreetly into a private, shady room at the rear. Soon afterwards a junior clerk delivered a short letter to Blasco; in this note Mendoza sought the official's permission to take the señora his wife, and naturally the Condesa, whom it might amuse, to the wild-boar hunt – unless, of course, he intended to accompany them himself. It went on to inform its perplexed recipient that the Condesa had expressed a lively interest in the event at the previous day's festivities.

Blasco knit his brows and pondered. Then he went to inform Bernadette and Carlota of this unexpected proposal and to advise against it. His prudent counsel met first with misunderstanding from Carlota and then, upon elaboration, with rejection. Certainly she would go. There could be no question of rejecting Señor Mendoza's invitation. It was most courteous of him to take her tedious complaints so seriously.

Blasco went across to the garrison officers' mess and discovered to his great relief that a group of officers would be joining the hunt. Certainly, said the adjutant, who was a major and would be in charge of their party, he would be delighted to keep an eye on Bernadette and the Condesa. Blasco thanked him, explaining apologetically that his horsemanship was not good enough for him to take part himself. He returned to Carlota and conceded, 'Very well, then. You may go with Bernadette. And you, Bernadette,' he added for his wife's benefit, 'are to mind your manners.'

'Bernadette and I will mind each other's manners,' his guest assured him.

Early next morning a collection of hats was swept into the air and magnificently flourished as the two ladies, accompanied by a groom, rode up to the mounted group of male huntsmen and female spectators who had already assembled. Mendoza, who had stationed himself at the edge of the brightly chattering party, was dressed in a black linen suit. He bade them a formal good-day and then, handing his spears to their groom, dismounted to check their saddles' girths. With unsteady hands he examined first Bernadette's and then Carlota's. Then he mounted and, placing his horse between them, escorted the two women into the forest to join the rear of the hunt.

Throughout the day he said little, and the few words he did speak were addressed to Bernadette. He took absolutely no part in the hunt. At last, when the sun had begun to fall behind the suddenly dark trees, Carlota said, 'I have seen far better hunting in the valleys of Madrid.' At this he requested Bernadette's permission to leave them to join in the last drive of the day.

'But of course,' she replied.

The Condesa said, 'Who knows, perhaps you will change my opinion.'

He took his position at the extreme right end of the line. In his black suit he stood out from the others, for by now most of the huntsmen had removed their jackets, which were draped behind them across their mounts' haunches. They rode in their shirt-sleeves, a scatter of white-clad figures to his left, many of them half drunk by this time. Suddenly, from some place ahead where the beaters were lost to view in the forest, there came a trilling cry followed by a stillness, in which the rustle of a leaf could be as distinctly heard as a pistol shot. The darkness was now growing rapidly.

There came a trumpeting. They could see the bushes moving as something thrust through them, and then the speeding hulk of a great bull boar was rushing straight at the horseman on Mendoza's left. Seizing his chance, the hunter spurred down

on it with a shout, tearing a strip with his spear along its body
that ran from shoulder to rump. But the boar wheeled round
on the blow, wrenching the weapon out of his grasp. Spurring
his mount more violently than ever, the disarmed hunter made
good his escape.

The boar went for Mendoza. He was ready for it. He had
already reined in his horse and remained motionless while the
tusker sped at him like a missile. Then it was on him. Mendoza
moved and, as if it had hit a wall, the hurtling brute stopped
short. For a long moment hunter and hunted stared at each
other along the spear. Then the boar was dead.

It was a full five feet in length, and they estimated the
weight at two hundred and sixty pounds. In the dusk, as they
gathered round to examine the kill, a drunken man said, 'It
was a lucky thing you didn't have time to think, Mendoza.'

'I had time in plenty, but it was only a boar, no match for
a man with a spear,' Mendoza answered, fixing his eyes on
the speaker, a foolish lieutenant recently arrived from Europe.

A sudden chill fell on the party. 'No, no, no,' the major
protested weakly. 'Bravo, señor! Very well done, very well
done indeed!' Other voices hastened to join in the congratulations, while Mendoza presented his quarry to Bernadette.
This meant the groom had to stay behind to load it on to
his horse, so, still riding between them, Mendoza escorted
Bernadette and Carlota back to the house in the square.

As they were riding off and were almost out of earshot, the
major, conscious that he must have seemed too ready to
placate Mendoza, passed some remark in a raucous voice that
raised a peal of drunken laughter from his junior officers.
Mendoza turned his head and stared in his direction through
the twilight. Then, turning back, he devoted his attention
silently to the two ladies. Throughout the ride he did not utter

more than occasional monosyllables, offered in response to the flow of conversation from Bernadette. Carlota spoke as little as he until they reached the gateway. Then she said, 'Thank you for today. What a pity the officers aren't up to it! Luckily one doesn't have to bother about them, don't you agree?'

'You do not have to, Condesa.'

He wheeled his horse round and rode through the now darkened streets to the house where the major lived. He took up his position in the shadow of the wall. Eventually the major came down the street accompanied by two captains, all very drunk until they realized who was there.

'Señor Mendoza!' the major greeted him. 'Is anything the matter?'

'Just now, when I departed in the company of Señora Bernadette and the Condesa, you laughed.'

'Merciful heaven! Not at you!'

'At what, then?'

'Eh, what? I was telling the others a joke.'

'Then tell it to me.'

'What?'

'Tell it.'

'It's not worth it. It's not very funny.'

'Nevertheless.'

So, miserably, in front of his embarrassed captains, the major fished up a joke and repeated it in the damp night air.

At last he finished. There was a pause. Then Mendoza asked, 'Is that the joke?'

Sheepishly the major looked at his companions and muttered, 'I must admit it sounded better the last time I told it.' The two captains exchanged glances and then looked away down the quiet street.

'I am glad,' said Mendoza, 'you have told me this joke. It convinces me that army life is not for me. You see, I do not find it funny. I think you should take care, major, not to repeat such jokes before civilians. Before the Condesa, for example. Yes, I would be very, very careful if I were you. Goodnight!'

Mendoza next met Carlota at a large riding party. Although they were in company, he seized an opportunity to get her to himself and made a grave avowal of his great regard for her. Then, before she could think of a fitting reply, he held up his hand.

'We belong to different orders, I know that. One day you will return to Madrid and make, perhaps, a fitting match there. I do not inquire when that will be. I prefer not to know. I am simply yours; you have only to ask what you want of me. It is enough for me to be by your side, like this.' He gave her a pale smile.

Carlota considered him and his inflexible bearing, and touched him with her whip. 'This is very unwise, you know.'

'The fault is mine. Where is the man who says that it is yours?'

'He will not say it to your face, but you cannot stop him saying it elsewhere. Nor can I stop you feeling as you choose.'

He was always strictly correct in his deportment, and besides she liked his rough talk and his hardness. As yet she did not realize that for her this grim man had opened a door in the fortress he had built around himself, and that once she had passed through, the door had closed behind her.

Just after the interview with Don Cabeza and Father Ribero,

a letter arrived from Felipe to say that he was coming home. Mendoza hurried round to tell Carlota.

'I should like to meet this little brother of yours,' she said.

'He is elegant, charming and refined. Not a man whom you would take to be my brother.'

'Yes? Take care, my friend, there is a difference between a charming letter and an upright man.'

Mendoza listened, and went by himself to meet Felipe on the waterfront. When the barge appeared and drew into the shore, he saw a slim figure which raised one hand to greet him. Stiff-faced, Mendoza raised his own in reply. The barge drew closer and, shading his eyes, he saw Felipe's eyes, the same detached, cool grey that they had been when he was three and Mendoza had fetched him his food beneath the high, lighted window in Cádez. His heart overflowed.

Felipe embraced him. 'Thanks, big brother. You see, I am come home.'

'You are welcome, little brother.' And then they fell into each other's arms.

When they were walking back to his house, Mendoza remarked, 'You do not wear a sword.'

'No gentleman wears a sword nowadays.'

'Indeed! A man without a sword is like a *capón* . . .' He broke off.

'What is it?'

'I remember when I first heard that. Gaspacho said it.'

'Have you met him again?'

'No.'

'You don't still bear a grudge against him, surely?'

'Yes, I do.'

'Big brother, you have not changed.'

After supper Mendoza, in his black waistcoat with a cheroot stuck between his lips, started humming a tune several times and broke off. He looked into the fire, got up and sat down again, when Felipe, touching his sleeve and looking curious, asked, 'What is it, big brother?'

'Listen, I am in love.'

'*Mi madre!* With whom?'

'The Condesa de Villasante.'

'The Condesa!'

'She knows how I earn my living.'

'Can I see her?'

'Tomorrow.'

'Pardon me, but what do you see as being the end of the affair?'

'She will go back to Spain.'

'And that contents you?'

'Nothing could content me more, little brother.' He looked pensively into the fire. 'We were born at the bottom; she was born at the top. If one can remember these things, one is content.'

'Yes?' Felipe spoke in a tone of doubt, for he had never known his brother to be contented.

Mendoza took Felipe, who was dressed in a brown suit, to meet the Condesa at an evening party. Felipe went, full of suspicion, and found his wariness reciprocated. She looked inquiringly into his eyes, and he peered frowningly back.

She was not, as Felipe had expected, his brother's age, but young and beautiful. Also, she was serious, animated, acute, deprived in Asunción of the same things he too felt the lack of: philosophy and music and the search for truth. At times a troubled expression clouded her face as she looked up at him, giving her a grave, even a wise countenance.

She had seen much, he was sure of that. She spelt no threat to his brother's tranquillity. Seating himself on a chair beside her, he turned to her with that air he had picked up from accomplished talkers who would throw off *bon mots* as if by accident and then apologize for being witty.

Carlota saw that he was handsome. Nay, to be fair, when he talked of something that interested him he was beautiful. Obviously he idolized his brother, yet not without a sensitive puckering of the brows for his anomalous status. Moreover, he was serious and cosmopolitan, with an excellent knowledge of the French writer Voltaire. He also talked to her about the English poet Alexander Pope, of whom she knew no more than the name.

Felipe was among the last remaining guests when Mendoza, crossing the candlelit floor, said, 'I think we should go now, Felipe,' and led him into the refreshing night air.

'Well, young brother, the cat has got your tongue,' he observed complacently.

'The cat has got my tongue, and with it my heart.'

And Mendoza said, in a hushed voice, 'There, you see?'

Many people scented scandal. Felipe and Carlota were closely watched, and many were the witticisms that were made about the two brothers. Bernadette, however, was the only person who realized that the foundation of a relationship both men had regarded as unshakeable was now being undermined.

As Mendoza, Felipe and Carlota went about their affairs together, Bernadette kept her eye on them. When Mendoza was called away, she noticed, as did many others, how Carlota and Felipe rode almost touching; and at a display of Italian fireworks, where they were seated far apart, neither had a glance to spare for the pyrotechnics, but each spent the evening gazing at the other. Blasco said, 'As long as they do nothing foolish – and you are there to prevent that – you need only watch.'

Felipe said to Carlota, 'I am of the same stock as my brother, though I have picked up mannerisms that remind you of the court.'

'Oh no. They are from the fashionable cafés. But what of that? They are good and they belong to you now.'

'I have no money.'

'Whereas I own a castle.'

'I am aware of that.'

She smiled. 'Which produces the rent of three large farms.'

'No more?'

'We can go back to Spain together and live off the rent.'

'What about your relatives?'

'What about the *hidalgos* here? They are all negligible.'

He kissed her hand. 'You are the most amiable person I have ever met. I embrace you.'

'Be careful,' she said, looking round.

A buzz of innuendo followed Mendoza around Asunción. Behind the sedate walls of private houses he was the subject of prattle, and an obscene joke in the corners of cafés. He did not notice. In fact, he rejoiced. It was as if these two, walled up in his mind, could indulge in nothing more than a brother-and-sister relationship.

Mendoza and Felipe attended a musketry competition organized by the messes of the garrison, where a number of marksmen shattered clay pans propelled on discs by Guarani. Felipe was just taking aim for his first shot when a door opened, and Carlota and Bernadette came in. He sent his first shot high over the clay pans and missed with all his others. Mendoza and a lieutenant of the guard competed for first prize, a silver tankard, which Mendoza duly presented to Carlota. To young Felipe, for it was a subject which he took seriously, Mendoza said, 'You must give your musket all your mind or it will let you down. You shouldn't let the Condesa distract you.'

There was a sudden quiet. It seemed that all Asunción was waiting for Felipe's reply. He looked at his brother sharply, but Mendoza's gaze was so guileless that he replied, 'On the day the Condesa can't distract me, I'll become a monk.'

Carlota, backing him up, said, 'On that day, Felipe, half the ladies of Asunción will become nuns.'

'Alas,' said poor Felipe, keeping it up, 'pure gossip. Mendoza is the lady's man.'

Mendoza quickly said, 'He is *this* lady's man.'

He made his way out of the courtyard with a darkened face, amid general laughter. Felipe went outside at once to join his brother, who asked, 'Did she say anything?'

'She blushed.'

'Blushed,' repeated Mendoza, and they walked home together without exchanging a further word.

———————

Carlota said, 'I must tell him.'

'Leave it to me.'

'He will not hurt me.'

'Do you think that he would hurt me?'

'I am not sure.'

'Then I must face him.'

'It would be like a boy facing a tiger.'

'Indeed? Then decidedly I must face him.' He strode off with Carlota after him.

'If you do this thing, I shall not speak to you again.'

'*Me cago en Dios,* I go now!'

'Goodbye.' He stopped. 'I mean it. Swear to me that you won't, give me your word. I will tell him myself.'

'When?'

'Tomorrow.'

The next day was the festival of the Guarani Madonna, which was made the occasion of a fancy-dress ball for those whose skins were white. Mendoza said to his brother, coming from his study and putting on his sword, 'Wish me luck.'

'Why, where are you going?'

'Wish me luck. Go on.'

'Good luck. But where are you going?'

He looked up at the sun, squinting, and then back at Felipe. 'I shall tell you this evening.'

He went to Blasco's house and asked to speak to Carlota, this time alone.

Blasco said, after a pause, 'I see. Wait here.' He led the way to a balcony, where Carlota softly entered.

Mendoza said, 'I have decided to put an end to this confusion. I have to ask whether you will marry me, yes or no. One word will make an answer.'

Carlota felt her blood draining away.

'The answer is no, I see. Forgive me.' So saying, he made for the door. She knew that now was the time.

'Wait.'

He stopped but did not turn round. She gathered her breath. 'I am to marry Felipe.'

The creak of a cart sounded from the street. He turned round. 'Felipe?'

'Your brother.'

He could not understand, came back and sat on the couch, frowning a little. 'But Felipe is a boy.'

'He is the same age as I am.'

He was struck by this. 'Of course, he is a man.'

'I love him, Rodrigo.'

He stared at her. 'Yes?'

'Oh yes, indeed.'

'Since when have you loved him?'

'Many months. I have been trying to tell you.'

He recollected certain incidents. 'So, that is what you have been trying to tell me.'

'Yes.'

He looked at her sideways, snake-eyed. 'Me you do not love?'

'Not as I love Felipe.'

'And how is that?'

'Gently . . . sensibly . . . That is the love that I need, Rodrigo.'

He breathed. 'Have I no need?'

She looked at him with fear and pity, wanting to comfort him but far more wanting him gone. 'You need so much.' She raised her hand to stroke his cheek, but with a hawklike speed he raised his own to cut it off. His face took on a masklike sadness, a grotesque grieving, like the strange Guarani carvings at San Miguel. He rose and made for the door again. She said quickly, looking after him, 'Rodrigo – you will not hurt him?'

He stopped and turned a face to her like the half-hidden grotesques at San Miguel, unforgiving, grinning like a wolf.

'Rodrigo!' She insisted.

He shook his head and left the house.

The city was thronged with Guarani, assembled for their Madonna. Carved out of a big piece of black marble by a Guarani hand many generations back, she was placed outside the Church of San Cristóbal, underneath a teak-wood frame to protect her from the rain storms. Mendoza, unseeing, tramped out into the country, walking blindly through the clearings and the brushwood, with his hand resting on his sword.

After a time dust clogged his pores, covering him with white powder. He took no notice. He felt inwardly dirty. His brother had befouled him with the woman he loved. All at once he stopped, halted by the thought that all the inhabitants of Asunción had been rejoicing over this. He started off again, and a branch whipped his face. He brushed it aside, thankful for the smart, and went on walking. His hatred was turned equally upon the guilty pair and the world at large. They were all false.

The sun was going down now. His farm was over the next rise; he would go there and sleep. The light of the fire lit up the surprised farmer who came to the door. Mendoza turned him out of his double bed and threw himself down there on his back, but could not sleep.

The farmer whispered to his wife, 'Do you see how white his face is, and the bloodstains?'

'I think he is mad.'

Mendoza came out of the bedroom and asked for a horse. He spurred the animal out of the farm and into the moonlight, with his sword dangling by his side.

As he drew near, he saw the walls of Asunción lit by torchlight from within, and heard the confused uproar of guitars and laughter.

Entering, he found the tumbledown shacks of the Guarani

servants on the outskirts of the town deserted, save for a few elderly natives dumped like heaps of old clothing. The rest were all assembled at the Church of San Cristóbal.

Mendoza rode through the bent little dwellings of tiled mud to the commercial quarter. Here, the outside walls of the houses were lit by candles, and mothers and children were standing in the doorways, looking up the street to where, out of sight beyond the turning, a chaotic din was sounding.

In Cabeza's house every room was illuminated. Inside it, and out in the street, people bizarrely dressed as birds, jaguars, heroes of the ancient world and satyrs were uttering strange cries and mocking laughter. The air was loud with the beat of guitars and the blasts of a trumpet. Those outside carried long torches so that the furthermost corners of the street were either glowing with light or suddenly plunged into blue-black shade. A dwarf, swathed in a shock of brilliant green feathers, came right up to Mendoza's bridle and grimaced obscenely, only to draw back at the sight of the rider's face.

Overtopped by a huge tasselled standard of the arms of Spain, Cabeza was whooping and clapping at the riot below. Mendoza looked at Bernadette, who was there with Blasco and all the other dignitaries of the town. She knew, of course. They all knew. He made his way into a side street, for he did not dare go back home.

The tiny square of San Angel seemed to draw him. He found it crammed to the walls with Guarani, all kneeling or prostrate before their Madonna. Not a sound escaped them. They faced the black Madonna. She was underneath a juniper tree festooned with flowers. Huge pots of clay had been arranged with a mixture of reeds and cotton waste burning in them, casting an eery light on the square. To the intoning of a Jesuit priest, they repeated a Hail Mary while a soft drum kept time. All hoped that their Madonna would come down and, by a miraculous magic and transcendent gesture, make them free.

Then they formed up behind the priest. The Madonna was eased out of her shelter, and they carried her away, four to each pole, still silently, out towards the first of the churches she was to visit before the night was through.

The square was empty now. The blast of a remote trumpet and the shout of a distant reveller were all that disturbed it.

There was an inn here which he had frequented in the days before he knew Carlota. He sat down outside it. Nobody came, so he banged his sword on the table. A maidservant emerged, stopped, looked at him, and retreated indoors.

A moment later the innkeeper came out, wiping his hands on his apron and saying, 'Welcome, Señor Mendoza – a thousand welcomes – it is quite a time since we last saw you here – this is an auspicious occasion – you don't join in the carousal up in town, then? – no, why should you? – it is idiotic, don't you agree? – thank God, the slaves have gone at last – you have been in the country?'

'As you see.'

'Does your farm fare well, señor?'

'Sufficiently.'

'You look thirsty – you would like a glass of wine? – I go now to get it – yes, in haste, señor, in haste.' So saying, he went back inside, preserving his usual deportment. But first he had cast a rapid glance up at the second-floor window.

Mendoza followed his glance. One window showed a chink of light.

Inside Carlota and Felipe were clinging to each other in the small walled space to which their world had shrunk, and she was crying. Earlier Felipe had searched the city for his brother and, not finding him, had become distracted. He would leave Asunción. After what had happened, how could Carlota bear to be seen in his company? He smashed a mirror. Then he set off down a narrow passageway to the poorer quarters of the city which Mendoza had shown him many years before, and proceeded to get drunk.

Carlota, told of his wanderings by her maid, went out in the dusk, dressed as a nymph with veils, and found him near the inn. With the whole town in bedlam they had taken this room on the second floor and made love. For a time that was all that mattered, but later he had to comfort her as she wept, rubbing her spine up and down with a strong hand and murmuring to her.

The innkeeper came out to Mendoza again with a bottle and two large stoneware mugs.

He called out, 'Here we are, señ—'

Mendoza snapped, 'Who is up there in that room?'

The innkeeper placed the goblets and the bottle softly on the table and did not meet his eyes. He shook his head.

'Pardon, señor, I have no idea.' Then he went back in and shut the door.

The square fell quiet. The shutters went up on the ground floor. The lights went out. He turned right round, looked up at the one lit window, and began to tremble. Slowly he got to his feet, went in, and tramped up to the second-floor landing. Felipe and Carlota heard his heavy tread on the pinewood floors.

'Listen,' she whispered.

The footsteps ceased. Outside the door Mendoza went to

the edge of the balustrade and scanned the moonlit roofs. His gaze fell upon the place where the outlying fields merged into the forest. Then he looked back over the roofs. The city was still brightly lit. What if it were not them behind that door? What he was on the point of doing would add a new indignity to the one they were already laughing at. The couple in the room heard his footsteps retreat and begin back down the stairs. But then they stopped. What if it was them? They heard his heavy tread come swiftly back to the door, and then it crashed open. The figure staring down at them looked gigantic.

He, for his part, took in two naked forms clasped loosely to one another. The two men's eyes met as if they had never met before. Then Mendoza spat full in his brother's upturned face, wheeled round and went away.

Felipe, sitting up in the bed, said, 'How did he know?'

'He thinks we have done this often.'

'Oh no! Rodrigo!' Pulling on a pair of breeches, Felipe dashed out in pursuit.

Mendoza marched blindly along the camino real to the square in front of Cabeza's residence. A few late revellers in their outrageous costumes, with Cabeza bidding them a tipsy farewell, stood talking there, making a bizarre contrast with the red mud and the carriages and the clattering palms.

Here Felipe caught him up and grasped his arm.

'Rodrigo, please!'

Mendoza stopped and said, 'Take your hand away!'

Felipe was shocked motionless by the menace in that voice. Mendoza wrenched himself free and then made off across the roadway in the direction of his home.

But an elderly gentleman in the costume of an ornate bird gave a nervous titter. Mendoza stopped. Here was the mockery which had been dogging him for months. He was up to the offender in two swift strides.

'You laughed?'

'Not I, señor. I did not laugh.' He appealed for corroboration. 'Did I laugh?'

'But yes, you laughed. At whom?'

'Señor Mendoza, you are quite mistaken, I did not laugh.' The gentleman licked his lips.

'That is a lie.'

Felipe said, 'Mendoza,' and his brother turned. 'Quarrel with me,' said Felipe.

Mendoza, though he looked as though this would entirely satisfy all his hatred for the world, said, 'No,' and turned back to his victim. Felipe tapped him on the shoulder and then struck him full in the face as he turned.

An officer of the guard thrust a rapier into Felipe's hand, but he had not time to find his guard before Mendoza ran him through with a thrust of his sword so accurate and violent that his brother was thrust backwards, to be pinned against the ornamental side of a carriage with two screaming ladies in it. So he died, looking into the face of his brother, who was forced to stand slammed up against his victim, not daring to extract his sword lest the other should fall.

Then two officers of the guard came, removed the sword and lowered the corpse to the ground. There was silence. Then the noise of the Guarani began to be heard. All Cabeza's hangers-on were witnesses, and Cabeza too. It was Felipe who had struck the first blow, so Mendoza could not be held accountable according to the law. But the whole of Cabeza's party drew back from him.

It was two weeks later that Gabriel received a letter from
Father Ribero, written in reply to one of his. Sebastian, who
had now found an easier way up the cliff, delivered it.

'A letter from the Father Provincial.' Gabriel opened it
carefully.

A dozen Guarani were watching Gabriel, as they did each
day when he sat down to make an entry in his diary, shaking
their heads. They still were awestruck at the art of writing.
The sight of print they were now used to, but the formation
of the characters by a moving pen was still magic.

'It is nothing,' Tanretopra had said. 'It is just a trick their
people have learnt.'

And Gabriel had replied, 'You are right. Perhaps you could
not learn yourselves, but your children could.'

'I have no children. Have you?'

About a week later a child took hold of Gabriel and led
him to where several lines of make-believe signs and symbols
were inscribed on the ground. The Jesuits were excited, for
they knew the Guarani were quick to learn. The musical
instruments they made, shipped to Europe, were pronounced
as good in ornamentation and tone as those made there. For
themselves, they had invented only canoes, long bows, spears,
cooking pots and simple looms and huts, and they were
irresistibly attracted by new skills.

This was the Jesuits' opportunity. They had built a camp,
with a little lean-to church and a small hut, by a Guarani
settlement. Antonio constructed an elaborate loom and
worked it painstakingly beneath the attentive gaze of the older
women. One day one of the women told him to get up and
change places with her. By the end of the day she had a
six-inch-wide strip of cloth woven on the warp. The brothers
were jubilant, but next day they awoke to find themselves

deserted. They stood discouraged among the abandoned huts and cooking places, and listened to the early-morning noises of the forest.

'Why do you think they have left us?' asked Sebastian.

Gabriel said, looking up into the ululating trees, 'It must have been Tanretopra; he hates us, and everything we bring. Perhaps he is right, save that we bring them the Blessed Word.'

They waited for a month and nothing happened. Gabriel said that evening, 'I fear we have failed.'

The next morning the Guarani were back. Unknown to the Jesuits there had been a fierce confrontation, with much shouting across the camp fires, between Tanretopra and his party on one side, and Hacugh and the older men on the other. Because of his skills with the bow, hunting spear and fishing lance, Hacugh had won.

On the morning that he led the tribe back, Hacugh saluted the Jesuits with, 'Here I am,' and received the answer, 'God be with you.' Gabriel told the others, 'Just follow their lead. Behave as though the past month had never happened.' All the tribe came up and greeted them, save Tanretopra. Gabriel went up to him and said, 'Here I am.'

'I do not see you,' Tanretopra said, ignoring his outstretched hand, and squatted down to watch.

Observed by the whole tribe, Sebastian and the five others began felling long scaffolding poles from the forest and dragging them painfully, inch by inch, towards the trampled earthenware foreshore by the river.

Breathless and exhausted, Antonio urged, 'Why don't we ask them to lend us a hand?'

Sebastian replied, 'We are the helpers, they are the helped.'

'Right,' said Gabriel, who was flat on his back.

When they had assembled twenty poles and begun to lash
two of them together, the Guarani laughed. One of the women
stamped her feet and, going down to the river bank, collected
some fine yellow reeds, immensely strong. She brought them
back to the Jesuits and laid them out to dry. They thanked
her, whereupon all the other women went down to the river,
collected the corded yellow reeds and laid them out to dry.
At the end of the day they were as tough as whipcord. Hacugh
inquired, 'What do you want to do with that?'

Gabriel turned to Sebastian and made him draw in the sand
an accurate picture of the uprights of a hut.

Hacugh and the others, gathering round, eventually asked,
'Will it stand up?'

'Oh yes.'

'In the rain and the storm?'

'There are much bigger ones than this that have stood up,
down there, for three generations.'

The braves reported this to the tribe, only to be greeted by
a shrieking diatribe from Tanretopra which lasted far into the
night.

Next day he was gone, and Hacugh reported to Gabriel,
'We will help you at your work and see if your Christ is pleased
with us for that.'

'Thanks be to God.'

'I have not said that I will serve your God.'

'He has plenty of time.'

'Maybe, and maybe not. Tell him that. We collect how
many of the poles from the forest?'

Sebastian looked reflectively at the poles. 'If only they were
thicker we could build an even bigger house.'

Hacugh looked at him ironically. Sebastian flushed.

'You make a fool out of yourself by trying to treat me like

a fool,' Hacugh said calmly. 'How much bigger do you want them?'

'About so big.' He indicated a size six times as large.

'Like that?' Hacugh pointed to a tall juniper growing in a clump nearby.

'That would do excellently.'

By the end of the day the trunk was lying on its side by the river, and the boys and old men had begun to trim its sides. In two weeks they had twenty more. When they got bored they went away, but always they came back. Then, directed by Sebastian, they began to erect the framework of a church, using the reeds to bind it. They seemed content to follow his instructions initially and then, having carried them out, performed similar tasks themselves. Fearlessly, they ran about high up in the roof-girders of the growing church.

Watching all this, Gabriel gave thanks to God. Setting his eloquence aside, he told them the story of the New Testament in the simplest terms. He found their questions about it probed his beliefs, forcing him to go much deeper than he had expected. Then the women came, posing even more basic problems. He was compelled to elucidate fundamental principles to justify the simplest articles of faith, so that he was lost in deep thought and prayer for days. Then he realized that they were teaching him, and loved them for it.

Tanretopra came back and installed himself some distance away in a dark, thatched shelter at the foot of a massive teak tree. He squatted there in a feathered head-dress, mixing the pigment of roots with blossoms and murmuring a harsh sing-song. Many tribesmen went to hear him and listened to his heart-rending incantation, painful and sad.

In the middle of the night Gabriel went to him, coughing

to give notice of his approach. He heard the shaman start awake, put on his feathered head-dress and recommence his melancholy song. Then he blew up the fire as his visitor came forward beneath the towering tree. Gabriel asked, 'May I sit down?' Tanretopra went on singing, so Gabriel sat down without an invitation, facing him. He waited for two hours, but still the sing-song did not stop. Then Gabriel drew out his little breviary and began to read. Immediately the high-pitched drone broke off, a skinny hand came swooping down on his book, and it was sent fluttering into the fire. Gabriel glanced at the breviary and snatched it out, dusting off the ash against his cassock. Tanretopra laughed softly.

'Well done, Gabriel.'

'What can I do to make you heed my words, Tanretopra? They are good for your people.'

'Good words, but false.'

'No. I may be false, but the words are true.'

For a few moments the shaman remained sunk in thought. Then, in a deep voice, he said, 'You have won, Gabriel.'

'Why won?'

'You have won today and may win tomorrow, but in the end you will lose. Do you not know this?'

'No.'

'Then you are a fool.' He resumed his harsh singing. Gabriel got up and returned to the camp, but still the painful singing followed him into the thick darkness, until the night sounds of the jungle drowned it.

That was how things stood when he received the Father Provincial's reply to his most recent report. With a long face he told Sebastian, 'He calls me to Asunción.'

It was a long-standing joke between them that Sebastian

looked forward to these visits to the capital as much as Gabriel dreaded them. He responded, 'I will come with you.'

Gabriel gave a shake of the head and made a grunting sound. 'Aye, if you like, then do.'

The next morning they set off, leaving Antonio in charge.

When they got to the Mission of San Miguel, they were met by Brother Ibaye, who had been left in charge of the great mission in Gabriel's absence. Gimlet-eyed, Gabriel sniffed into every crevice. He called for the accounts and asked many probing questions. Ibaye had the answers at his finger tips. At last Gabriel closed the last account book with a sigh of satisfaction.

'All correct,' he said. 'Oh, most orderly!'

Ibaye was a Guarani with lovely olive-brown skin. He answered, 'Did you think that I would cheat those of my own colour?'

'Oh no. I thought you would incline a little to their side. Instead I see that you have kept the accounts strictly according to the rule.'

'I see. You did not think that I and my people were capable of being faithful to the rule?'

'I ask your pardon. Bless me, Brother Ibaye.'

'I bless you.' He looked proudly at Gabriel and swept out of the little chamber. Left alone, Gabriel jumped for joy. Then he caught sight of a frieze of little brown faces watching him from the veranda. He cleared his throat, put on a pedagogic air and pushed his way out through them, for, in fact, he had no idea how to treat children. They followed him about, fascinated, clinging on to his cuffs, sensing that he was himself a child, with a saint's bravado.

It was raining when Gabriel and Sebastian reached Asunción, paddled by half a dozen Guarani. The low clouds scudding with the wind emptied their contents all day and all night upon the city, whose streets were full of mud, and whose walls ran with racing water. They tramped hurriedly along the empty streets to the entrance of the Provincial Superior's residence, and Sebastian pulled on the bell. After a while the door was opened by a brother who, when he saw who they were, came out into the rain and insisted on bearing their rolls up to the first-floor rooms which had been prepared for them. Then he brought two rough cassocks and two big jars which he filled with water, one soapy and one clean, in front of the roaring fire.

Father Ribero greeted Gabriel with a smile. Gabriel bent to kiss his Superior's ring and then, at the other's invitation, seated himself with an inquisitive glance of his sharp blue eyes.

Ribero returned his glance, thinking, 'How blue those eyes are! Is that a sign of something? Or is it just a badge with which God has marked out that island race – well, no, not God – yes God, God.' Yet again, he smiled. 'How are things above the falls?'

Gabriel, who disliked these smiles, replied, 'Insects and twigs, Reverend Father Provincial.'

'And how many converts?'

'None.'

'I see.'

'But many who are almost ready.'

'How do you know when they are quite ready?'

'They tell me themselves.'

Ribero frowned. He thought that Gabriel's regard for the Guarani as individuals was excessive. Mass conversion was good enough.

'Tell me, are they as you expected to find them?'

'No. They are far more sophisticated.'

'Sophisticated?'

'There is, for example, a shaman called Tanretopra. I have to pit my wits against him continually.'

'You don't think that it would have been better left as it was, with the Mission of San Miguel as the last outpost on the river?'

'No, Reverend Father Provincial. Do you?'

'I do think so. But you are the one in the forest. I have agreed that you should start another mission stretching from the head of the falls up to Portuguese territory, to be called the Mission of San Carlos.'

'Reverend Father Provincial, God's peace be upon you. As for us in the forest, we will do our best, guided by the rule of Saint Ignatius and under the superintendence of Christ.' He got down on his knees and crossed himself before again sitting down.

Ribero continued, 'I am anxious about your successor at San Miguel, however.'

'Here it comes,' Gabriel thought. 'I am sorry,' he replied. 'Why is that?'

'What is his profession?'

'He is an agriculturalist.'

'Not a soldier or a musician?'

'No, an agriculturalist,' Gabriel repeated. But why beat about the bush? It was better to have it out in the open. 'As an agriculturalist he is not handicapped by the colour of his skin.'

'Then let him remain.'

Gabriel spread out his work-hardened hands with an expression of puzzlement. 'But naturally. What else?'

'You know what I mean, Father Gabriel. Do you really

think this man qualified to take over the great mission?'

'None more so.'

'Has he any notion what the world outside the missions is like?'

'I do not know.'

'Is he completely subject to the Order?'

'Reverend Father Provincial, he would perform whatever you commanded without question; and that is more, *culpa mea*, than I can say for myself.'

Another ironic little smile from Ribero. 'I appoint him.' The smile vanished. 'May he follow in your footsteps and do as virtuously, Father Gabriel.' He extended his hand and Gabriel rose to kiss it.

Ribero became the host. He went round to the glasses and bottles near the blaze of the crackling fireplace.

'Wine? From the Captain-General's own stock. Excellent!'

He poured out two glasses, holding up his own to the leaping firelight to view its colour.

'Ah! How rich! You have heard of Condesa Carlota de Villasante? She has been staying with Blasco de Bigorente these twelve months past.'

'No. Why?'

'You know Rodrigo Mendoza?'

'Indeed.'

'And his brother?'

'I know that he has a brother.'

Ribero raised his eyebrows quizzically. 'To be precise, he *had* one. Let me tell you what I know.'

When Ribero finished recounting the tale, Gabriel said, 'They sound like a well-assorted trio. Why are you telling me all this?'

'She is here, waiting for you to see her.'

'Me? Why me?'

'I suppose she will tell you that.'

'I will not listen. This is merely a device to squeeze the last drop of excitement out of it.'

'But I am asking you to see her.'

'Because she is a de Villasante?'

'Perhaps. Remember, this day I have done you a favour.'

'In that case, Reverend Father Provincial, take it back.'

'I command you to see her.'

'I can be very hard with the guilty.'

Ribero smiled. 'Not always, perhaps!'

Motioning his visitor to stay, Ribero rose and left the room, still smiling. For an angry minute Gabriel sat there, waiting without curiosity or any other sort of interest. Fashionable suffering did not concern him. His duty called him to battle on a plainer field. Nevertheless, no sooner had Carlota glided silently into the room than he was impressed. The features of the pale woman who now composedly seated herself in front of him in the firelight, though youthful, had already settled themselves into a mask of resignation. He coughed irritably.

'Well, what do you want of me?'

'I want nothing, father. It is Señor Mendoza who wants something.'

Gabriel's expression was stony. 'I know that he has killed his brother and that the law cannot touch him. Now he seeks absolution too. Is that it? Well, I can't help him. God forgive me, I loathe him. Tell him so.'

'I thought the Church could help anyone.'

'There are better helpers in the Church than I.'

'He is lying here in the hospice.'

144

'Then let him be cast out, so that another can take his place.'

'You cast him out.'

This made him raise his eyes to look at her. He gave her a faint, cryptic smile. 'It seems that you love this man.'

'Not love.' She shook her head. 'Fear,' she said.

'Yet you are anxious about his spiritual welfare.'

'Father, listen if you please.' She told him of Mendoza's love for her, and also all that he had done for his brother out of love.

'I see.' Gabriel frowned. 'Has not one of the other brethren already seen him?'

'He does not wish to see the others. He will see only you.'

'He seized five people from the tribe above the falls, did you know that?'

'That may be why he wants to see you.'

Gabriel yielded. He would see Mendoza once and only once. Carlota walked back through the rain to Blasco's house. There was nothing left to detain her in Asunción. She would return without delay to Spain – but not to Madrid, not to court. Her story would be common gossip there already. She would go back to her castle and perhaps – why not? – to marriage if some tolerable *hidalgo*, who no longer expected very much, found her worth the risk.

Gabriel too went out into the rain, to the hospice. A lay brother took him to the cell and the heavy door was shut behind him. He had to peer about, for there was no light. When he became used to the dimness, he saw that the walls were running with damp. He seated himself on the only chair and looked at Mendoza, who was lying naked on the bed. Mendoza returned his gaze but otherwise did not move a muscle, until he followed Gabriel's eyes to his sword, leaning in the corner among a heap of dirty clothes.

'You took five men from the tribe above the falls.'

'Yes.'

'Where are they?'

A pause; then, 'Dead, I expect.'

There was silence except for the crash of rain on the tiled roof and the plaintive howl of the wind outside. Then Gabriel got up and examined a cheap wooden image of the suffering Christ. 'This man is implacable,' he thought, and the strain of his task weighed on him physically.

'To whom did you sell them?'

'I don't remember.'

Gabriel resumed his seat, tilting it on its back legs this time, balancing himself against the damp wall with his hands stretched out behind him.

'And you feel no remorse?'

'If I said I did, would you believe me?'

'No.'

'Then it was a foolish question.'

Gabriel gestured at the damp walls. 'What's all this about, then?' he asked with hostility. 'Remorse for your brother?'

Mendoza looked at him; his eyes were set remotely deep in their sockets, but he answered, 'Yes.'

'Then why hasn't God forgiven you?'

'I don't know.'

'Perhaps it is not remorse but regret that you feel.' The haunted eyes took on a wary look. 'Do you know the difference?'

'No.'

Gabriel experienced a flood of exultation. He thought he saw his chance to make Mendoza recognize his need of grace.

'Regret is only for the consequences. A lecherous husband regrets that he married a plain girl. A usurious banker regrets that he didn't charge more for his loan. And you regret that the man you killed was your own brother. Of course you do. Who wouldn't? But to feel remorse you must renounce the deed itself. The very deed must revolt you. Does it?'

Mendoza, still looking at him, made no response.

'How did you do it? With this?' He went to the corner where the sword was leaning and took it, glittering, like an instrument of justice in his hand. 'You enjoyed doing it.'

Mendoza muttered, 'I don't need your forgiveness.'

'No man can be as good as you must be with a thing like this unless he enjoys it.'

Mendoza looked at the blade, his breath beginning to come short.

'Take it,' Gabriel urged him. 'Are you frightened to take it?'

Mendoza grasped it and weighed it in his hand. At once his impassivity began to crack. Even as he opened his mouth to deny the charge, he was aware of a surge of irresistible power in his arm and shoulder, and knew that when he had driven that heavy blade into his brother, in and up, what he had felt was joy. He lowered it, replacing it gently in its scabbard, and went to look out of the tiny window into the night. He said nothing.

'Well?'

The mute figure did not appear to have heard. The silence remained unbroken. Gabriel waited for two minutes, during which his ardour was somewhat cooled.

'Well?' he repeated. 'What is your answer?'

'Then I am damned.'

'This sinner did not wait to be condemned!' Gabriel thought. 'And what are you going to do about it?' he asked.

'There is nothing I can do. I feel no remorse.'

This was what resulted from attacking the sinner and not his sin. Gabriel realized that he had contrived his own defeat. His own argument had been turned against him. He appealed to the sentimental image on the wall for assistance, but the figure of Christ only replied, 'Go on.'

'I have lost the way.'

'Go on.'

Taking the baselard by the hilt, he said in his thoughts, 'This is a heavy burden,' and Christ replied, 'Yes, he is relentless, that one.'

Suddenly Gabriel asked Mendoza, 'Are you prepared to carry this thing, your pistol and musket, powder and shot, above the falls?'

'Yes. What for?'

'The chief is there.'

'He will kill me.'

'You can turn back.'

'I shall do it.'

Gabriel left without more ado, and next day took no particular notice when Mendoza presented himself at the place by the river where the Jesuits had moored their canoes. He was dressed simply in shirt, breeches and boots, not like a conquistador, and he carried his weapons like so much luggage in a bundle slung over his back.

But all the other members of the party knew who he was and had heard the story. The Guarani paddlers slipped him dark glances out of the corners of their eyes and kept out of his way.

Sebastian was furious with Gabriel for imposing this incubus on them, but his protest received a short reply. Grimly, he offered the newcomer a paddle. It was his duty, as he saw it, to contribute his own strength to the voyage. It was also his pride. Conscious of his own power, Sebastian counted on driving the canoe continuously round to starboard, but Mendoza kept sweeping the canoe to larboard instead, until just when the furious Sebastian, red in the face, was about to ask Mendoza to slacken his stroke, the offender, frowning to himself, slowed down.

The shades of evening were already falling on the forest when they came to the first of their resting grounds. Mendoza hoisted his bundle of weaponry out of the canoe and, after a moment's thought, tied it to his waist. It must have weighed a hundredweight of steel and lead, but he did his fair share of the work. The others looked significantly at one another and at Gabriel, but the latter was looking elsewhere. Mendoza ate his food in silence and then, ignoring the conversation between the brothers and the Guarani, turned on his side. He could not sleep, however, and his eyes were as wakeful as ever when the firelight faded and the rest were overtaken by oblivion.

When they awoke in the morning, he was already up fanning the fire, with his bundle still beside him. Gabriel looked him full in the face and said, 'Good-day. *Dominus vobiscum*,' but he uttered no word in reply. While they said morning prayers, he threw himself on to his back, sitting up to take breakfast only when they had finished. Once in the canoe he guided it forward all day without a word.

Although he remained silent, after a week he sat up in the shade of the trees to listen when they said their prayers.

'Here,' said Sebastian, offering him a book, 'take this.'

'I cannot read,' Mendoza answered and rolled over on to his side.

For two days they stopped at the Mission of San Miguel where Ibaye gave an emotional greeting to Gabriel, who brought him the news that he was now the new head of the mission. Some of the brothers were jealous of Ibaye, in view of the colour of his skin, saying that he was not fit to take command of whites, but others were agreeable and all alike were swept up in the service when Gabriel, beneath the huge vault of the church, announced the appointment. All knew that they were eavesdropping upon a communion between Gabriel and God. Standing at the back, with a large space cleared around him, Mendoza saw why Gabriel was revered.

When they went on upriver, they left the Guarani but took on two new Jesuits. When he could speak to them in private, Sebastian told them that Mendoza was a little mad, but made no mention of the madman's spiritual condition; and now, when they said their prayers, Mendoza stood up for the first time. In response to Gabriel's gratitude, however, he replied, 'Your prayers mean nothing to me. It is just that I feel more comfortable this way.'

It began to rain, and they came to the place where the peaceful flow of the river was impeded by huge blocks of basalt which extended far away upstream – nobody knew how far. They dragged the canoes far upshore for fear of floods, and packed the lightest of their provisions into portable bundles.

Mendoza gazed over the rain-soaked landscape, stretching always uphill, till it was lost in the seemingly immovable clouds that capped the mountains. Sebastian saw how he jerked the enormous load of weapons on to his back and brought up the rear. In an hour or two he had dropped behind, out of sight.

When they started a blaze of twigs in a clearing, high up in the hills, Mendoza was still not there. With an air of preoccupation, Gabriel was reading. Nobody spoke. Then, silently, Mendoza appeared and lowered himself and his bundle to the ground. At once all the brethren started chattering, only to stop the moment he got to his feet to fetch armfuls of wood for the fire, still lugging his load along with him. When the meal was ready he consumed his plateful and then made as if to sleep.

Next day Sebastian watched the rain-drenched bundle bumping, sliding, wrenching and straining on Mendoza's back. When Mendoza stopped for a rest, he asked him, 'How long do you suppose you can go on with that? It must weigh a hundredweight.' But Mendoza did not answer. He was scanning the next ascent.

That evening he appeared to fall asleep in the folded roots of a big ash tree. Gabriel said quietly, 'Good. He sleeps.' But Mendoza, without opening his lids, replied, 'No, he does not.'

When Gabriel and Sebastian went over to their sleeping places, Sebastian asked, 'Father, how long must he carry that thing?'

'I want him to drop it, but he must decide himself when that will be.'

A scarlet millipede, six inches long, was where Mendoza's hand came down to help him up among the trees. He cursed and threw the twisted, involuted shape to the ground. Sebastian saw the blue-black of the sting on his wrist and quickly pulled his own knife from its sheath.

'Here, let me do that!'

But Mendoza only got a poniard out of his bundle and, holding his wrist against a tree, sliced into it this way and that. Then he wiped the blade and replaced the poniard in the load.

Sebastian said: 'Better bandage that,' but Mendoza was already off on the ascent of the cliff, with his bundle clashing and banging against the rocks. The rain flowed down in rivers.

Next day the sky, a level sheet of dirty grey, disgorged itself. Within minutes the wet ground was slippery. Mendoza's face was white and leaden with fatigue, but he slithered relentlessly along with his swaying burden, like a heedless automaton, up slopes and down. He had fallen behind. Only Sebastian was with him. All at once Mendoza was jerked off his feet. The bundle had got caught in a low forked branch and he would not let go.

Sebastian could bear no more of it. He drew his big knife and slashed the fastening. Thudding into the mud, the massive load began to slide downhill the way they had come, impelled by its own weight. It started slowly, but then, gathering speed, vanished over an edge into dead ground. Standing there in the crashing rain, Sebastian stared at his companion, but Mendoza did not look at him. He turned back without a word.

'Let it be,' shouted Sebastian. 'Do you want to kill yourself?' There was no answer. Mendoza was already out of sight. 'Do you think God wants you dead?' he called. No answer came from the pouring trees.

Retracing his steps, he came to the edge of a slope where, looking down, he saw Mendoza crouched in a puddle, surrounded by all his weapons. He had succeeded in collecting them, but was now staring at them as if he did not know what they were. At last, very deliberately, he spread the cover of his bundle out flat and began to collect everything on to it, methodically placing his pistol in the centre, then arranging his armour and, in their exact positions, his musket, poniard and sword. Only when the four corners had been folded in and the rope retied did he look at Sebastian for the first time.

His face was a blank white circle of skin, with pits, in which no light shone, in place of eyes. For several seconds Sebastian stood without moving, receiving that deathly stare. Then he turned back to the track to rejoin the others.

That night Sebastian told Gabriel, 'He'll never let it go.'

'What makes you say that?'

'I let it go for him.'

'That was foolish of you. Has he got it back?'

'He has. But he was going to kill me.'

'Was he? That ought to please you, brother. He knows no other way of showing his affection.'

Next evening they were back within sight of the river, now flat and calm beneath the setting sun. Sebastian checked the canoes. The Jesuits waited until Mendoza had sunk, exhausted, into rigid unconsciousness. Then, in one united body, they made their plea to Gabriel through the senior among them. 'Father, we are all of one opinion. He has borne his burden long enough.'

'I thank you for your opinion, but I do not share it,' he informed them. 'Christ laid that burden on him and Christ will take it off. Happily we are not a republic but an Order. I am in charge. May the Divine Care watch over you all during this night.' Then he unwrapped his oboe and wove a musical incantation over the dark water.

Next morning when they pushed off upstream on their rafts, Mendoza took a pole as usual, but made no response to suggestions that he should abandon his load, so that in the end they left him to himself. The thunderous falls were at last in view, and they reached them the same day. The Jesuits gazed into the drifting vapour and then at Mendoza who, standing apart, was staring at the cross. Gabriel knew from his set, livid face that the man was locked in a grapple to the death with Christ, relishing the justice of it. He would never seek to palliate his guilt, or weep, or turn to the Church for mercy. Realizing this now, Gabriel saw the error he had made in entering Mendoza in such a contest. He had underestimated the man's strength. He had overestimated the coercive power of hardship. He saw now that Mendoza was ready to force himself to breaking point. Death was what he sought. Frantically Gabriel prayed for guidance but received none.

They camped for the night. At daybreak Gabriel sent the rest of the party ahead with Sebastian in charge, but himself remained behind with Mendoza, out of touch, bringing up the rear at a distance. Gabriel kept ahead of Mendoza until they were half-way up the ascent, where he waited in the mist for the other to labour up and join him. Then he made no move to carry on. Without a word Mendoza lay down on his belly like an armadillo that had emerged from the forest, and drank muddy water from a hollow. Hair, body and face, all were smeared with slime. When he finished drinking, he rolled over and stared at the waterfall.

Gabriel said, 'You will kill yourself. You know that.'

'Not if you order me to put this down.'

'You yourself want to put it down.'

'Not until Christ has shown mercy.'

'Cannot you show mercy?'

'On whom?'

'On me, if you prefer it so.'

Mendoza rolled back on to his stomach. 'Did you not think of that earlier?' He stood up, shakily, and resumed the climb, with his dripping burden hammering the back of his legs and catching in the thorns that grew out of the cliff face.

Towards the end of the day Gabriel began to think about

their destination. 'What will happen when you meet the chief?' he asked. 'What will you do? Have you thought of it?'

'Will he be there?'

'I think so.'

'In that case, I shall submit myself.'

'To be murdered?'

'Yes.'

Mendoza stayed there in the gathering dusk, while Gabriel went on ahead to where Sebastian and the others had lit a great fire, and Hacugh, together with a company of warriors and children, had already joined them. When the greetings were over, Hacugh demanded, 'What is the silence?'

Gabriel looked inquiringly at Sebastian, who shook his head. Nothing had yet been said. He took Hacugh to one side. 'There is one who comes later.'

'Why later?'

'He is called Mendoza.'

Hacugh scanned the head of the falls. 'He comes alone?'

'Yes.'

'Why is he so far behind you?'

Gabriel explained about the bundle.

'Last year he took five of us. What has become of them?'

'Dead, probably. You will never see them again, that is for sure.'

'Then he must die and I shall kill him.'

'If you murder him, then I and the other brethren will have to leave you.'

'I shall be sorry for that, but I shall kill him.'

Then Hacugh went to get his spear and warn the other tribesmen. They talked in low voices. Hacugh went to his boat and took out his head-dress of parrot-feathers. He put it on and went to stand in the shadow of the rocks.

Sebastian came and stood with Gabriel. 'Tell me what to do.'

'I have lost my way, Brother Sebastian,' said Gabriel. 'Just stay with me.'

'Gladly.'

Thus they all stood for two hours in the darkness. Suddenly Hacugh stiffened. The ring of metal had sounded from the cliffs below. Brothers and tribesmen together, all froze. Five minutes later they heard a louder clang. 'That is the bundle I told you of,' said Gabriel in a low voice. Hacugh grunted, too intent for speech.

There was not much longer to wait. They could hear Mendoza approaching all the time now. The clinking of his load was continuous and soon they could also hear his laboured breathing. The group of Jesuits heard a stir in the undergrowth just down the slope and saw Hacugh moving stealthily forward with his spear raised. He halted and stood poised to stab. Sebastian glanced at Gabriel for a signal, but Gabriel gently raised his hand in a gesture forbidding interference. Flat on the ground, hauling himself along, dragging his lurching, grinding bundle behind him like some trailed excrescence, with his face only a few inches above the mud and stones and roots over which he was dragging himself, Mendoza encountered a human foot. Then he saw its fellow. The feet were dark and bare. Rolling over on to his back, he found himself staring up into a pair of coal-black eyes.

'Is this the one I met before?' asked Hacugh.

'Yes,' Gabriel answered.

Frowning, the chief stooped to examine the mud-caked face out of which a pair of red-rimmed eyes stared back at him relentlessly. Then he straightened himself and surveyed the prone, mud-coloured body in its entirety. He took a step to the bundle and picked it up. Surprised by its weight, he put it down again without opening it.

'He has brought this thing from his home?'

'Yes,' Gabriel confirmed.

'He must be strong.'

'Yes.'

'Why has he brought these weapons here?'

'He has no more use for them,' Gabriel explained. Turning to Mendoza, he asked, 'What happened to the slaves you took? Are they all dead?'

'Yes.'

'What?'

'Yes, they are dead.'

'What does he say?' asked Hacugh.

'They are all dead, the people that he took from you.'

'It is a foolish thing to drag those weapons through the jungle. He could have left them, having no more use for them.'

'He is still attached to them, although he has no use for them.'

'You joke. Do not think I have forgotten the debt he owes me. I have not forgotten.' Hacugh's hand closed on the hilt of his knife. Sebastian darted forward, but Hacugh only cut the cord that joined Mendoza to his burden. Seizing the bundle, he carried it over to the river bank and halted there. 'Come here!' he called to his companions. 'Feel that!'

'He is strong.'

'Yes, potent and evil.'

'I have not forgotten!' With a mighty heave Hacugh slung the enormous weight away from him. There was a splash, and then the water closed over it. Nobody moved and there was a moment's silence. Then Gabriel started to laugh. Laughter shook the whole of his spare frame throughout its length. Sebastian joined in, and then the other brothers. The Guarani too began to laugh, delighted to have occasioned so much pleasure, although ignorant about how this had been achieved. Slowly Mendoza sat up and looked from one group to the other. Then his body too began to emit a sound that might have been sobbing but was indeed laughter. He gazed at the dark river into which his burden had just disappeared, then covered his face with blackened hands and laughed and cried.

Worn out, he was not permitted to paddle when they pushed off upstream for the mission station but was laid in the bottom of one of the canoes. Passive and supine, watched over by a Guarani boy who was studying him closely, he too studied the moon riding with her stars beyond the festooned trees that leaned far out over the river. He saw enormous moths navigating through the dark, and heard the yells of monkeys and the snorting of wild pigs. It seemed to him that he had never noticed any of this before. His sleep was dreamless.

When he awoke, he opened his eyes to a blinding blue sky and turned his head to find himself the target of the gaze of a frieze of children along the river bank. He had been left to have his sleep out in the canoe. Seeing that he now moved, all the children fled except the boy still with him in the canoe who had been left to keep a watch on him. Boy and slave-trader stared at each other aimlessly. Then he tried to sit up. His whole body shrieked for mercy. He did not groan, but he sank back. Then he tried again. Gabriel, coming to the landing, saw the boy crouching down in the canoe behind Mendoza and Mendoza gently trying to ease himself up. Gabriel joined him to tell him where to go to wash, and all the children followed him to watch him bathe his body in the

clear pool and rinse out his clothes there. Then, squatting at
a discreet distance, they watched him eat.

'What shall I do now, father?'

'I cannot say.'

'Should I go back to Asunción?'

'The river is always there.'

'But what do you advise, father?'

'You could stay here.'

'I will stay here until I have made up my mind.'

'You are wise. You need time. You must consider.'

Loitering at a distance, Mendoza watched the Guarani
closely. They were building a church and some big huts. The
women were beating wild cotton that they had gathered in the
forest.

Realizing that it was impossible to prevent these new developments, Tanretopra had taken to joining the crowd of
men, women and children which collected every day to watch
the Jesuits say Mass. When the ceremony was over, he sat
and argued with Gabriel.

'Why did God make the Devil?'

'The world God created is not without suffering. The
Devil prefers suffering to happiness. Suffering is the Devil's
choice.'

'Then why did God create a world with suffering in it?'

'He wanted to create a world in which we could worship
Him.'

'And so?'

'Unless there was the Devil, we could not turn from the
Devil to God. Men have to choose.'

'Then let them know that God has given the Devil power.
It is the Devil who commands prowess in battle.'

'Yes, you are right. The Devil has great power.'

'And you also say that God takes women's graces for his share – tending and pity and self-sacrifice.'

'And love.'

'But I choose men's virtues. I choose bravery. I choose endurance.'

'Those are Christ's virtues. What have you to say of cruelty and cowardice and deceit?'

'They are great virtues when the Devil commands. Great virtues, great!' The shaman struck an authoritative posture. 'The Devil will win!'

'That depends upon how many rally to his standard.'

'Multitudes rally to him, and they are right to do so. Tell me why your towns and farms are built upon the backs of slaves.'

'Alas, I do not know.'

'I know.'

'Then tell me.'

'It is because you people are cunning. You worship the Devil in secret and pretend that you worship this Christ.'

'So the brethren and I are liars?'

'No. You are the true believers. You serve the Devil's worshippers. You form the screen they hide behind when they do the Devil's will.' Tanretopra suddenly pointed at Mendoza, standing on the edge of the group. 'He knows what I say is true.'

Suddenly Mendoza found they were all looking at him.

'Well then,' Gabriel invited, 'speak up!'

'There are many servants of the Devil in Asunción,' Mendoza said. 'But there are true servants of Christ as well. Back Father Gabriel with all your might. This shaman is false. He is telling you lies.' In the silence which ensued he left, having nothing more to say, and went to the brothers' hut, where a bed had been allotted him. He stretched himself out on it. He had said nothing which he did not truly believe.

After that, as the days went by, Mendoza gravitated to the children and the women, away from the men. He watched the babies riding on their mothers' hips, asleep, or being bathed in the pool. His harsh features relaxed at the sight of them. At first when their mothers spoke to him he did not reply but turned away after a swift, curious glance. At first too he discouraged the children who followed him everywhere he went, trying to understand him. He answered their curious gaze with a threatening glare that drove them all away except Babuie, the boy who had watched over him in the canoe. Babuie was not afraid of his opaque stare but looked straight back at him with puzzled eyes. Not that he stared at Mendoza perpetually. Sometimes he found Mendoza's doings boring, and on these occasions, to Mendoza's wonder, the boy simply fell asleep.

Babuie would sometimes pole a hollow log across the river. One day he challenged Mendoza. 'You can't do that! Watch him,' he told a circle of his friends who were also watching. 'He thinks that he can do it, but he can't.'

Mendoza went down to the hollowed log at the water's edge, took up the pole and, squatting in it, launched out on to the river with an easy shove. As soon as he stood up to punt it, over it rolled, plunging him in. A score of times he tried in vain to re-embark. Then, rising to the surface after his last attempt, he saw the small watchers on the bank all rolling with laughter. He joined in. Then they came rushing to help him and show him what he had to do.

One day Mendoza and Babuie were watching an old woman

working a loom when she asked the boy, 'What is it he wants?'

'He wants to know how you do it,' answered Babuie.

'Is that so, Mendoza?'

'Yes.'

'It is not man's work.'

'I know, but I am not a man.'

'Sit there,' she invited. 'I will show you.'

He was astonished by the women's skill in communication, their patience and methodical ways. After he had received his first lesson in weaving, the old woman inquired, 'Would you like to see how it's done properly?'

'Yes.'

She put him alongside five girls in a weaving team, showing him how to play his part, and then called other women to come and see him at it. He found it a restful occupation. It employed that part of his mind which had been brooding endlessly on the death of Felipe.

Next the old woman showed him how to stir the huge pots of food for the men when they returned from hunting or gathering honey. 'How long does it take?' he asked, breathing hard.

'You can keep on with it as long as you like,' she told him, 'but you must go on without stopping. If you want a break, you must hand over to another woman. But it is not man's work after all.'

'I am not a man,' he declared again. Watched by a silent crowd of women, he kept on at it for hours, because it employed that part of his mind which would otherwise have been in Hell.

One morning he awoke in the early sunshine to find a young woman kneeling beside him. She pressed her hand to his lips, enjoining silence, and then led him by the hand through the silent village to a hut where many women had gathered. The woman seated him on a raffia mat.

'Mendoza, take off your clothes,' said a very old woman. He looked at their faces. They were all grave, so he obeyed, pulling off the cassock which he now wore to reveal his white skin, marred by many wounds. These they examined closely, inquiring how he got them. Some came from fighting with Guarani, others from fights with his own people. 'This is a warrior,' the old woman declared.

The space around him was cleared and the old woman ordered a pot containing a sticky black fluid to be held beside her. Then she was handed a stick of bamboo with a fanned-out bristle at one end. With this she very cautiously painted a wide stripe down the left side of his face. This she followed with three minor stripes down the right-hand side. 'That is good,' the spectators said, and they crowded in closer to watch while further lines, serpentine but firm-edged, were painted down his rib-cage and down into his groin, and then round his arms and legs. In conclusion lines were painted round his scars. By way of benediction he was then offered a young girl. He kissed her and said, 'I am not a man.' Then, after making a profound obeisance to the old woman of the tribe, he went out.

'What does this mean?' he asked Sebastian.

'It means that the tribe accepts you. Can you not now, through Christ, accept yourself?'

'It is not in my power.'

The men took him hunting. Shouting, they steered a hog to where he stood drawn back like a bow with his spear at the ready. It was fizzing with rage. He made no move. The hog halted to stare at him with bloodshot eyes and then ambled off into the forest with tail high and rump thrust up.

'Why didn't you kill it?' Babuie demanded.

163

'I do not know. Forgive me,' he said to the assembled hunters, but the eldest of them nodded and turned away.

'I have no faith in all this,' Gabriel told Sebastian.

One day Mendoza went into the forest. He looked up and saw tree-tops with monkeys playing in them meeting a hundred feet above his head. He looked down and there was Tanretopra, seated at the foot of a tree.

'You are not a Christian,' he said. 'I have been watching you.'

'Yes I am. I am a Christian.'

The shaman raised his hand to shake a finger at him. 'Take care. This Christ may be only a little god, but a god is what he is.'

'He is the one God. All other gods are devils.'

Tanretopra grinned at him. 'You do not believe in Christ at all.' He rose to his feet and disappeared into the forest, but his voice declared, 'The Devil is your god.'

'That may be so, but still the only God is Christ,' Mendoza called after him.

Gabriel had taken good care to explain to the Guarani that at their Masses the brethren consumed the blood and flesh of Christ himself. As a result they held the Jesuits in awe, watching in strict silence when they administered the sacraments to one another, but they could not be persuaded to take the Mass themselves.

'Why will you not take the Mass?' he asked Hacugh. 'It is a joy. It is an honour.'

'Why does not he?' Hacugh pointed to Mendoza.

'Because he has committed a crime against God, and does not believe he is forgiven. Is that not true?' He appealed to Mendoza.

'Yes, that is true. And it is nobody's concern but mine.'

Hacugh's expression became watchful. 'I will take it when I see you take it.' He nodded and turned away. The other men followed him.

Gabriel asked Mendoza, 'Is your judgement higher than that of the Society of Jesus?'

'It is in such a case. I learned that at my mother's knee. Is it not so?'

Gabriel drove his fist into his palm and answered, 'Yes, it is. But still, you are mistaken. I who have watched you say that Christ has forgiven you. I beg you to consider that.'

Mendoza went away to think. There were only two who could judge his conscience: himself and Christ. But what if he were to be received into the Society of Jesus? As to whether he was fit for that, not he but Father Ribero in Asunción was the appointed judge. And if he were judged fit, then that could only mean Christ had forgiven him. In this way his problem could be solved for him by someone else. He had watched the happy brothers joking together, and realized that they were all united in obedience. It would be a good life here, among the Guarani, with the brothers to keep spiritual watch over him. Perhaps he would be permitted to stay, not as an ordained priest but as a lay brother, having taken his vows. It would be good to die at the mission, without ever having run the risk again of doing what was unacceptable to Christ.

In his tiny cell enormous insects veered into the candle flame, to fall dead with shrivelled wings; a ceaseless whispering of wind could be heard from the leaves outside, and there was the steady croak of frogs. He repeated a passage he had conned from Sebastian's Bible: 'Though I have all faith, so that I could remove mountains, and have not love, I am nothing. And though I bestow all my goods to feed the poor, and though I give my body to be burned, and have not love, it profiteth me nothing.'

If Christ accepted him as a lay brother, He would accept him as a being capable of love. 'Love suffereth long and is kind; love envieth not; love is not puffed up . . .' Love, say, for the Guarani. They told the truth. A black beetle banked in through the window and droned on towards the flame. He blew out the candle and listened to the beetle careering around the cell. Then came a steady drone that sank into silence. It had escaped, and his heart took flight with it.

'When I was a child, I spake as a child, I understood as a child, I thought as a child; but when I became a man, I put away childish things . . .' Catalina, his mother, had told him that.

'But now abideth faith, hope, love, these three; but the greatest of these is love . . .'

He went to Gabriel's cell, to present his request in the name of his love for the Guarani.

Gabriel was incensed. He lit his candle and asked, 'Now what in the name of Michael has put this into your head?'

'If Christ accepts me as a lay brother, I shall know that he accepts me at the Mass.'

Heavens above, but the fellow was no better than an idiot! 'But it wouldn't be Christ who accepted you. It would be only Father Ribero in Asunción.'

'That I know.'

'Then don't you know that if you made your application he would judge you as one man judges another?'

'But Christ would speak through Father Ribero.'

A man with the heart of a child! Gabriel asked Mendoza searching questions about Felipe and Carlota and the souls he had sold into slavery and the helpless girls he had violated. Then he warned, 'If Father Ribero did permit you to take your vows, you would start right at the bottom and almost certainly remain there. Do you realize that?'

'It would not matter to me.'

'I will write to the Provincial Superior, seeking his opinion.'

Mendoza went, leaving Gabriel to ponder the irony of the situation. When the Guarani saw Mendoza take the Mass, they would all take it too and proclaim themselves Christians. Mendoza had been guilty of enormous crimes against them, but in their mind he had a special place. He despatched a long and complicated letter to Ribero.

It took several months to reach Ribero, who roared with laughter at the array of saints and fathers whom Gabriel had mustered, first on one hand and then upon the other. It was clear that the writer longed for the request to be granted, and he obliged with an affirmative response which cost him two hours' effort in the composition, as he knew it would be gone through with a mental toothcomb. In common with the other Jesuits who knew Gabriel, he regarded him as a nagging saint.

On receipt of the letter Gabriel sent for Mendoza. 'Are you still sure?'

'Yes, father.'

'Well, now it has come. Go away and spend tonight thinking it over. In the morning you will be received.'

So next morning, in the presence of all the Jesuits and the assembled tribe, Mendoza was received as a lay brother and took the Mass. Then Hacugh also took the Mass, and many other Guarani after him, and Gabriel thanked God.

Mendoza lay down and slept. He dreamed of Felipe, who was dancing, and of his smiling mother washing the cane matting. Next morning, upon awaking, he knew that they approved of what he had done. His thoughts turned then to Carlota, and he was thankful when the blaze of memories faded away.

Hacugh presented himself to the shaman. 'I am a Christian.' The shaman gave him a piercing look, nodded and turned away. That day he moved a short distance out of the village and, with two others to help him, built himself a shelter with a matting roof, high in a tree. There he sat day after day. He was there when the sun came up and when it went down, sometimes alone, sometimes with the other two staring at him.

With a sober expression on his face, Sebastião José de Carvalho e Mello, known to history as the Marquês of Pombal, backed out of the bed-chamber of His Majesty King José I of Portugal, and then, when the door was closed, smiled up at the ornate ceiling. He returned the salute of the officer on guard outside the royal door, and proceeded with a firm tread beneath a row of lamps illuminating a series of paintings in which pompously benign generals, watched by angels, were depicted in the act of extending clemency to the kneeling or prostrate figures of alien wretches, ignorant of the True Faith, whom they had just defeated. Carvalho, who regarded the True Faith as an irrelevance and the Church as an obstruction, found these glorifications of the servants of the Crown old fashioned. Here in Lisbon, on the third floor of the royal palace itself, he wondered whether subsequent memorials to his own service would display the same provincial taste; for Carvalho – still only fifty-one years old and decidedly the most useful man to know at court – prided himself on his cosmopolitan sensibility.

His views upon religion were particularly *au courant*, and he stopped to stare contemptuously at the portrayal of an event being celebrated by heavenly trumpeters, while on earth below them enraptured bishops were simultaneously thanking God for it – to wit the nativity of King João V of Portugal, which in Carvalho's view had been a national disaster. The bishops struck him as stupid looking: stupid but also crafty, like all clerical advisors, he told himself, especially Jesuits. Carvalho was no deist. Provided people in authority did not take it seriously, in his opinion religion probably did more good than harm. What harm it could do in high places, however, he had witnessed to his cost during the reign of the credulous dotard the baby in the painting had grown to be.

In his last years the fat, incompetent, devout old man had been invisible within a crowd of pale-faced clerics who had deliberately prevented him from even glimpsing the service-able Carvalho, waiting in the wings. Well, wherever he might be now, bad fortune to him and all success to his chubby successor, the rosy-faced José I, whom Carvalho had just left snuggling down with his mistress in the royal bed. When he was heir-apparent, José had chosen Carvalho to be his confidant; devoted as he had always been to the less energetic of the deadly sins, he was not hard to humour now he was on the throne.

So reflected Carvalho, recalling the scene in the royal bed-chamber, while at that same moment, in the said bed-chamber, his royal master lay back with lips parted to admit the cherries fed to him, one by one, by a choice companion. If Louis of France could conduct his amours in public, so too, José had regally decided, could he. All that mattered was to make it absolutely clear who was in the saddle. He smiled domineeringly and congratulated himself on the lesson he had just taught Carvalho. Carvalho might be very clever, but he would rack those brains of his in vain to work out how his master had found out about the secret meeting he was off to have with the envoy from Brazil.

'Goodnight, Carvalho.' He had waited to deliver his thrust until the lamps had all been lowered and his minister was about to leave him to his pleasure. 'By the way, as you're just going to meet him, remind the envoy from Brazil that he takes leave of me tomorrow in the morning, not in the afternoon as we arranged at first. Which brings me to another point, Carvalho. I'd like to be informed officially when you arrange meetings like this in future, instead of having to rely on my other sources to find out what you are getting up to.'

The astonished minister could not conceal his consternation. His response, the King recalled with pleasure, had been gratifyingly confused. Well, it would do him good to realize that a monarch had more ears than other people. As the woman (whom he had decided to make a duchess) pressed herself against him, King José decided to reward Carvalho's secretary, his source on this occasion, with a little cash. He rolled over and said, 'No, sweetheart, we'll have some wine,' finding that statecraft made him thirsty. In point of fact it was Carvalho, now passing down the corridor to his suite of rooms, who had himself instructed his secretary to betray his private meeting with the Brazilian envoy to the King. Evidently the fellow had been convincing. He must remember to congratulate him; congratulations spoke louder than coin, and the King would be bound to pay the rascal something in any case. It would be overdoing it to reward him twice over for one trick.

Another thought followed. Suppose his secretary decided to change sides in earnest? There was nothing to hinder him. But the fellow knew what was good for him. He, of all people, knew where the real power lay.

When he got to his rooms, the minister found the envoy was already waiting. He bustled in, offering wine, and then settled down to listen to the familiar arguments. The envoy was a member of the Council of Brazil, and these Brazilian councillors all said the same thing. This one came fresh to the customary performance but had no new notes to sound. He opened by lamenting the diminishing supply of silver and gold to the royal treasury. The mines were down to a mere trickle now. Heaven knew where it had all come from in the first place! But the problems of the royal treasury, he declared angrily, were of no interest to the grandees of Brazil – if you could call them grandees when there was not a single one of them who could be pictured in a European court. Descendants of mere traders or civil servants, they put on what they absurdly imagined to be aristocratic airs. Of course half of them passed their entire lives without paying civilization a single visit.

But their rusticity was only a source of amusement. What caused concern to the loyal subjects of the Portuguese King was their attitude to the colony. They seemed to think it belonged as much to them as it did to the Crown; and, as they were on the spot, no project, however beneficial to the treasury, had the least chance of succeeding if they did not like it. Unless their selfish interests were involved, no problem caused them any concern. Take the slave-trade, for example. As long as slaves were available, they cared nothing about where the slaves came from. The scandal was that in Portuguese territory nearly all the suppliers were foreigners. Take Sacramento. The slavers docking there flew the flags of every sea-going nation except Portugal: England, France, the Low Countries. As a result the profits of the trade all went abroad. Thank God at last for the Treaty of Madrid! Things would start to get better once all those thousands of Guarani the Jesuits kept secluded on their missions in Spanish territory were brought on to the market.

Courteously, impassively, Carvalho inclined his ear. This bit was relatively new, but he had heard it before as well. He was learning nothing, but then he had not expected to do so. What mattered was to send the speaker away with the belief that he had a friend at court who understood him. This he proceeded to do by thanking his visitor for clarifying his ideas with illuminating arguments and unrivalled information. Carvalho rose and, as a mark of favour, personally conducted him all the way to the farthest door and remained there to give him a farewell wave as he disappeared into the gloom of the corridor.

Carvalho quietly closed the door and consulted his pocket-watch – made in Augsburg. It was half past twelve. In another half hour a visitor the King knew nothing about was due: the last of the day and the most important. He had arranged a meeting with the Jesuit Father Altamirano, who stood as high in the inner councils of the Pope as in those of the General of his Order. This was going to be an encounter with a foe worthy of his steel, the meaning of whose words was not to be discovered in a dictionary but by looking behind them. Well, Carvalho was ready. The first important step in his career had been taken in diplomacy.

He returned to his salon and sat down comfortably to wait, folding across his chest the muscled arms of a man who had been a keen swordsman in his early manhood. With his confident bearing and his autocratic stare, standing six feet in his stockinged feet, he made a formidable figure – a fact he frequently confirmed before a looking-glass. It was not, however, his physical presence which created the strongest impression. From his youth what everybody had been struck by was the sense of some unquenchable fire in him. Impatience and resentment had left their mark on him since then, but the flame within had not gone out. Age was powerless against it. It was burning upon the altar of ambition.

His first attempt to make his mark had been as a hanger-on of aristocratic rowdies. When he arrived in the capital, to the neglect of his small estate, he found the Duke of Cadaval had earned a reputation by rioting in the streets at night with a gang of regimental officers, so the young Carvalho attached himself to them and did his best to behave no less disgracefully than his models. Nobody was more feared by shopkeepers. The Duke of Cadaval took note of him accordingly. Nevertheless, despite his convincing impersonation of a lounging bully, he loathed the role, and vowed that when his day came, as he was sure it would, he would stamp out privileged delinquency.

What sharpened his hatred of his lordly accomplices was their refusal to accept fully his claim to be one of them. As a Carvalho he was a member of the nobility of the sword, but they regarded him as nothing better than a farmer. He loathed them all, realizing they did nothing with all their privileges. Yet how he envied them for not having to earn their power! What bliss to be a member of one of the dozen ruling families of Portugal! To have enjoyed unchallengeable authority from the moment of his birth, even if he had been born a half-wit, as so many of them were. Inter-marrying down the centuries, what else could be expected?

It was not only envy that he felt for them. There was disgust too at the spectacle they presented, eating with fingers which they then wiped on damask napkins worth one year's income of an honest tradesman, or a year's rent for a fine town house. Many of them could not even read and write. They mismanaged their estates. They could not even drink without incapacitating themselves. They knew little of Brazil and nothing of the world outside it. They had to ask the King's permission if they wished to go abroad, but hardly any did in any case: outside Portugal they knew of no families blue-blooded enough to consort with. And yet these squalid no-bodies were repositories of unquestioned power – together with the ecclesiastical hierarchy!

The ecclesiastics were even more dangerous, however. They were more cunning, and the superstitions they fostered enabled them to maintain a steady stranglehold on the privileged. This was particularly true of the favourite confessors of kings, princes and dukes, namely the Jesuits. When death was approaching some royal sinner sweating in abject fear, a Jesuit could make him do exactly what he wanted. Those schemers knew what they were doing when they took such pains over education. It was madness to entrust responsibility to anybody who believed in Hell.

Ironically, it was by means of the only ecclesiastical connection in his family that Carvalho contrived to break into the outer circle of power. The only use the Duke of Cadaval could find for him was to toss him to the constables when the needs of justice called for the infliction of punishment on an aristocratic scapegoat. So he abandoned his first patron. Remembering that his uncle on his mother's side was a priest, he started to pay strict observance to evening attendance at his church, allowing himself just the hint of a smile at his own behaviour. His approving relative rewarded his hypocrisy by bringing him to the attention of no less a person than the late King's confessor, a Jesuit who saw through him immediately. Continuously promising that something would be done for the young careerist, this devious cleric kept him idly dangling for three years. Nevertheless, he was dangling where he wished to be. He seized this chance to study the ways of great ministers and ecclesiastics, and the spectacle of power stoked the blaze of his ambition higher. In the end, tired of being trifled with, he went back to his modest estate in a rage.

But life in retirement was impossible for him now. The passion to succeed was only intensified by the boredom which outdoor pursuits and solitary reading in his library failed to relieve. Fragments of court gossip trickling into the depths of the countryside served to remind him of what he was missing. Inevitably he was driven back to Lisbon, where he looked about him with an eye which was now as coldly calculating as success demanded. It alighted on Teresa Noronha, strait-laced and grave-faced, in no way pleasing to the officers but, as he realized, ready to fall in love with whoever might make a plausible show of being in love with her. Another fact he registered was that she was a niece of the Conde d'Arcos.

It took him just two months to reduce her to readiness to elope. He carefully weighed up the odds and decided to risk it. They married and retired to a small country estate, from which she wrote pleading letters on his behalf to her uncle. For months Carvalho waited to see which way the dice he had cast would fall. It might have meant life-long banishment from Lisbon, but in the end the Conde d'Arcos summoned him to a family meeting where, after a thorough dressing-down, he was offered the post of Minister Plenipotentiary to the Court of St James.

He knew he had his wife to thank for this, but he did not take her with him to the embassy in London. She had served his turn, and at last his foot was on the ladder. After all, he had never loved her.

Those who had sent him had not the least idea what use he could be to Portugal in England, a far-off corner of Europe, not to be compared with Spain, for example, or France, let alone Portugal herself, mistress of half the globe. English monarchs were not even Catholic, but members of some petty ruling house of a minor Protestant state in Germany. Their aristocrats, for the most part, were a crowd of *nouveaux riches*. A man might rise by his own efforts to become one of their viscounts, or even a duke like the soldier Marlborough. It was a thoroughly upstart kingdom. Carvalho ought to find it to his taste.

It burst upon him like a revelation. Unlike his masters, he was not reluctant to draw comparisons between the empire of Portugal, crippled by conventions he regarded as preposterous and rituals he found superstitious, on the one hand, and the bustling, noisy, energetic and above all prospering kingdom of England and Scotland on the other. What if the blood of the royal house of Hanover was not to be compared with that of Hapsburgs and Bourbons? In this particular kingdom the salient point about the royal house was that it was of no account. The business of government was in the hands of people who saw the direction in which their country had to move in order to achieve prosperity. Even the English equivalent of great aristocrats devoted their energies to their estates, enlarging their heritages by improving yields and livestock. Some of them even employed machinery in their fields. And there was no shortage of money. Instead ingenious ways and means had been devised to make it available – not for the poor, of course, but for enterprising people who knew how to set money to work, for this was a commercial kingdom. In England you found no antique regulations of the kind that were regarded as so sacred in hide-bound Portugal. The merchants might not be in charge of ministries – they were too busy making fortunes – but the whole kingdom was run in their interest.

He found his ceremonious manners stood him in good stead. Apparently the English thought of his country as a relic of the days of chivalry. He contrived to turn this condescension to his own advantage. Alas, he had no English, but luckily French was acceptable in enlightened circles and he spoke it fluently. He learned to speak the name of Newton reverently, and came to understand that his old instinctive distrust of the Church did him great credit. He did learn one English expression and made it his watch-word: *self-interest*. It meant the same as selfishness but was commendable, as he had always secretly believed even in Portugal.

He was not so interested in philosophy, however, as in the competence of bankers, the acumen of brokers and the ingenuity of new manufacturers. Fascinated, he observed a novel world springing up of turnpike roads, canals, shipyards, mills, glass-houses, kilns and breweries. He vowed that this was going to be the future of Portugal as well, if he had anything to do with it. Self-interest was the key, and that was something he understood thoroughly.

On his journey back to Lisbon, at the end of five stimulating years, he was filled with admiration and envy at the spectacle of the Thames Estuary. It thronged with shipping activity of every description, from great Indiamen to colliers' ships, flying many different flags and sailing to and from all quarters of the world.

In the course of his residence in London he had repeatedly received intimations, occasionally laughing, sometimes contemptuous, but to him always humiliating, that his own country was no longer a power of any account. It was merely the decrepit ruin of a bygone kingdom with an empire hanging on to it, waiting to be taken by a more efficient state. He dug his nails into his palms and vowed that Portugal would regain her proper place in Europe, thanks to the firm hand of a master at the helm – which would have to be his own.

Back in Lisbon he found nothing had changed in his absence. Ignorant of the way things were in the rest of the world, and oblivious of the cleansing breeze of self-interest which was blowing away the cobwebs of superstition in the rest of Europe, ecclesiastics joined complacently with aristocrats in a petty display of useless pomp, effecting nothing, ignorantly devoted to the antiquated rites that spelt their doom. Particularly offensive was the display of ecclesiastical power at court, where João V had become the willing puppet of creeping priests. The ministers had no policies worth the name. All they were capable of was a repetition of manoeuvres which had already ceased to be relevant in the previous century.

But woe to any man who questioned them! Woe in particular to the ambassador freshly returned from a den of thieves and money-lenders, even if he had impudently contrived to connect himself by marriage to that pillar of the establishment, the Conde d'Arcos. He spent a few unhappy months at home in the company of his wife, and then came to court to find himself an outcast. He made the only move open to him and began, as stealthily as possible, to devote his attention to Prince José. Perhaps in ignorance of this development, or perhaps, more probably, to thwart it, he was sent on an obscure mission to Vienna. Once again he left his wife behind, though not without a scene this time.

On arriving in Vienna, he was chagrined to discover that his mission did not entitle him to the ambassadorial status he had enjoyed in London. His chagrin was not only due to loss of dignity; there were practical disadvantages too. He was no longer immune from proceedings for debt. As a result nagging anxieties were added to the agonies of thwarted ambition, an ambition which he began seriously to consider abandoning for country retirement in the style of an English squire. It was at this stage, as he liked to say later when people hung on his words, that Fortune did him the one solitary favour which she ever granted him: the wife he had left behind in Portugal conveniently died.

The convenience was romantic. He had fallen in love and his love was passionately returned. The young woman who found this mature and sombre lover irresistible was not in a position to improve his financial fortunes. She was poor, but that did not prevent him from loving her. She was also a Hapsburg, which was a more serious obstacle. It meant his suit could not succeed without the approval of the Empress Maria Theresa. Inquiries to the Queen of Portugal, however, elicited the information that Carvalho's blood did just marginally qualify him for the honour he sought, and he returned to Portugal with a partner he could share his inmost thoughts with. No longer as tempestuous as before, he soberly set about securing his position with the heir-apparent, Prince José.

Suddenly King João was stricken with a flux. His death took time, however. It was not until over a year later that he was gathered to his forebears. Meanwhile, month by month, to Carvalho's secret fury the King's Jesuit advisors prayed night and day for the fat old man's benighted soul, and all the court made a great show of joining them in their petition. Prince José held himself most meekly. Carvalho walked warily. Nevertheless, remorselessly, a new faction was forming around them and growing so that when, at the very end, the dying man gave signs of recovery, there was widespread concealed alarm. But the signs proved deceptive and at the age of fifty-one Carvalho at last found himself in possession of the power he had so long been conscious of deserving.

The late King had done little to merit a heartfelt response to the tolling and chanting which now filled the air. Knowing how little affection he had inspired, Carvalho sneered at the mourning that overspread the entire court. There was no time to waste on hypocrisy. Those whom the new King had called to power must bestir themselves to drag the kingdom into the light of day. The first task was to destroy the influence of the Church.

He was appointed Minister for Foreign Affairs, the Empire and War. The new Prime Minister was a very happy choice, being an innocuous dotard whose antique presence would serve as a cloak for innovations. The only other minister who ranked above Carvalho was a courtier of the old school, whose interest in society was confined to pedigrees.

The field was clear for Carvalho and he had his programme ready. At home he started by tackling the immediate debts the old King had incurred as a consequence of his munificence to the Church. The time-honoured way of dealing with such a burden was to perpetuate it. Carvalho's was to clear it. Then, faithful to his early memories, he clamped down on gentlemanly street rowdyism in a series of harsh edicts which he then made sure were strictly enforced.

Pope Benedict XIV, whom he suspected to be an atheist, had rewarded João V with the title of 'Most Faithful King'. Carvalho's first foray in the field of foreign affairs was to claim that José I now inherited this honorific and, accordingly, refuse to accept missives from His Holiness that were not properly addressed. This was no more than a mild foretaste of the treatment he was to hand out to abbeys and religious orders at home. A more serious diplomatic problem was posed by the Treaty of Madrid.

As he had inherited this agreement with Spain from his predecessors, he had initially been tempted to abrogate it. The Treaty sought to end the long-established friction between the two empires in South America. Carvalho at first could see no harm in permitting that friction to continue. Upon closer examination of the terms and circumstances, however, he perceived that the Treaty was to Portugal's advantage at the expense of Spain. Centuries ago a pope had taken a pair of callipers to divide a map of the world into two halves, one for each of the two Catholic kingdoms, drawing an imaginary line between Brazil, which went to Portugal, and the Río de la Plata, which fell to Spain. The recently concluded Treaty of Madrid shifted this boundary. Portugal was to lose the haven of Sacramento to Spain. In return Spain was to transfer to Portugal certain territories which included the areas occupied by the Jesuit missions.

Portugal, Carvalho calculated with the eye for profit and loss which he had acquired in the city of London, benefited by both halves of the exchange. Even the loss of Sacramento must be accounted a gain. In the first place, although a port it contributed nothing to the treasury. It was also of no commercial benefit to Portugal. The only people to make commercial use of it were the English, French, and Dutch slave-traders about whom the envoy had just been enviously complaining. Moreover, as he also learned from three naval captains whom he took the trouble to consult, the place was a nest of pirates which an up-to-date administration would have to eliminate.

That would be a difficult and expensive business, calling for a full-scale naval expedition. Far from being a source of revenue, therefore, Sacramento constituted a heavy liability and that was not what colonial possessions were for. Fortunately, if the liability was passed on to the Spaniards, they could be counted on to meet it; although the pirates of Sacramento plundered Portuguese and Spanish vessels impartially, the position of the Spanish port of Buenos Aires would cause Spanish trade to suffer most.

The surrender of territory by the Portuguese, therefore, landed the Spaniards with a liability. The surrender of territory by the Spaniards, on the other hand, endowed the Portuguese with an enormous asset. Carvalho found it hard to believe that the Spaniards would execute it in good faith. To make sure, he cautiously sounded out the opinion of Spaniards who were on the spot by establishing contact with the Spanish Captain-General at Asunción. He found this dignitary, whose name was Cabeza, enthusiastically eager to become a subject of the Crown of Portugal, for reasons of self-interest which were after Carvalho's own heart. A further point of sympathy was hostility to the Society of Jesus.

The Jesuits, as he now learned, had caused an artificial shortage of slaves in the colony by keeping thousands of Guarani tribesmen in their missions and thus off the open market. The existing Spanish law forbidding slavery was bad enough, and the settlers were counting on the Crown of Portugal to abolish it. Nevertheless, it was possible to escape the prohibition in practice while observing it in the letter. What could not be infringed were the peculiar rights granted to the Jesuits by the Crown of Spain, because the Jesuits were there to protect the Guarani. As a result thousands of Guarani idled their lives away under Jesuit protection instead of making a contribution to the prosperity of the colony by working properly for the industrious settlers. As long as the colony remained a Spanish possession there was nothing the Captain-General could do to rectify this deplorable state of affairs. For this reason the colonists all hailed the Treaty of Madrid as their salvation.

Cabeza was a curious fellow. A fourth-generation colonial, apparently he did not feel the slightest desire to visit Europe. But he was clearly going to be useful. He had an eye for essentials. For instance, he had already estimated and reported that taxes on the land now belonging to the Jesuit missions could be raised to ten times their present sum as soon as the Jesuits were deprived of their control over them. He was a good Catholic – quite devout apparently – and yet commendably possessed by a banked-down fire against Saint Ignatius Loyola and his mischievous Order. Carvalho reflected with satisfaction that their enemies were increasing every day. Madrid itself, Carvalho was sure, would be secretly relieved to see the last of those missions. They were a bulwark of the old paternalistic order and had no place in the settlers' more up-to-date view of what the colonies were for.

The Jesuits, however, still remained to be dealt with. There ought to be a special section of the law dealing with sanctimonious meddlers who thought they were a law unto themselves, to make it easy to place them where they deserved to be, out of harm's way. Gaol was the proper place for people who tried to create a state of their own within every state prepared to tolerate their presence. They even collected their own revenue! Well, he would be happy to knock one more nail into their coffin. South America was really the only place where they still counted as a force to be reckoned with. Everywhere else they were adroitly giving way without appearing to do so. They knew that their days were numbered, just as their priestly claptrap had at last gone out of fashion. (Of course, if truth were told, they had never believed a word of it themselves. Carvalho had a deep respect for them as politicians.) In private nowadays, if their tastes inclined that way, or even publicly when it suited their purposes, they were not above revealing an acquaintance with the new philosophy.

In these circumstances he held a good hand. The Pope knew very well what was brewing in the courts of Europe and did not want to provoke a crisis over the issue of the Society of Jesus; the General of the Order also wished to avoid this. His response to the Treaty of Madrid, therefore, had been to depute a special representative to visit South America and ascertain the Treaty's consequences for the Jesuit missions. In view of the general situation it was not hard to guess what the answer to this local question had to be. Naturally it would have to be a lengthy process. No doubt there were significant local interests inclined to the *status quo* to be considered. That was why the veteran negotiator, Father Altamirano, had been selected for the operation.

Carvalho had not yet met Altamirano, but he had collected information, including the detail that the preferred indulgence of this priest, despite his almost venerable years, was dalliance. Also, according to reliable informants, he was not above taking a bribe. This corrupt priest was not only the trusted agent of his General, but also privy to the inner councils of

the Holy Father, so he must know which way the wind was
blowing and could be relied upon to reach the conclusion he
was being sent across the ocean to arrive at. In any case, if he
chose not to cooperate . . . Seated now in his salon, awaiting
the arrival of this very special dignitary, Carvalho struck the
globe beside his chair a smack in the region of Asunción that
sent it spinning.

Altamirano, approaching at that moment down the gloomy
corridor, treading softly in the wake of a tip-toeing under-
secretary, did not affect the dark habit that might have been
expected of him. Indeed, the figure he cut was suited to
more vivacious, brilliant surroundings. Due allowance, he was
thinking, should of course be made for official mourning for
the defunct King – a deplorable creature! Nevertheless, the
total lack of social activity in Lisbon as early as midnight did
compel certain comparisons – for instance, with Versailles. He
allowed himself a smile of reminiscence, which he prudently
converted into one of gratification as he followed the under-
secretary into Carvalho's antechamber.

His guide departed to announce their arrival, carefully
closing the door behind him, leaving the alert Jesuit to look
about him. It was a businesslike space, with a row of chairs
to accommodate a considerable number of people summoned
– or maybe seeking – to see the minister, and compelled to
wait hours for the privilege. At the long desk with a bell
on it he pictured an overworked secretary, delighted by his
position, sitting all day. There was a painting on one wall.
Moving to examine it, he found it – even though the artist, as
he noted with approval, was a Frenchman – dull. The subject,
a group of councillors, was admittedly unpromising, but a

perceptive brush would have made something more amusing of it.

Suddenly Carvalho stood bidding him good morning in French from the door of his salon and then advanced into the antechamber to take his hand. The under-secretary stood inconspicuously waiting at the inner door, so he could close it quietly behind their backs as they entered the salon.

Carvalho indicated an upright chair and stood waiting, a masterful, erect figure, for his visitor to be seated. 'Forgive me, father, for detaining you one moment. I must deal with this while it is still in my mind.' He picked up a document from a table. Altamirano, outwardly respectful, inwardly entertained, watched Carvalho's performance as he wrinkled his brows at the paper. Meanwhile the minister was assessing the papal representative. He had often sneered at the Jesuit Order's military pretensions, but there was something in the settled expression on this one's face that reminded him of an experienced commander. He signed the document carefully and put it on a pile. Then, seating himself and casually crossing his legs, he asked, 'Have they made you comfortable here in Lisbon?'

Altamirano realized that the man who had made this polite inquiry knew about the girl awaiting him at his lodging. 'Thank you. My Order has arranged everything as it saw fit. It is most considerate of you to think of my comfort, with so many other things to keep in mind.'

'Ah yes!' Sighing, Carvalho riffled the pile of papers on his desk. 'Alas, all this has to be got through before I see the King tomorrow morning.' Ruefully he shook his head, and shrugged his shoulders.

Courting scrutiny, Altamirano looked about the room and

nodded in the direction of a picture behind the desk. 'That looks interesting. May I?'

'What? Of course.'

The Jesuit rose, and with a natural gesture picked up a candelabrum from a side-table on his way to examine the painting.

'It's by Martin Schaffner,' his host informed him.

'Really!' Altamirano exclaimed with studied surprise. 'Was it, perhaps, your personal choice?'

'None of the paintings was my personal choice.'

So there was nothing to be learnt from them, the other reflected. Carvalho knew how to secure himself from observation. He sat down with an air of frankness to meet another polite inquiry.

'I trust your passage to Asunción has been taken care of?'

'By your admiralty. Yes, many thanks.'

'I have been corresponding with Cabeza.'

'Cabeza?'

'The Captain-General in Asunción.'

'Thank you for reminding me.'

'He is in favour of the transfer.'

'So I should hope, Senhor Carvalho.'

'I mean, as it affects the territories at present administered by your missions.'

'I see. Thank you for explaining.'

'So, you see, you should have no difficulty in reaching a decision.'

'If only the question had been settled in the Treaty – then there really would be no difficulty.'

'Then you are of the view that the will of Fernando of Spain still presents a difficulty?'

Changing his position, Altamirano seemed caught by the painting on the far end of the room. 'That really is a masterpiece. By Tiepolo, isn't it? Superb!'

'Indeed.'

'Superb! Yes, your splendid admiralty have seen to everything. Do you suppose the voyage will prove as onerous as they make out?'

'I would say the burden the Holy Father has entrusted to you is not a light one.' Altamirano fluttered his hands deprecatingly, with a rueful smile. 'But Fernando of Spain was always an obedient son of the Church,' Carvalho went on.

'Of a certainty, yes.'

'Then do you think we have to be governed by his will?'

'Is there a provision in it that you wish to ignore?'

'Perhaps you will ask Cabeza.'

'Assuredly,' Altamirano answered in his frankest style. 'I am going to Asunción to ask questions.'

'Then you will hear from Cabeza that the missions should be included in the colony.'

'Indeed? And that would involve several hundred thousand natives, I am told.'

'You are told? You surely know.'

'My dear sir, I know nothing without being told.'

'There are about three hundred thousand natives on the missions.'

'If you say it, then it must indeed be so,' Altamirano smiled thinly. 'No wonder the *hidalgos* are so ready to change kings.'

'As the Treaty, may I remind you, requires them to. And you must understand that, as matters stand, these mission natives make no contributions to the treasury.'

'Yes, I believe I have heard that. And what do all these natives on the missions do?'

'Grow maté and make musical instruments, apparently, in the mission workshops.'

'Well, it sounds as if it should all be very interesting to see.'

'But what is your opinion? Should the mission lands be part of the colony or should the mission natives be allowed these special privileges for no good reason?'

'I shall listen to every opinion on that subject at an open hearing when I get there.' So saying, Altamirano closed his mouth in another smile, an innocent-looking one, seemingly unconscious that the question he had just avoided was the only one which really interested either of them.

Carvalho tried a new tack. 'There is another side of the bargain, as you must know. On our side, we are giving Sacramento to the Spaniards.'

'Yes. Tell me, what sort of place is it?'

'A nest of pirates.'

The Jesuit nodded. 'So I have been told.' A thought appeared to strike him. 'I shall beg the captain to keep a sharp look out when we approach those shores.'

'The pirates will give you a wide berth, don't worry.'

'Thanks to your naval escort. I am most grateful for all your help, and also for this instructive meeting. One thing I have heard already,' Altamirano continued very smoothly, 'is that this part of South America produces a steady stream of gold. Can this be true?'

One of Carvalho's qualities as a statesman was an ability to distinguish the possible from the absurd in rumour. 'No,' he said flatly. 'You only hear that because whenever the word "gold" is uttered, His Majesty's advisors prick up their ears.'

'Very naturally too,' commented Altamirano, shooting a glance at the other out of the corners of his eyes. 'Not all your royal master's advisors are as disinterested as you.'

'I am not a man to dismiss the thought of gold lightly,' the minister assured him. 'Gold is always a welcome addition to the treasury, but where could this gold they all talk about be coming from? Not from the earlier inhabitants. The Río de la Plata isn't Peru. You'll find no ancient ruins there that used to be ablaze with bullion, and there aren't any mines in the jungle either. Even if the gold was lying there, waiting to be extracted, the natives wouldn't know what to do about it.' He shot a sharp glance at his questioner. 'Unless it were on the mission lands and the holy fathers showed them how to get at it. There is a story going to that effect, you know.'

'I assure you, there is no question of it.'

'As if you would tell me, if there were,' Carvalho thought. 'I know there is no gold there on the authority of the unfailing laws of nature.' Aloud he agreed, 'I believe you, although it does need something like a gold mine to explain the high returns you get on those missions of yours. They all seem to make half as much again as comparable plantations. If they aren't running secret gold mines, how do they do it?'

'Until I have been there and seen for myself, I can have no idea. Why don't you tell me what Cabeza has to say about it?'

'The explanation is simple, according to him. The missions have taken all the best land.'

'And do you believe him?'

'I have no means of knowing. No servant of the Crown is permitted to enter a mission, not even Cabeza himself, the Captain-General!'

'In accordance with an enactment of King Fernando, that is so.'

'As you say, by an enactment of a bygone king. It is by a similar enactment that slavery was made illegal in those territories,' Carvalho pointed out, 'but surely you would not contend that slavery will continue to be illegal when the Treaty of Madrid comes into effect.' He smiled his most superficial smile.

'Slavery will, of course, become legal,' Altamirano agreed, returning his smile, 'in the territory transferred to Portuguese administration. The question which still remains, alas, for me to settle is whether the mission lands should be included in that territory.' He sighed.

Carvalho felt the time had come for him to show displeasure. He frowned. 'In your honest opinion, is there really a serious possibility of a decision against inclusion?'

'Senhor Carvalho,' Altamirano answered, mockingly wagging his finger, 'you can hardly suppose I am travelling half-way across the world in my declining years to decide a foregone conclusion.'

'But nevertheless, just on the face of it, you must find yourself inclining one way or the other.'

Altamirano tugged his waistcoat. He was beginning to enjoy himself. 'Unfortunately,' he confessed, 'I find I have two turns of mind.'

'Indeed!' Carvalho responded drily. 'Which turn inclines you to exempt the missions from our administration, may I ask?'

'My theological turn.'

'And will you take it with you to that public hearing you'll be holding in Asunción?'

'Undoubtedly,' the Jesuit said, again tugging his waistcoat.

'I am never without it. But then again, my other turn of mind is always with me as well.'

'And what do you call that one?'

'My other turn of mind is distinctly practical,' Altamirano gravely informed him.

'And what would that one incline you to?'

Altamirano again wagged his finger. 'Oh, as to that I must wait and see. It will depend on the advice of practically minded people on the spot. I'm sure the colony is full of them, and they will all attend my meeting and tell me what to do.'

'I promise you, they will tell you to abolish the missions, so that the whole area can be opened up to enterprise.'

'Thank you, thank you. I shall store that promise away. But of course I must also listen to what any theologically minded people have to say to me. I expect there will be some of them as well.'

Carvalho sat back in his chair and looked at his visitor with alarmed respect. He had hoped to catch an inkling of the directive Altamirano had been given by the Pope, but found himself no wiser than he had been at the start of the interview. Indeed, he was now less sure about it. And no doubt he had also received additional instructions from his General.

'A glass of wine?'

'With pleasure. From a Portuguese vineyard?'

'Spanish. If it does so fall out that you have occasion to withdraw your missionaries from the colony, whereabouts in Europe will you put them?' he asked, approaching his opponent with the glass he had just filled for him.

Instead of answering, Altamirano held his wine up towards the candelabrum and asked what region it was from.

'Granada.'

'Your health!' Altamirano took a sip. 'Oh, excellent! I

remember being particularly appreciative of a wine from Granada in the days of my youth.'

'Would you perhaps take them to Rome?' Carvalho persisted.

'The missionaries, you mean, if they have to leave? I fear that Rome as it is nowadays might give some of them a shock.' He shook his head humorously.

'Please believe we could arrange something very acceptable for them here. You may count upon it.'

'Thank you. Oh, thank you. That is most kind. I shall certainly remember that – if the need should arise, of course.'

'A generous endowment, and their labours will be clerical, not physical. They will be assigned to study.'

'And teaching?'

'Preparing men for the business of life is no work for priests. My own opinion, I must tell you frankly, is that your Order is too much involved in secular pursuits – even in state affairs sometimes.'

Altamirano made an exaggerated show of thinking this opinion over before responding, 'Ah well, you and some others may be right to say so. I must confess, however, it is a view I do not share.'

He leaned forward in the manner of one who is prepared to learn, provoking his host to a prolonged harangue in which he dwelt particularly on the Jesuits' predilection for the spiritual guidance of the great. The memory of this tirade later caused him some dissatisfaction.

Altamirano bowed his head appreciatively. 'I have heard it said,' he admitted, 'that in France things sometimes are indeed as you describe, but until I heard this from you I had no idea that it was going on in Portugal too.'

'In Portugal,' Carvalho continued tartly, 'there are even

men of a certain rational frame of mind who go so far as to say that if it knew its own best interests the Curia itself would curb the activities of your Order, lest calamity befall the entire Church as a result of the presumption of a small but dangerous section.'

Altamirano, who was aware of the precarious situation of his Order, recognized this as a serious warning. Stretching back in his seat, he rested his wine glass on his stomach and said, 'As it has been left to me to judge for the Church in this particular matter, you can rely on me to judge ecclesiastically, not Jesuitically.' His smile this time was sweet.

A clock over the fireplace struck two. 'I must leave you to your bed,' Altamirano said, 'unless you have more advice to offer me.'

'We have said all that can be said at this point, don't you think?' replied Carvalho. 'Later, perhaps, when you have reached your decision, we may have more to say to one another. My bed, however, is another matter. Before I can give it my consideration there are more matters which His Majesty desires me to attend to.' He indicated the pile of papers on his desk.

'I am more fortunately placed,' Altamirano confessed, thinking of the attractive young creature waiting for him at his lodging. 'I will leave you to your endless labours.' He rose and went over to examine the Tiepolo again. Then he turned round to face his host. 'Impressive,' he said, thus summing up his personal impression of the minister, whom he also hoped was not immune to flattery.

Carvalho rang a little bell to recall the under-secretary from the antechamber, and Altamirano was ushered out with several 'God be with you's' for his coming voyage. Outside his coach rumbled over the flagged court and rattled under a threatening arch; then he was halted while a young officer of the guard poked his nose into the carriage.

Altamirano sat thoughtfully. Carvalho had not attempted to conceal his hostility and had delivered a threat he might well be able to execute. He would engineer a concerted move against the Society of Jesus throughout Europe if he did not get his way in South America. Altamirano knew that if it did reach that point, Carvalho would probably succeed. On the other hand, he had also indicated – for what such hints were worth – that if the missions were subjected fully to the terms of the Treaty of Madrid this catastrophe would at least be postponed. He decided to write a categorical report on the conversation to his General, and a less frank but no less forceful letter to His Holiness the Pope. Portugal must now be numbered among the enemies of the Faith, whatever claims might be made on behalf of its King to an honorific papal title.

Considered simply as a man, Carvalho, bureaucrat as he so boringly was, had all the tell-tale characteristics of the parvenu. Witness his pretence of ignoring admiration of his paintings while so obviously enjoying it. As a bureaucrat, however, he was also dangerous – one more sign, Altamirano reflected, of the enormous change which had come over Europe since he had chosen his career. In those days the director of a royal or ducal conscience had been a force to be reckoned with. Defending the Order had not been a grim battle in those days but just an agreeable intellectual amusement.

Nowadays, though monarchs still occupied their thrones, kingdoms were ruled by men like this one, and a religious order was too antiquated a mechanism to be incorporated in the new machinery of government. If he instituted a concerted move against the Society of Jesus throughout the courts of Europe, Carvalho was very likely to succeed.

Of course the Order itself had made things easy for him. Concentrating all its efforts on making itself indispensable to the old order, it had rendered itself suspect to the new one. He struck the window jamb of his carriage with his gloved fist, attracting the footman's attention, so that he had to change his gesture of impatience into a thoughtful stroking of the window through which he now peered into the night. Somewhere out there in the murk was the fleet that would carry him to Buenos Aires, across the at first storm-tossed and later sultry South Atlantic. This was the first inordinate journey he had undertaken for the Order and the Church. He was getting old, as he would not forget to mention in his letter to the Pope.

Altamirano had no faith in the simple cures of the spirit. Some twenty years ago he had tried treating the sins of the flesh he had no trouble in acknowledging with prayer. The attempt had been in Rome, and he remembered the unresponsive silence in the vault above him when his experiment had ended. Then, all at once, everything was shattered by a clamour of bells. Well, if critics of the Order wanted suitable targets, his case would suit their book. He smiled at the thought and, removing his wig, pressed his cheek against the embroidered linen lining of the carriage interior. A moderate meal of figs, white wine and duck awaited him in his room, followed by temporary solace in the arms of a woman who doubtless deserved a less venerable companion – more supple, less subtle – but who would still find the ageing man who had engaged her for the evening could enjoy himself.

In the royal palace the man he had just left was now the only person still awake, save for the night guard and his under-secretary. Carvalho, drinking deeply now, had shifted the candelabrum on to a side-table so that he could examine his Tiepolo in comfort. He was sure now that it was a masterpiece. Not that he was a connoisseur of painting, but he was a judge of men, and he knew his recent visitor's admiration had been genuine. The fact that the Jesuit had also been using it to create a conversational diversion was incidental. Tiepolo was a master! Strange how good Italians were at everything nowadays except the one thing needed – power! He decided to have some more Tiepolos brought into the larger suite of rooms which would be his before the year was through. It was situated at the end of the opposite corridor and contained eight rooms, twice as many as Pedro de Mota's four and what was more it had a balcony.

He foresaw the day – indeed it was almost come – when the proudest aristocrat would leap to his feet at the announcement of Minister Carvalho's arrival, whoever else might be present. His was the hand on the tiller of the ship of state, and soon the time would come when everyone would realize that the vessel had changed course and that thanks to Carvalho, Portugal was again one of the foremost nations, strong as Prussia, prosperous as England. He would be rewarded with a dukedom at least, perhaps a princedom.

After all, King José was already planning to make a duchess of his whore. One way or another, certainly, he must be raised above mere dukes, for unlike them he would have earned his title. He bared his teeth in a grimace which even his wife had never seen and, listening to prolonged applause accompanied by drums and trumpets, remembered how the ancient Romans had expelled their kings. Kings were not necessary. In ancient Rome men like Carvalho had been declared dictators.

This was not the first time these lunatic aspirations had invaded his mind, usually so cool and practical. The smothered fires threatened to scorch his brain. He had been forced to wait too long for his day to dawn. To relieve the blind force that agitated him, he got up and strode up and down the room, recovering a touch of ceremony with each turn, backwards and forwards. Then he stood still, drew himself up to his full, splendid height and condemned all his opponents, clerical and aristocratic, to death by hanging or at the stake. Suddenly he directed a guilty, cunning look in the direction of the door, reached it with long, swift strides and flung it open. The under-secretary at his table in the antechamber contrived to look genuinely busy before looking up, startled. Resuming his normal air, Carvalho recovered his equilibrium too and shut the door, reminding himself to be more careful.

Back in his office, his mind a blank, he sat at his desk and picked up a paper. Altamirano, of course! A typical Jesuit! There could be no knowing what was hidden in a mind like that. People talked of church mice; why didn't they talk of church chameleons? He chuckled. What a labyrinth of sophistry that lecherous, avaricious old sinner's conscience must be! (For Carvalho, all ethical questions were simple. He solved them on the spot by rule of thumb.) What he had in his hand was the last letter his agent had forwarded. It was Cabeza's fulsome welcome to the Treaty of Madrid.

The worthy Captain-General's thinking was obvious, of course, but sound. He was counting on the Treaty of Madrid to increase his colony's prosperity by releasing restricted land and labour into the open market. It was wonderful how self-interest could teach an unthinking man to see things for himself – things which the deepest thinkers of the Church were blind to. Dispensing with the aid of hypocritical claptrap, he was ready with one bold stroke to cut the knot that priests, entangled in theology, could never rise to. It must have called for enormous effort for this obscure Spanish settler to jettison the prejudices bred of ancient enmities and old traditions and voluntarily transfer his allegiance to Portugal. Indeed it was one more proof that the real law of peace was the law of the market. It was absurd that the decision about the missions did not lie in the hands of the Captain-General on the spot. If it had been a question of an English colony, he was sure Altamirano would not have been permitted as much as to set foot in it. That the final decision of a practical question should finally be left to a priest was intolerable, and now, after their interview, Carvalho was no longer even sure which way that decision would go! Well, whichever way that Jesuitical cat happened to jump, he could prevent Altamirano from doing any damage. Drawing a sheet of paper towards him, the minister began writing additional instructions to the representative he had sent to Asunción to keep an eye on the implementation to the Treaty of Madrid.

Three months later in Asunción this letter was opened by its addressee – Hontar by name – in the Captain-General's residence, where he was a guest. Senhor Hontar, thin and elegant, homosexual, with a long, humorous, sad-eyed face, sighed in anticipation of disagreeable reading and gazed out upon the exotic garden with distaste. The heat was stifling, and he wished he was back in Portugal where – a failed diplomat with a pedigree receding into the fourteenth century, ministered to by a valet who understood his tastes – he could live comfortably enough on an income which, though slender, permitted an elegant if unostentatious style of life. The confidence Carvalho had displayed in him by despatching him to this barbarous region, although flattering in its way, had been unwelcome. Failing a posting to Vienna or some almost equally attractive capital, his preferred residence was his villa in the foothills not too far from Lisbon. Here, on the edge of the jungle, he dabbed his sceptical, sweating face and tried to guess what Carvalho could be up to this time. As the newly appointed Minister of Foreign Affairs was fifty-one, he was in a hurry. Worse still, he was eager to wield a new broom and consequently Hontar would put nothing past him. Carvalho's views might well be sound, for all he knew or cared. No doubt the upstart worked hard and well, in the new efficient style. To Hontar, however, modernity was no recommendation. Long ago he had decided he had been born at the wrong time. In his own pondered opinion, he should have lived in fourteenth-century Venice, a grey-bearded savant living in a cool apartment by the sea, flocked to by muscular sailors straight off the wharves from middle-eastern voyages, and strapping soldiers fresh from frightful wars.

But here he was instead, in Asunción of all places, and involved in a dirty business, which contributed almost as much to his discomfort as the heat. The contents of the letter in his hand proved worse than he had feared. He was dismayed to learn what lengths Carvalho was prepared to go to in a final reckoning. What could it be, he wondered, that enabled a man to contemplate drastic decisions? Surely honour was not worth it – if you called it that – nor even wealth! Could it be the fellow actually believed he was called upon to be some sort of instrument? There was no denying a new spirit was abroad. It was no longer just a case of being greedy. There was something actively destructive in the air, and Carvalho had somehow caught it. What made it worse was that he was bound to win. Even if they tried to make a stand, the Society of Jesus would find they had no backing. But they must have realized that already.

All of which meant it would be interesting to watch Father Altamirano, who had just arrived, playing his difficult hand, because now his real opponents were his own people, the Jesuit fathers from the missions, whom Hontar had watched assemble at their house here in Asunción over the past weeks, in readiness for the public hearing that had been arranged. Grim-faced, resolute men he found them, men who would defend their position inch by inch. The new spirit received no welcome from priests like that.

Carefully assessing the actors who were to take part in the coming drama, he had already taken note of the Irishman, Father Gabriel. It was extraordinary to find such childlike eyes in an old face so ravaged by suffering. Even more extraordinary, though, was the one who silently dogged his footsteps: the Jesuit with a dark, scarred face who, despite his habit, looked downright dangerous.

The summons to Asunción to assist in the presentation of the missions' case had reached Gabriel two months ago at San Carlos, the new mission he had established above the falls. 'What question can there possibly be?' he asked Father Ribero as soon as he arrived. 'There is no argument on the other side.'

'His Holiness has despatched Father Altamirano, who has his complete confidence, to listen to both sides of the debate with an even mind,' was the warning answer.

Gabriel peered at the carved face of the Provincial Superior for a sign. 'Do you think it possible he might actually decide to close the missions?'

'What I think is that you need to make your arguments convincing.'

'I see. And may I tell this to the other brothers, father?'

'That was the purpose of this conversation.'

So Gabriel told Sebastian and Mendoza.

Two years had passed since Mendoza had taken his vows. Since then he had been at peace, working quietly, devoting his attention to the work of building and learning to read piecemeal at night. From his first arrival he had been adored by the Guarani children and accepted by the braves for the man he so recognizably was. The women also trusted him. He exchanged his inmost thoughts with all of them, and listened to their replies in a way that even Gabriel could not do. He frankly discussed with them whatever question happened to be uppermost in his mind.

It was not without some envy that the other brothers saw how easily he pursued conversations with the Guarani on the shadowy forest tracks by day and by the fire at night, and how the Guarani always stopped talking if another brother came near. Antonio in particular took it badly. He had always wanted to be close to the precious hearts of the converted.

At last he complained to Father Gabriel about it.

'Building is what you put him in charge of,' he pointed out, 'not the care of souls.'

'That is so. But it is Christ Himself who, in the end, appoints the pathway.'

'This,' Antonio said firmly, 'is not Our Lord's devising, no, certainly not. There is no denying Mendoza is a murderer, and now he holds new converts in the hollow of his hand. It is not right.'

'Then you should tell him so.'

Antonio found Mendoza at work in the forest, sat down

and explained to him all afternoon what was so objectionable about his intimacy with the Guarani converts. Meanwhile Mendoza worked away silently at several felled trees and listened to his words with concentration. The sun was low before Antonio finished with the declaration: 'A brother must do the work that he is set, not invent his own duties.'

'I am not helping them with their difficulties,' Mendoza explained, 'any more than they are helping me with mine.'

'If you have difficulties, you should seek help from Father Gabriel or some other brother.'

Mendoza laughed and said, 'Brother Antonio, some of my difficulties are very minor. It is those that the Guarani help me with.'

'And what about *their* minor difficulties? Should you be helping them or should it be Father Gabriel?'

'Father Gabriel, of course. But they talk to me to prepare themselves to go to him, because they would rather start by talking to an equal.'

Antonio, astonished, protested, 'An equal?'

'I hope I am their equal.'

Brother Antonio fell silent. Then, in a pious voice, he consented, 'Of course. We are all their equals in the eyes of the Lord.'

'But also in the eyes of men I am their equal. That is why they can talk to me of the sort of thing that happens to ordinary men.'

'What things are those?'

'I suggest you work next to me tomorrow. Perhaps they will chat with you as well.'

But when Antonio did work next to him the Guarani did not come at all. When he slipped off, they came back immediately.

'You have told them to stay away from me,' Antonio accused him.

'They keep away from you because you scare them.'

'Me, scare them?' Antonio, frail and tiny, was indignant and amazed.

'Yes.'

'How?'

'They say you are severe –'

'But how?'

'They think that you are a misery, a moper.'

'Nay, truly – do they say that of me?'

'They all do.'

'Perhaps they are right.' He puffed his cheeks in his unhappiness. 'A moper. How would you describe a moper?'

'A moper cannot help a man to decide how to treat his extra wives when he becomes a Christian.'

'I see. And what do you tell them a man should do?'

'I do not know, they just discuss it with me.'

'What do they say Gabriel is?'

'A man who has Christ inside him but does not realize it.'

'Well,' said Antonio, 'that at least is true. And what do they say you are?'

'I only know they say that I build well. Now I have told you all I know. Shall we get back to work?'

'Yes, let us. You have shown me a great sin that I was unaware of, and I thank you.'

'I thank you too. I will remember what you said.'

Antonio was excited when he repeated all this to Gabriel. 'I think,' he declared, 'I really and truly think we have some sort of saint among us.'

Gabriel flung both his hands up in the air in irritation. 'One minute you tell me he's a murderer, not fit to be a member of our Order, and the next thing I know here you are telling me that he's a saint. Well, I tell you he's neither, but there's no denying he's fit to be one of us for all his faults – and his virtues too, if it comes to that.'

Gabriel realized that Mendoza's virtues were a soldier's, not a priest's, but after all, Saint Ignatius Loyola, the founder, had once been a soldier too and thought of the Order as Christ's army. In his eyes the missions were Christ's forts, outposts in a holy war. As for Mendoza, Gabriel, like the Guarani, was ready to accept him for what he was. Mendoza himself struggled with his weaknesses – and in particular with illiteracy. He would stay awake at night with pen and paper to sweat over a primer by firelight. It was a long, hard struggle for him to learn his alphabet, and when he had done it he found it no less difficult to join letters into words. The ease with which the Guarani children accomplished it filled him with admiration.

When he received Father Ribero's summons to Asunción, to assist at the assembly Father Altamirano wished to hold to enable him to ascertain the truth about the missions, Gabriel knitted his brows. Everybody knew the truth already. Enemies spread calumnies about the Guarani – not all of them calumnies, perhaps, but the obvious intention of such stories was deception. Everybody who knew about the missions spread their fame abroad as bastions of Christ's Kingdom. Altamirano must surely know this. What was his purpose, then, in calling this meeting?

The summons instructed him to bring with him any companions he thought likely to prove useful. He decided on Sebastian and Mendoza. Altamirano would be able to see at once that Sebastian was incapable of lying, a straightforward, stalwart, horny-handed ex-commissioned officer of a foot regiment. Mendoza, in his flesh and blood, was living testimony to the existence of the slave-trade, and in his words, should he speak at all, could bear awesome witness to Christ's readiness to employ the missions in his service. It was night when he announced his decision, and the brothers were all seated round a fire. Sebastian blushed scarlet when Gabriel laughed out loud at his schoolboy attempt to conceal his gratification by pulling a long face. Mendoza, however, was deadly serious when he shook his head firmly and said, 'Father, let me stay as I am.'

'You must not stay as you are. It is time for you to spread your wings a little.'

'I do not know how to speak. Take one of the others.' He gestured towards the others.

'You will not have to speak, except perhaps in ordinary conversation, and I shall be there.'

'I do not wish to set foot in Asunción.'

Gabriel looked at him, understanding, and said nothing immediately in reply; but, taking an opportunity to move apart with him a little later he murmured, 'You don't believe you have been forgiven for the death of Felipe?'

Mendoza did not reply at first. His face was expressionless, but Gabriel held his gaze. The crackle of the fire sounded very loud. 'As long as I am here, I feel forgiven. That is why I do not wish to leave,' he said at last.

'You fear that in Asunción certain feelings might return.'

'Yes.'

'God's mercy is everywhere.'

'Father, let me be.'

'You cannot pick and choose the form God's mercy takes.

I will speak to you again about this in the morning, after I have meditated on it.'

Lying in bed that night, Gabriel realized how deep had been Mendoza's wound and how shallow his own sympathy had been not to realize that before. If he did not come to Asunción, Mendoza's wound would cripple him. He prayed to Christ that he might be shown how to proceed, and in the darkness he could tell how much Christ cared. His prayer, however, was not answered. He was still at a loss the following morning when he urged Mendoza, saying, 'I beg you. I beg you to come.'

'No, Father Gabriel.'

'It is most important. I need to have you with me at this gathering.'

'I regret it very much, father, but I must say no.'

Gabriel shuffled his feet. 'Very well, then, I command you.'

'Then I obey.' Mendoza scowled. 'That could as well have been said last night.'

'That means you know it to be right,' Gabriel insisted, pleased.

Mendoza only said, 'Perhaps.'

'Tell Hacugh I need him too, and a pair of his braves. And we shall also need Babuie.'

This was the boy who had adopted Mendoza from the first day of his arrival. Gabriel wanted him to sing the canticles he had taught him, for his voice was very pure.

'I will tell them all,' answered Mendoza and walked off, leaving Gabriel to thank Christ, who foresaw all, for making obedience the first vow of the Jesuit Order. It came unhesitatingly to Mendoza, who saw a chain of command passing from God through Gabriel to himself – a chain that was a life-line

– although it was through the Guarani that the peace of God had come to him.

But when they arrived in Asunción, he followed at Gabriel's heels, with his face sunk far into his collar and his eyes unseeing. The conquistadores sought him out, swaggering, and one called out, 'Hey there, Mendoza,' but he gave no answering sign.

The *hidalgos* and their ladies nudged one another at the sight of him, remembering the scandal, and Cabeza took the opportunity to remark that if it had been left to him to decide, the fratricide would not have got away with his atrocious crime. 'As things are at present,' he reminded them, 'I am still hamstrung by the antiquated enactments of bygone kings of Spain, but I can promise you, ladies, things will soon be very different.'

When Mendoza visited the spot where he had slain Felipe, he found a load of melons had just been dumped there.

Ribero took the assembled Jesuits through four rehearsals for the coming meeting, to make sure they made the best possible case and to anticipate any attacks on the missions. Discussion on these occasions was keen, but Mendoza sat through them like a stone, simply shaking his head when Ribero at last asked him directly for a comment. Gabriel was appointed chief spokesman. By the day of Altamirano's arrival they were fully prepared.

Accompanied by a flotilla of small boats, decked with the flags of Spain, Portugal and the Vatican, he arrived seated imposingly in a state barge, to the accompaniment of trumpets and drums. He made a sweeping gesture of greeting to the crowds watching from the waterfront and from moored lighters. All sorts and conditions had gathered for the occasion – *hidalgos* and their ladies, tradesfolk, clerics, including the visiting Jesuits, and last of all, yet outnumbering the others, a host of half-naked Guarani. The *hidalgos* removed their hats as Altamirano, supported by his secretary, got unsteadily to his feet to dispense a universal blessing. He had already raised his hand when the mob of natives shifted in a mass before his eyes; he paused, impressed and startled, while they knelt. This spectacle left him uneasy. He told himself how explicable it was. They were converts. They were pious. Naturally they thought of him as their saviour come from Rome, associating him, as a Jesuit dignitary, with the missions. Nevertheless, what perturbed him as he gazed for the first time, fascinated by those platelike faces with their gem-hard eyes, was a sense of quite impossible proximity, as if he wished to flee from them but could not leave.

Once he was ashore, the fathers from the missions were presented to him one by one, and as they bent before him in turn to receive his blessing, he took note of their eyes. There was one blue pair in particular that reminded him of eyes equally clear and youthful in a worn face, although the owner of these remembered eyes had been elderly, unshaven and white-haired. They were the eyes of his first teacher, eyes so transparent that they continually revealed the old man's feelings, whatever they were, to the perceptive boy. He remembered the face too now, gentle, usually melancholy but occasionally smiling, and the long neck, shrinking into the vestment below it. The slap of the water of this American river against his boat carried him back to his Italian boyhood in a villa by a narrower stream beneath a more opalescent sky. For a moment he could even hear the frogs. Undoubtedly, he told himself, he was fatigued. It was a very long voyage he had been sent on.

It was in that village beside a river that the feet of Altamirano had been guided to the path that had brought him where he was now. He had become a consummate negotiator, thanks to the example of a pious simpleton. Each year when the family was in the country, his father used to call the village priest in to teach him the elements of the doctrine of the Church. 'Because,' he used to say, 'this priest can do no harm.' This priest was the old man with the expressive eyes. In the village the hale and hearty accounted him a fool. A shepherd should not allow his flock to fleece him if he values their respect. Altamirano, who always enjoyed being with him, regarded him as a kind of clown. When, for example, he tackled the old man on the way the villagers used to rob him, he received a passionate explanation of how much they needed the money in reply. A story from the Bible then followed as usual and, also as usual, was listened to attentively.

It seemed that telling Bible stories, which he did irresistibly, was the only form of discourse the old man had mastered. When two self-styled philosophers who had heard of his simplicity – an upholsterer and a goldsmith's clerk – came from the local market-town to bait him, they had no difficulty in completely baffling him. To the great delight of the villagers, whenever he tried to answer one of his inquisitor's questions, the questioner seemed always able to answer him back, and even the priest himself seemed to expect it. His view was that his real business was plodding the roads on visits to the sick or sad or dying who prized his company.

So did Altamirano, and when the priest died he had gone to his house and wept, burying his face in the old man's vestment, comforted by the familiar smell. It was then, after a week of silence in the villa, that he had informed his father he was going to be a priest himself when he grew up. His father, surprised, understood the reason and took care not to forbid him or ridicule him. There would be time enough for him to get over it. Later he realized that this ambition might have to be taken seriously, and paid a visit to a relative who was a bishop. He returned favourably impressed.

'There may be something in this idea of yours,' he said when he returned. 'I shall make inquiries.' He did so, and the eventual verdict, Altamirano recalled, had been, 'You're a clever boy. If you are still inclined the same way at the end of the year, a priest you shall be, and if anybody laughs at you, then he's a fool.' Altamirano recalled how at these words he had nearly changed his mind.

It was his mother's delight that had held him to his choice. She took this decision as a blessing conferred upon her constricted soul by the Virgin Mother.

His own admiration for artless love did not survive the education he received at a Jesuit college. His original resolve was lost there, but his personal resolution grew. Here in Asunción, however, in an unsteady boat, at last he felt his resolution weakening.

Ceremoniously he was handed ashore, to be accosted rather than welcomed by a rude fellow, gorgeously dressed, who planted himself in front of him with an exaggerated bow and the words, 'Good-day, Father Visitor-General. I am Cabeza, the Captain-General. Allow me to present to you Senhor Hontar.'

That had been three days ago. On arrival at the Captain-

General's residence he had announced his need for rest, but now the assembly was only one day away, and he was due to have a preliminary discussion with Cabeza and Hontar. The latter, having completed his rereading of Carvalho's instructions, folded up the minister's letter and buttoned it inside his linen coat. Quite unnecessarily a major-domo was waiting to conduct Hontar across the boarded first floor on which he was accommodated, down the marble stairway and across the flagged ground floor, to the room occupied by his fellow-guest, the Reverend Visitor-General. Descending the stairway, he saw two Guarani in livery planted on either side of it in the hall below. In honour of the European visitors they were wearing throttling cravats, but their feet were bare and their impassive faces betrayed no flicker of recognition of the significance of the event which they were witnessing.

Altamirano, in his room on the ground floor, was watching Guarani servants and labourers preparing the courtyard outside for the assembly tomorrow. Cabeza, who had already presented himself, had opened the door that led on to the courtyard from Altamirano's room, and was shouting at them. Descending the stairway, Hontar flinched at the sound of the Captain-General's raucous voice, and pitied himself for being tied to such an ally. He would have preferred to be associated with his opponent, he reflected, admiring the distinguished Jesuit's style as he entered his room. Altamirano casually relieved himself of an elegant buff coat and laid it on a table to reveal an admirable waistcoat and fine cambric shirt. Now, at a cough from the major-domo, he turned in the doorway with studied informality to greet the man whom in his own mind he thought of as Carvalho's watchdog.

'I wonder how long it will be before I tire of watching these natives,' he said. 'There's something very strange about the way they never look at you.'

'At you, father, surely they must gaze.'

'Not at all. They may have the utmost veneration for my office –'

'Of course they have!' barked Cabeza, coming in from the courtyard to join them.

'Yet I have not caught as much as a passing glance from one of them. Last night they unpacked my books.' He picked up an elegantly bound volume which Hontar noted was by Voltaire. 'I hoped that they would handle the bindings carefully, and so they did, but they also kissed them.'

'Naturally,' explained Cabeza, 'because the books are holy.'

Altamirano showed the book in his hand to Hontar. Embossed on the cover was a nymph, surrounded by admiring animals.

Cabeza, squinting at it, said, 'You read such books?'

'A priest must be able to recognize evil,' Altamirano informed him, with a sober face.

'I do not allow any book into the Province if it attacks Mother Church.'

'Would there were more of you!' Altamirano commended him. Clearly this ruffian was not aware of being a hypocrite. He supposed himself to be devout. 'Can we have privacy?' he asked, nodding at the door Cabeza had left open to the courtyard. The Captain-General obediently went and closed it. While he was doing so, the Visitor-General seated himself unhurriedly in the highest chair. Then, with a gesture more of authority than hospitality, he motioned his two visitors to seat themselves too.

To Hontar's irritation, Cabeza spoke first. 'Will you be sailing back on the same vessel?'

'That depends on how long it will take me to reach a conclusion.'

'No more than two days, I'd say. The *hidalgos* certainly can't afford more than a week away from their farms, you know. In any case, there aren't any problems I know of for you to settle, and there's nothing of consequence in these parts that I don't know all about. If there's anything that you don't understand, you may as well tell me now. I'll clear it up for you before you start.'

'Why, look!' Hontar intervened quickly. 'A monkey!' He rose from his chair and stole softly to where the tiny creature, wearing a bright red turban, was clinging to the curtains, peering at him inquisitively. 'Does he bite?'

'It's a she. It belongs to my wife. It's quite safe,' said Cabeza.

Hontar stretched out his arm. The creature hesitated. Then, with a flick of its tail, it climbed on to him and nestled in the crook of his neck, examining his ear. Hontar, pleased, delicately resumed his place, making a soothing noise. 'So,' Altamirano told himself, 'this one's a sentimentalist.'

'Do they travel, Don Cabeza?' Hontar inquired, stroking the pet.

'No. They usually die on the voyage.'

'I'm sorry to hear it. You'd be worth a gold coin in Lisbon, my little friend.'

'Presumably,' remarked Altamirano with a stare, 'that is why they do not travel. They prefer to stay in a place where they have no market value.'

This was his first reference to the issue of slavery. The time had come to make them realize he was not just a papal underling.

'But she never tries to escape from here, does she?' Hontar asked Cabeza.

'Never!' came the answer, delivered with a hostile glare. 'Now can we get back to business? Visitor-General,' he turned back to Altamirano, 'as I just said, if there's anything you want ironed out, best tell me now before the hearing starts.'

'Surely,' chimed in Hontar, 'the Visitor-General already knows that he can count on your assistance in every way, is that not so, father?'

The response caught him off balance. 'About this letter from Senhor Carvalho you have just received.'

Hontar stiffened and thought, 'How has he got his information? Or is he just guessing?' He uncrossed his legs in an effort to relax and answered, 'Thank you. It was delivered safely.'

'May I be told about such of its contents as pertains to my business tomorrow?'

'The answer to that is simple. Nothing, nothing at all. The letter was about my next appointment, not this one.'

'Ah, so? And what is that to be?'

'Unfortunately he doesn't say,' Hontar managed to answer with an easy laugh.

Altamirano thought, 'He dare not tell me. My worst fears are confirmed. There is no point in any of this.' And he sighed at the prospect of the next day's charade. 'These natives,' he asked, 'the Guarani – what are they like as a people?'

'Ignorant,' Cabeza answered.

'And yet,' Altamirano pursued his question, 'when I was watching them working outside just now, they were far more anxious to preserve your splendid furniture from damage than your Spanish overseer appeared to be.'

'Of course,' Hontar confirmed, with a warning glance at Cabeza. 'They are the craftsmen.'

'Indeed?' The visitor ran his finger over the elaborate carving on his chair. 'This was not shipped from Spain?'

Again Hontar glanced at Cabeza, but the Captain-General was not a total fool. 'No, Reverend Visitor-General,' he said smoothly. 'It is mission work. So is all the rest of the furniture. These people can make anything, just as long as they've been given something to copy. Without that, though, they're helpless. As I often tell visitors like yourself, they didn't even know what a wheel was, before we arrived on the scene to show them one.'

'In the forests where they live I suppose they had no need of one.'

Cabeza reflected that this was typical Jesuitical talk. 'All the same,' he sneered, 'the wheels have started turning now!'

Hontar, who had identified one quotation from the Captain-General in Carvalho's letter, reflected that the minister might even adopt this gem as his motto. Aloud he observed, 'Naturally, the local population are attracted by the amenities of a superior civilization. Naturally too, Captain-General, you cannot imagine the fascination your strange country and its people hold for visitors from Europe like the Reverend Visitor-General and my humble self. I blush to confess it, but before the Treaty of Madrid was negotiated I did not even know that such a place as Sacramento existed, let alone that it was a haunt of pirates. Have you heard about Sacramento, father?'

'Yes,' said Altamirano, 'from Senhor Carvalho in Lisbon.' He began to stroke his leg. Hontar watched him curiously. What was coming now? 'He also spoke of gold. Is there much gold these days, at Sacramento?' Altamirano's eyes flashed as he asked the question. Hontar, who was not avaricious, was amazed.

Cabeza's manner too changed at the introduction of this interesting new subject. Suddenly he became hesitant. 'I do not know.'

'You mean, then, it is not impossible there is some?'

'No, it is certainly not impossible.'

'Where could they get the gold in Sacramento?'

Cabeza looked unpleasantly sly. 'There are those who say there are mines on the missions.' He shrugged.

'What do the brothers themselves say?'

'They deny it, of course. But I must say, Reverend Father, that there are those who do not believe them.'

'Do you?'

'I am bound to,' leered Cabeza. 'Am I not?'

'Any gold mines on the missions,' said Altamirano, 'would have been accounted for.' He looked out of the window and reminded himself that somewhere out there, before the end of that distant forest he could see was reached, lay the city of El Dorado.

'Amazing!' thought Hontar, watching him. 'He's too clever to believe the rumours, but he believes in the dream.'

When his visitors had left, Altamirano, discouraged, said to himself, 'I shall be leaving on the next sailing, just as that animal said.' The word 'animal' reminded him of the monkey. It was still there, but it refused to come to him as it had gone to Hontar. 'Hontar is no fit servant for Carvalho,' he thought. 'Cabeza is his man. He wouldn't sully his lips with the name of Newton – supposing he had ever heard of him, which is not likely – but all the same he is in tune with the new philosophy, there can be no doubt of that. Just as there can be no doubt the Order will survive it. The Order must. But survival,' he reminded himself, 'will call for the sacrifice of much that would be worth keeping if the world were a different place. My life, as I see now, has involved much sacrifice of this kind, and those brothers I met when I landed must sacrifice the simple, skilful people they have brought to Christ. They must do it for the sake of the Order to which they belong and to which they have sworn obedience, but how am I to tell them?' In his mind he felt a pair of eyes upon him. 'That will be my sacrifice. In order to obtain their obedience I must sacrifice their fellowship.'

He felt calm but tired, and above all else wished to be alone, but that night the Guarani were presenting a pageant in the main square. It was an annual affair, Cabeza told him, arranged by the nearest mission, but this year, in view of the coming assembly and the arrival of so many visitors in the city of Asunción, it should be worth attending. Cabeza was going himself! Altamirano had already explained to Ribero that he could not go to their house in Asunción to celebrate Mass there, much as he longed to do so, because he had come on behalf of the Pope and must on no account appear to identify himself with one of the parties in a case in which he was the appointed judge. To refuse to grace this occasion as well would be to promote distrust – premature distrust – so he joined the Captain-General's party.

Darkness had fallen hours before they arrived, and the square was crowded as far as the side streets: *hidalgos* and officers and their families in the front, tradesfolk at the sides, and a solid mass of Guarani at the back. Even before they left the residence, the Captain-General's party could hear the din, which rose to a roar as they joined other, less distinguished

figures on a temporary gallery. All the visible trees or walls
had been decorated with flowers. Their arrival was the signal
for the pageant to begin.

Altamirano soon gave up the attempt to understand what
it was all about. There was enough to engage his attention
without attempting that. He could have listened to the orchestra all evening. It astonished him with its precision. A massed
choir sang. There was also a moment when a clear space
beneath him was invaded by horsemen in fantastic costumes
– not savage but strangely sacerdotal.

A Jesuit appeared at the top of a tower, where two torches
were suddenly set ablaze, turning all eyes in his direction. The
music died down and there was silence. In a resonant voice
the Jesuit said a prayer in Guarani. Altamirano could sense
the devotion in the listeners below him. Then it was over and
a noise like the sea sounded across the square. Suddenly
Altamirano realized that thousands of faces had turned in his
direction, and he knew what they expected. He bowed his
head and blessed them.

In the early morning a small crowd of watchers had already
gathered in front of the Captain-General's residence, from
which the flags of Spain, Portugal and the Vatican were
hanging listlessly against a dull grey sky suffused with cloud.
They saw the Jesuits arrive, two by two, led by Father Ribero.
By the back streets came the up-country Guarani, led by two
Jesuits who disappeared into a side door. The *hidalgos* and
their ladies came on horseback – even a few in coaches –
leaving their mounts under the trees outside, heads drooping,
in the care of grooms. Confident that the decision would go

their way, they called out cheerily to one another. For them it was something of a festivity.

Altamirano came, flanked by a choir not of Jesuit origin but from a local church, singing a psalm. When he entered the courtyard to take his seat facing them, the entire assembly rose. The choir completed the psalm and then the prior of the Franciscans said a prayer. Altamirano stood, and with an expressionless face looked across to where Ribero sat in the midst of ranks of Jesuits, on benches ranged to the same side as that on which, crowded into a corner, a group of up-country Guarani, all but naked, had been placed.

He then turned his head to direct a smile at Cabeza and make a friendly gesture to Hontar, both of which were acknowledged. They were seated in the front row of the *hidalgos*, their wives and daughters. The arrangements had been good. Satisfied that everything was perfectly in order, he was about to make his opening statement, inviting each interested party to make its case fully, because justice was only possible after everything had been taken into consideration, when Ribero asked permission for a choir of recent converts to make an opening contribution. He was confident the Captain-General would agree that sacred music would help on this occasion. With a shrug Cabeza signalled agreement, but then instead of introducing a full choir Ribero summoned a small boy from the group of up-country Guarani. There was a slight delay while the child sought permission from a Jesuit who was standing there apart from the others, in whose care he appeared to be. As he came forward, the introduction of a Palestrina solo was heard from a harpsichord and the boy, lifting his flat expressionless face, began to sing. It was as if he were a natural spring and the notes were water, even softening Cabeza's surly look. Altamirano, however, knew well such skill was not spontaneous, and marvelled that the training necessary should be available in such a place. Even now the singer's eyes were fixed on somebody who was unobtrusively directing him. Following the boy's glance, with a shock of interest and recognition Altamirano found that he was staring at the worn face and limpid eyes that had transported him to his childhood on the day of his arrival. Gabriel was discreetly conducting from his sleeve.

When the boy had brought his piece to an end in a trill of quiet notes, Altamirano told Ribero it would give him particular delight to hear the same singer render the same composer's Plenum. Ribero bowed his head and consulted Gabriel in an undertone. Then both turned to the boy. '*Sí*,' said Babuie, in answer to a question in Guarani, and without accompaniment proceeded to sing the ecclesiastical music. Altamirano, astonished, watched peace descend on the crowded courtyard – on all but Cabeza. Pulling angrily at his collar, the Captain-General scented some sort of trap. Altamirano saw Hontar frowning a warning at him to be patient. He knew he had only to wait.

In sudden hostility to the pair of them and what they stood for, he clapped loudly when the child had finished, and the ranks of Jesuits enthusiastically joined him. The *hidalgos* and their womenfolk did not. Hontar, however, deprecating any whiff of demonstration, clapped too. The Visitor-General watched the boy return to his place among the up-country Guarani next to a single Jesuit, to whom he now held out his hand. The Jesuit handed him a little monkey, such as had so captivated Hontar, which clung immediately to his arm.

Altamirano attacked Cabeza with a question. 'Captain-General, was that the cry of an animal we just heard?'

'Reverend Father, a parrot can be taught to talk.' The retort

earned a volley of shrill laughter from the *hidalgos*' wives.
Altamirano looked at them and in their faces saw scars resulting from years of wresting from a hostile environment the
goods and services they could never enjoy at home in Spain.

'Are parrots here so melodious?' he asked.

A man's voice called out, 'Yes, father. A brute beast can
be taught anything, with a whip.'

At the word 'whip' there was a murmur of rejection from
the Jesuits and of approval from the *hidalgos* and their womenfolk. Father Ribero suppressed the Jesuit clamour. 'Good,'
thought Altamirano. 'You have authority. I shall need you
later.'

Cabeza rose truculently to his feet and stood with legs
apart. He thought of himself as a settler. He had never cared
twopence for the Crown of Spain, and no longer had to
pretend to.

'Reverend Visitor-General,' he began unctuously, 'we have
just heard a child of the Guarani sing and it appears Your
Reverence was much taken with it. Very well, but before
Your Reverence goes on to make a big mistake, I'll just
describe the barbarity that produced that little angel. I am
able to tell you because, as anyone who lives here can see at
a glance, it's one of the untamed ones from above the falls,
and in that part of the world things still go on the way they
did everywhere in the Río de la Plata, before we arrived and
brought the twin blessings of religion and trade here. Up there
the Guarani live like beasts.'

A burst of applause sounded from the *hidalgos* at hearing
their spokesman call a spade a spade. Encouraged, he went
on. 'I'll tell you this. If what we heard just now was not an
animal with a human voice, then it was something lower. It
was a human with animal vices!' He paused to hear his wit

applauded. 'No, worse than that even, for it has vices any beast would flee from. Reverend Father, let me tell you just one thing about these people. Even here in your very presence they've got practically nothing on, as you must have noticed. Well listen to this. When they get back into the forest up there they'll go around stark naked. You ought to see the state they get into, all smeared with earth and scratched with branches! In other words, as I said they live like animals!'

The women behind him had often discussed the Guarani's gross indecency, but that did not prevent them from displaying outrage anew. Some shook their heads with pursed mouths, while others broke into exclamations. Cabeza continued, 'What's more, they don't live in human homes. In fact they don't live in any particular place at all. They turn up in some corner of the jungle, kill everything that moves, eat, and then wander off to some other part. While they are there, they just pile up a few branches and huddle underneath.'

He turned to appeal to the *hidalgos* behind him and there was a rumble of agreement. He was enjoying himself hugely. 'Do they have arts? Well, I must admit they can chip stones and they can squeeze clay. They also weave a kind of crude cloth from wild cotton. I'll grant them that. And then there is their painting. They paint their naked flesh all over with dots and stripes, let's not forget that! But that's the sum total of the arts of the Guarani. Which reminds me, talking about sums, they can also count. Yes, like this!' He held up one hand and displayed his fingers. 'One, two, three, four and plenty! Anything over four, is plenty. Plenty! Can you believe it?' His supporters joined him in a fit of cackling laughter.

'Can they cultivate the soil? Some of them scratch around with digging-sticks on patches of land they have cleared by slashing and burning. Then, when they've emptied all the goodness out of the soil, they wander off somewhere else and start again. This, Reverend Father, is the condition from which we have rescued them, and I defy anybody to deny it.' Jutting out his lower lip, he stared across at the Jesuit ranks, while his supporters cheered. His prime audience, however, Altamirano, while continuing to make a show of inclining an attentive ear, showed no sign of shock or outrage.

'Reverend Father and Visitor-General, I do not wish to weary you, but before ending this pitiful list I must inform you of one or two more details which tell their own story. For instance, one thing they do go in for is lethal weapons. They have clubs and swords and bows and arrows, and what is more they take a lot of trouble over them. Some of their bows are eight feet long. Their swords have basket hand-guards. Their arrows have barbed heads and, if they are war arrows, I am sorry to tell you that they are tipped with human bones. Savage? They want to be savage! When they paint themselves the way I've already told you, they add jaguar ashes to the colours, on purpose to become like beasts of prey.'

Gabriel, the Jesuits' chosen spokesman, turned his lean, burnt face to Ribero, but the latter shook his head and whispered, 'Wait.'

'The two things they devote their lives to are drunken orgies and cannibal feasts.' Even Altamirano seemed shocked at this. Gratified, for he was prepared for this, Cabeza produced something he had brought along in his pocket, wrapped in cloth. It was a piece of hard meat. He held it up. 'A chop from a tribal hero,' he said, and paused to let them all look at it, before concluding, 'That's all I have to say for the present. Such, Reverend Visitor-General, are the converts which the Jesuits would have you believe are equal in the eyes of God with us!'

He sat down to a storm of applause. The *hidalgos* drummed their handsticks on the pavement.

Ribero got to his feet and said, 'As the world well knows, we Jesuits, who cleansed the Church of Jansen's heresy, accept – nay, we maintain – there can be no salvation where there are no good works. Nevertheless, we are confident that the Guarani will be numbered among the redeemed, which is to say that they have souls as acceptable to Christ as are our own. This does not mean that we deny that they are sinners. But such we also freely confess ourselves to be.' The entire gathering nodded. Ribero was known to be the cleverest theologian in the Río de la Plata. But what had this pious truth to do with what Cabeza had just said? 'Father Gabriel,' announced Ribero, 'is best qualified to comment on the remarks we have just heard, because he directs San Carlos, the mission above the falls.'

Gabriel came quietly forward. Again Altamirano felt the presence of his old teacher. 'This man's conscience,' he thought, 'is as clear as day. The work of God is all he can contemplate doing.'

'As Father Ribero has told you, Reverend Father, my mission is up-country, above the falls,' Gabriel began. 'Here, where we are now, below the falls, this Province belongs to Spain, under the protection of the Captain-General, but above the falls it belongs to the Guarani under God – and the Crown of Spain.'

'I see where you are,' thought Altamirano. Aloud he said, 'I understand that Portugal too was awarded territory in the mountains.'

'Reverend Visitor-General, indeed that is so, but although none can say with authority where the division runs, there is no doubt that it leaves the land beyond the falls to Spain. The falls, Reverend Visitor-General, were placed there by God to be a barrier. Standing above them and looking down, a man can have no doubt of that. Reverend Father, I have to tell you that up there the Guarani behave very much in the way the Captain-General has just described, but as to their precious souls the evidence is in their music.'

'*Their* music?' interrupted Cabeza, staring round at the *hidalgos*. '*Theirs?*' he repeated to Gabriel. 'The savages above the falls? When you arrived up there, what instruments did they have?'

'The gourd rattle and the stamping tube.'

'So!' said Cabeza, turning round again to share the joke with his followers. 'The gourd rattle and the stamping tube. From these we see their wonderful gift for music, do we?'

'No, indeed,' Gabriel conceded. 'When first the Jesuits came among the Guarani,' he explained to Altamirano, 'we found they would not stay to listen to the Holy Word of God, but they were drawn by the evening canticles – though all they had known so far themselves of music was, as I said, the sounds of the gourd rattle and the stamping tube. Hearing the strains of rarest music – Charpentier, Scarlatti, Lully – they laid down the weapons which the Captain-General has listed and came out of hiding. The first Jesuit fathers travelled up the river with their instruments, on rafts, to play to them, and the Guarani came and stood knee-deep in the water to get close to them and listen. Then later the fathers would speak words to them and tell them the Holy Story. I can show the Reverend Father various old texts from which this can be verified.'

Cabeza said, 'There is no need to see old texts. Everybody knows that those old Jesuits used music to impress the natives. What does that prove?'

'I must admit, Father Gabriel,' said Altamirano, 'much as

I relish these stories of our ancient forebears, I cannot accept them as evidence to be assessed by this assembly.'

'Of course not. They are only old wives' tales,' commented an *hidalgo*.

'But I also have living evidence,' said Gabriel, and related how, when he first ventured above the falls, he had established contact with the Guarani with his oboe, and how they had come out of their hiding places to listen first to his music and then to the Word of God.

Sneered Cabeza, 'Obviously they had already heard some. They must have sneaked down below the falls to one of your missions and heard one of your choirs.'

'No, on the contrary. Far from going down to where we were, they wanted to have nothing to do with us. There was bad blood between us, in fact.'

'How so?' queried Altamirano. 'What bad blood?'

Gabriel looked at Father Ribero, who nodded. So he told them of the martyrdom of Julien, who was the first to carry the Word above the falls.

'And are these the same people?' asked Altamirano. He pointed to the group of Guarani.

'Yes, father. And yet they are not the same, thanks be to God, and the power of music is His work!'

'And it was you yourself who went?' asked Altamirano admiringly.

'Yes,' said Gabriel. 'That is how I know for myself that they are spiritual beings.'

'Spiritual!' exclaimed a hard-faced woman, as if somebody had insulted her. 'As you have just heard from a man who knows them like the back of his hand, Reverend Father, the natives are perpetually drunk.'

'Sometimes,' Gabriel said swiftly, 'it is true that they are drunk. I have also heard that the Captain-General goes to the trouble of sending all the way to Europe to stock his excellent cellar with wine which must surely have the same effect on those who drink it as the liquor that the Guarani brew has on them.' He cocked an Irish eyebrow at the Captain-General, who was forced to look away, and even many of the *hidalgos* laughed, for Cabeza's drinking was renowned.

Hontar decided to come in. It was the first time he had opened his mouth that morning, but the time had come to return Altamirano to a sense of realities. He had become too interested in this dangerous witness. The time had come.

'Father, have you established a mission up there permanently?' The question was addressed to Gabriel, but it was Altamirano it was aimed at. It was an unpleasant necessity, but clearly he needed to be reminded who had the whip hand.

Gabriel looked at him, puzzled, and asked, 'How does that concern you?'

'Why, father, as representative of the Crown of Portugal at this assembly, it is a question of legitimate interest to me. If you have established a mission there, in effect you have annexed the territory above the falls for us.'

'We do have a mission there,' Gabriel stated. 'I am, however, surprised to learn, Excellency, that you know in advance what conclusion the Reverend Visitor-General will reach at the end of this assembly.'

'Ah, no!' Hontar protested. 'No, no, no. I am distressed if I have conveyed such a wrong impression to anyone present, Reverend Father.'

Altamirano, who had understood this intervention very well, was fuming at it inwardly, but with a forgiving wave of his hand he answered mildly, 'Pray do not distress yourself.'

Angry as he was with Hontar, he knew that if he was to save appearances he must not allow the formidable father now before him to make his case so well. 'So you deal with the untouched Guarani, Father Gabriel,' he said to him, apparently encouragingly. 'Tell me, do they indeed employ the system of counting Don Cabeza explained to us just now?'

'All Guarani count that way.'

'Then how are they able to make a splendid chair like this, or this magnificent table?'

'Well, let us take that table as an example. There would be no difficulty about the length and breadth. They could measure those all right. The problem would come with the curves on the legs. They would have to trace round them to make a pattern they could transfer on to a piece of timber. Then, that way, they could reproduce it in the finished article. And so on, with the other curves. There is really no limit to what they can do, using methods like that. In the Mission of San Fernando they have constructed an organ, complete with the stops and listening pipes.'

'What you mean is, they can copy someone else's model,' Hontar pointed out. 'You see how it is, Reverend Father, as scriveners are to poets, so they are to Europeans. It seems the Muse disdains them. They can do nothing without a master copy.'

To his annoyance, his contribution was received with applause and more thudding of sticks. In the belief that the cool voice of reason sounded better than the hot tones of prejudice, even when they were saying the same thing, he had deliberately forestalled Cabeza in order to make the very point the latter had made the previous day. Much to his chagrin, though, the *hidalgos* were completely satisfied. 'Nothing!' they echoed him. 'They can do nothing!'

The combative father, who, Hontar thought, had already dealt neatly with Cabeza over the matter of intemperance, now paid the diplomat the compliment of picking up his reference to poetry. 'If any Muse has visited you, Excellency,' he began, 'and inspired you with a practical idea that I could pass on to my Guarani for them to copy – I mean something that would be as useful in the forest as accountancy is useful in the town – I beg you to impart it to me now.'

'Alas,' Hontar said drily, 'the Muses have always shunned me for some reason. But to return, with your permission, to the question we are supposed to be considering, you cannot deny the reason why your Guarani have turned to you for guidance is that they recognize the superiority of what you have to teach them – be it music, be it joinery – over what they have achieved themselves, even in the very forests they and their ancestors were born in. In other words, they acknowledge Europe's natural superiority – even in using their own local materials, for example, to erect buildings they could never dream of for themselves.'

Impressed by this philosopher, the *hidalgos* started whispering among themselves. Disgusted, Cabeza pulled at his lower lip and looked sulky, feeling eclipsed.

'I suppose,' Gabriel reflected aloud, 'if what you say is true, that would make the Guarani my bond-slaves, wouldn't it?'

'If that is the word for it,' said Hontar.

'It is a word whose meaning is well known to your countrymen,' answered Gabriel, seizing his chance. He would explain the origin of the Jesuit missions. Without that knowledge Altamirano would not understand the need for the missions' special privileges and immunities. 'Your countrymen were very quick to decide that *slave* was the proper word. I am speaking of the Paulista *bandeirantes*, as we call them

Reverend Father, men from São Paulo in Brazil. They used
to raid Spanish territory here, looking for slaves for their
plantations; they headed bands collected from the wild Chaco
Indians, half-trained *mamelucos*, who are men of mixed race,
and also negroes – all violent, desperate men for whom there
was no honest, settled way to live. They raided the Guarani
villages, killing many and carrying off the others into slavery.
There was terror everywhere, and there was good reason for
terror, but its effects were horrible. Fleeing their villages, the
Guarani had to kill their old people and the feeble and infirm,
because they would not be able to keep up with the speed
of flight. I am telling you the truth completely. And these
Portuguese called themselves Christians, Reverend Father.
Small wonder the Guarani flee from us, when they hear that
we are Christians!'

'This is ancient history,' Cabeza objected. 'You have embarrassed Senhor Hontar. We have a treaty with them now. That
is why we are here.'

'Is this information relevant to our inquiry, Father Gabriel?'
Altamirano inquired.

'It bears directly on the Treaty. It explains why the kings
of Spain saw fit to give our Order special rights and privileges,'
Gabriel answered. 'At the time I speak of, the Jesuits were
the only Europeans who attempted to protect the Guarani.
They sent letters to the courts of Spain and Portugal, complaining about what was happening. Nothing was done, however,
by governments to stop the Paulista *bandeirantes* before it was
too late. By the time order had been restored and the Province
was safe, the Guarani were no longer to be found in their
villages. Many of those who had not been killed or captured
had taken to wandering in the forest where they would be
safe.

'There was another thing the Jèsuits did besides writing letters. They did not help the Guarani resist by force, but they took many thousands of them to safety. They established mission settlements for them in the fertile regions of the Paraná and Uruguay rivers, where they could live in peace away from the Portuguese, and prosper. As Senhor Hontar has explained to us so clearly, by coming to these missions the Guarani have unmistakably acknowledged the superiority of Europeans – as in their situation who would not? And it is true they have acquired many skills on the missions: animal husbandry, poultry-breeding, agriculture, weaving, carpentry and joinery, pottery, tailoring, boat building, architecture . . .'

A suspicious-looking *hidalgo* interposed: 'Mining and metal refinery.' His tone was deeply significant. Altamirano pricked up his ears and waited.

Gabriel paused. 'Do you mean gold?'

'I did not mention any particular metal.'

'Whatever metal you had in mind,' Gabriel informed him, 'you will find none of it on any of the missions. I have heard talk of gold arriving in Sacramento. Some gold may do so. I do not know. What I do know is that any gold there may be in Sacramento has nothing to do with any Jesuit mission. Quite simply, we run no mines.'

Many there resented him, some even hated him, but nobody disbelieved him.

'I thank you for explaining the history of these missions,' Altamirano said. 'That was most helpful. Tell me one thing more about them. To whom do the mission lands belong?'

'To the converts.'

'Don Cabeza, is this true?'

The Captain-General shrugged. 'Perhaps.'

'Perhaps?'

'I cannot say. How can I when I am not allowed into a single mission? If I wanted to enter one for any reason, I should have to apply to its Father Superior for special permission. So what is going on inside them is something I can only guess at.'

Altamirano turned to Father Ribero for an explanation.

'King Fernando decided that the Guarani should be administered completely separately from the Spanish settlers, in their own interests, which he thought were best entrusted to the Society of Jesus. And that is why, in my opinion, both the spirit and also the letter of his legacy require that the missions be excluded from the terms of the recent Treaty, whose application to this question we have gathered to discuss.'

'In this connection,' Gabriel added firmly, 'it must be remembered that, although they may no longer call themselves *bandeirantes*, slave-traders are still operating legally in the territories belonging to the Crown of Portugal.'

They had reached the nub of the problem more rapidly than Altamirano had expected or desired. But at that same moment Cabeza, who had been listening with growing impatience to a discussion from which he felt excluded, rose to his feet and, striding up to the table behind which Altamirano sat separated from the body of the meeting, burst out, 'Reverend Father, this could go on endlessly. I don't see any point in it. I therefore beseech you –'

'There is no point in beseeching me,' Altamirano told him. 'I am not here to please you in particular or anybody else. My duty –'

'Nevertheless,' Cabeza impatiently insisted, 'I implore you to stop this talk and give us your decision now, at once!' Then, having delivered himself of this request, he remained standing there, as if he expected his wish to be granted immediately.

Altamirano stared at him, biting back the crushing reply that rose temptingly to his lips, but which would later make it harder to do what he had to do. As a result he found he had nothing to say at all and avoided looking at Cabeza. The mere sight of the man robbed him of his normal self-control.

The Captain-General's sudden prominence caused Mendoza, sitting with the Guarani in their corner, to raise his head and stare at him, remembering. His visit to Asunción had affected him as deeply as he had feared. He was haunted by the murder of Felipe as if he had committed it repeatedly, and not only by that act but also by the long succession of other horrors which had preceded it and which he now realized he would never forget either. He would have done better to disobey Gabriel. There was nothing for him to do here but suffer. What could a man like him contribute to the conversation over there at the Reverend Visitor-General's table? If Cabeza had looked back, he would have trembled at the sight of Mendoza's dark shadowed eyes contemplating him so steadily from his scarred face, but his own glare was aimed at the indifferent profile of the most distinguished person present. A moment later Mendoza lowered his eyes lest Gabriel, who had taught him the first Christian message, which was forgiveness, should see them. Only Babuie saw.

Hontar, who already respected Gabriel, again cursed the luck that had given him Cabeza as an ally. It was easier said than done to ignore Cabeza, he reflected, but well worth attempting. He addressed Altamirano.

'Reverend Father, earlier this morning we heard a charge of cannibalism which, in view of what Father Gabriel has just told us, I find hard to understand. Can he explain it?'

This had the effect of taking Cabeza's eyes off Altamirano.

'It's true,' declared Cabeza, pulling his wrapped meat out of his pocket again and showing it. 'If you want the details, they eat their enemies' muscles and testicles.'

Gabriel said quietly, 'Reverend Father, the truth of the matter is that they are guilty of a childish identification of a man's muscles with his strength, just as some of the faithful at church here in Asunción confuse the virtue of the Blessed Virgin with her image.'

'Nobody is to be blamed for an honest confusion,' Hontar agreed. 'But it is not permissible to eat human flesh. Is the truth that they do eat it?'

'I will put the question to them,' was Gabriel's reply. So saying, he went across to where his Guarani, with Hacugh in their midst, were deep in amicable conversation which he had to interrupt. He spoke briefly to them and they all joined in a common reply, adding to one another's words and amending them. Gabriel then put another question to them, apparently a summing up in which all concurred. 'They are very clear about this,' he reported, turning towards the others. 'What they say is that they did once eat the flesh of enemies but no longer do, being now persuaded that the spirit is something separate from the flesh. Moreover, they no longer wish to do it, as it is against the wishes of Christ, who they hope will act as their protector from the Spaniards.'

'The Spaniards?' Altamirano exclaimed.

But before he could pursue that question, an *hidalgo* had risen to his feet and asked accusingly, 'Why doesn't he ask them why they kill their own children?'

Altamirano glanced confidently at Gabriel. 'I suppose this is just another story,' he suggested, 'like the gold?'

Gabriel's eyes sank to the flagstones. 'No,' he admitted. 'This is not just a story. This is true.'

There was total silence.

'Then what need is there to hear more?' demanded Hontar.

Gabriel replied, 'There is need to hear the explanation. The Guarani who do this thing are those who live in the woods, the ones you call untamed. Because of the danger they are constantly in, their women can never have more than two children – one for each hand. If they have more, they cannot run away. Of course, with bigger children it is different. They can run on their own. I will tell you from whom they are running. They are running from us.'

Sitting among the *hidalgos* was an old lady. Gabriel's attention had been largely concentrated on Altamirano, but she had caught his eye because he liked her face, although it was clear from her expression that she disagreed with him. She had shaken her head suspiciously when he had dismissed the idea that there were secret gold mines on the missions. When he had compared devotion to the image of the Blessed Virgin with cannibalism, her face had stiffened with contempt. At this point, however, she surprised him by rising to her feet, supporting herself by gripping the back of the chair in front of her, and declaring in a high voice, 'In case that sounds like evil calumny, I would like to say, as an old woman, that I know it's partly true, I have heard my father speak of it. They had to kill some of their own children in that way when *mamelucos* were after them.' She sat down carefully, having done her duty.

'Who knows what truth there is in the stories of those days? Both empires were still settling down and nobody knew what was what. Both sides believed lies about each other, if you ask me. What matters now is that everything is going to be quite different, thanks to the Treaty we are here to serve.'

Cabeza turned and bowed ceremoniously in the direction of Hontar, who rose to his feet to return the courtesy.

'Nonsense,' Gabriel responded coldly. 'It makes no difference to them who drags them into slavery. Listen to the word of the Guarani.' He turned back to them to question them, but the courtyard broke into an uproar as the *hidalgos* tried to stop the Guarani from answering by shouting them down. The Jesuits too had erupted. Half a dozen fathers had risen to their feet in support of Gabriel's allegation and were trying to make themselves heard. Watching the scene with detachment, Altamirano saw how at first even Ribero hissed and signalled a return to discipline in vain. There was, he noticed, just one saturnine, scar-faced brother who, alone among the others, remained impassive, staring at Cabeza.

Following his glance, Altamirano saw that Cabeza was receiving some sort of swift advice from Hontar. A few seconds later the Captain-General waved his arms and bellowed for quiet. The *hidalgos* fell silent. The Jesuits had already done so, and in the resulting calm Cabeza was addressing Altamirano again.

'Reverend Visitor-General, in the territory which his Catholic Majesty has entrusted to my hands, there is of course, no slavery, nor has there ever been since the days of Fernando. The institution of slavery is permitted in the territories of our Portuguese neighbours . . .' (Here he broke off to bow to Hontar.) 'A fact, to my mind, much misunderstood. But here in Spanish territory plantation labour are *encomienda*; that is the system.'

'Exactly,' confirmed a settler. '*Encomienda*.'

'In strict accordance with the laws of Spain and the precepts of the Church.'

He was sitting down, well pleased with a sense of his own style and applauded by Hontar's murmur of assent, when the scar-faced Jesuit raised his face, looked across at them both, and quietly said, 'That is a lie.'

A sigh ran round the hall, followed by perfect silence as Cabeza, in instant fury at this unlooked for insult, glared into the steady eyes of the man who had uttered it. He remembered that many a man had looked into them as he was doing now, just before he died. Drawing himself up with theatrical hauteur, he blustered, 'In the name of the Monarch whose majesty I embody, I demand an apology. A gentleman ignores challenges from priests. Their cloth protects them.'

'Don Cabeza, this assembly can judge for itself who my cloth protects.'

Revealing the bull-like set of his head, Cabeza snatched off his powdered wig and flung it to the floor. 'By God!' he raged. 'I will not suffer this,' and under the cover of this declaration escaped by striding off into the shelter of his residence.

Hontar rose slowly. 'Reverend Father,' he said quietly, 'I feel compelled, most unwillingly, to observe that the worst enemy of your Order could not have hoped to witness such damning proof of its contempt for temporal authority. Your priests here seem to consider themselves a law unto themselves, citizens of a state within a state.' So saying he made his own more stately exit in the wake of Cabeza, whom he joined in the hall. Cabeza was heavy with outrage. Hontar was laughing silently to himself. 'Perfect,' he whispered. 'That could not have been better.'

'What did you say? Are you mad?'

'You don't understand. Come here. Just listen.'

Even through the closed doors, the angry voice of Altami-

rano could be clearly heard, calling on Father Ribero, Gabriel
and Mendoza – whom, like a schoolboy, he addressed as YOU
– to accompany him to his private room.

'That little flash of temper,' Hontar confided, 'was exactly
what the Reverend Father has been working for all morning.'

'So? Why is that good? He's against us. He's a Jesuit.'

'And therefore we can count on him to be obedient.'

'To his Order, not to the King of Portugal.'

'To his Order, yes, but above all to the Pope.'

'Perhaps. But the most important thing to remember when
you're dealing with a Jesuit is that you can't count on him for
anything. Nobody really knows the sum total of the orders
that he's got.'

Meanwhile Altamirano had passed straight out of the courtyard into his ground-floor apartment, taking Ribero, Gabriel
and Mendoza along with him. Without more ado he began
questioning them sharply.

'What is your name?'

'Mendoza, Reverend Father.'

'And how long have you been a brother?'

'Two years, Reverend Father.'

Altamirano scrutinized the bone-hard face with its narrow
eyes, clamped mouth and scars. 'And what were you before
that?'

'A slave-trader, Reverend Father.'

'So, Father Gabriel, you admit slave-traders to our ranks?'

'Yes, Reverend Father,' Gabriel replied, 'as in the Old
World the Order recruits soldiers.'

'There is no comparison. And why bring him to the
assembly?'

'To tell about the slave-trade, Reverend Father.'

Altamirano seated himself and considered the figure before him. Mendoza stood meekly, with eyes cast down, each arm thrust into its fellow's sleeve. 'Brother Mendoza,' he ordered, 'you will apologize to His Excellency Don Cabeza, and you will do it in the open hall, for all to see.'

'Yes, Reverend Father.'

'Now go.'

Mendoza went out and closed the door behind him. He did not resume his old position out in the courtyard which he knew of old, but moved across to a flight of steps leading to a balcony, along which he withdrew. Babuie had seen him and made to join him, but he shook his head.

Altamirano asked, 'Will he obey?'

'Like any other brother,' Gabriel told him.

Then he spoke of the old Mendoza and his gang, and their eruption into the placid world above the falls. He went on to tell the story of the two brothers' love for the same woman, with its tragic outcome. Last of all he explained Mendoza's bitter struggle to atone, which had made him the most docile member of the mission. Listening to Gabriel and watching his compassionate expression, Altamirano again recalled his old teacher, who, to him at least, had always seemed noble in the threadbare clothes that contrasted so starkly with the splendour of his father's villa. But then he remembered Hontar and Cabeza outside, waiting for the next move, and returned his attention with a sigh to the present.

'Well, whatever your plans may have been, Father Gabriel, this brother of yours is no longer in a position to carry them out. I trust you understand that.'

'I acknowledge it, Reverend Father, which makes me wonder what it is I can have brought him for,' said Gabriel.

'What do you mean? You could not have foreseen his fit of spleen.'

'But Christ must have foreseen it.'

'Christ?'

'Yes, Reverend Father.'

'You are talking like a zealot, Father Gabriel.'

'I may not speak of this with Your Reverence?'

'No. I wish to see no further sign of this enthusiasm.'

Father Gabriel looked at him and then slowly nodded.

After an inner imprecation Altamirano asked, 'Is it true the Spanish here have slaves?'

'Yes. They call them *encomienda*, but it means exactly the same thing. The *encomienda* get no wages and are taught the truths of Mother Church.'

'By whom?'

'Such priests as work for Don Cabeza.'

Ribero added, 'As for the Portuguese, the last time their *mamelucos* made a raid, carrying off four thousand into slavery, the raiding party included two justices from São Paulo and two aldermen. We Jesuits have been expelled from all Portuguese settlements. These facts appear to us as reasons against inclusion of our missions in the Treaty of Madrid. I draw them to your attention, Reverend Father, in case you too judge them relevant.'

'And Don Cabeza connives at all this?'

'And profits by it too.'

'I understand,' said Altamirano. Then, closely watching their faces, he said, 'Many of the settlers seem convinced that there are gold mines on the missions, Father Gabriel. Do you know why this should be?'

'These gold mines are a myth, Reverend Father, based on

the ancient histories of Mexico and Peru. But come and see for yourself,' Gabriel invited.

Altamirano's immediate response was to flinch at the prospect of a further trip up the interminable river. 'No, no. That is impossible.' He saw Gabriel look at him again and lower his eyes and Ribero nod again, as if his reaction was only to be expected, and demanded irritably, 'What is at stake here, as you see it?'

'The work of Christ,' said Gabriel.

'The man must be a simpleton unless he is some sort of saint,' thought Altamirano and demanded, 'Where were you born?'

'In Ireland, Reverend Father.'

'Ah, yes.' He looked thoughtful, recalling that one Father Hildebrand, distinguished by a fly-away head-piece and an infinite knowledge of papal edicts, had come from Ireland too. 'Now I will explain to you what is actually at stake – nothing less than the sheer survival of our Order, do you understand? Not only here but throughout Christendom. Furthermore, by comparison with the courts of Europe, your jungles here in South America are well-kept gardens.'

Ribero lowered his brows to protect his eyes from his Superior's stare and murmured, 'Ah yes, indeed,' but Gabriel asked quietly, 'Father, are we not the soldiers of God?'

Altamirano, bereft of a reply, stared at him, pushed back his chair and strode to the half-shuttered window just as Hontar and Cabeza chanced to pass by. Cabeza was saying vehemently, 'Christian amity between two empires is far more important than the work of a mission. That is what I maintain, with or without the approval of a Reverend Father.'

Altamirano's face betrayed no sign, but he was listening with interest for the answer.

'Don Cabeza, be assured the Reverend Father has been sent here by His Holiness the Pope to do a certain thing and he will do it, never fear, only provided we are prepared to help him. Patience is all I ask of you. And try to be more modest. Do you understand?'

'Well, I will wait a little longer,' was the reply and the speakers re-entered the building.

Conscious that others might also have overheard that compromising interchange, Altamirano turned to show a troubled face to his two companions and then fell to pacing noisily up and down the resounding floor until his features had recovered their customary composure. 'Father Gabriel, make sure Mendoza understands what is required of him. See to it at once.'

Gabriel went up to the gallery, away from the others, and seated himself beside Mendoza while Ribero and Altamirano proceeded to resume their places in the courtyard. 'Now listen,' he said quietly, 'you have undertaken to do a deed. Perform it now, before the whole assembly, on your knees.'

'It was a lie he spoke. Why should I apologize?'

'It is an order.'

'I will do it, father.' But then, as Gabriel was moving off to rejoin the others, he added, 'But it will still be a lie.'

Down in the courtyard where Gabriel again joined the Jesuit ranks, the meeting had reassembled in a murmur of conversation which suddenly died into silence as Mendoza too reappeared in their midst. All eyes were fixed on him as he went over to Cabeza, sank to his knees and, with arms outstretched, said, 'Humbly, and without reservation, I ask you to pardon my presumption and my insolence.'

Cabeza turned to the *hidalgos*. 'Very well. Why not? As I said, a man of honour cannot quarrel with a priest.'

'Which makes my insolence doubly impertinent, and your

pardon doubly courteous,' came the response, at which Hontar half smiled. Then, addressing himself to Altamirano, Mendoza continued, 'Reverend Visitor-General, I ask your pardon too.' Next, turning to the Guarani, he said in their language, 'I ask your pardon, also.'

'For what?' said Hacugh.

'For insulting His Excellency.'

Hacugh looked at Cabeza, and weighed him up and down. 'That needs no pardon.'

A ripple of amusement stirred the Jesuits and the one or two others present who understood Guarani. Gabriel said hurriedly, 'Reverend Father, may he resume his place?'

Dismissing a pang of envy at the glimpse he had caught of a different world, Altamirano brusquely signified his assent and the meeting was resumed. As he often did when he was about to make a crucial move in a conference, Hontar crossed his elegant legs and said, 'And now, Reverend Father, may we be honoured by acquaintance with your attitude to the transfer of the mission territories from Spain to Portugal? Because,' he said, turning to Cabeza, 'unless we know the Reverend Father's sentiments we shall find ourselves, a year from now, still parleying here.'

Cabeza grunted, 'Very true,' and looked expectantly in Altamirano's direction. The Visitor-General nodded sagely and declared, 'From the moment I departed from the Holy City, the question which has brought us together here today has been continuously in my mind, although, as many of you will know, it is a hard business crossing the Atlantic Ocean and, as you all know, the journey upriver here is far from pleasant. I am also aware how difficult it has been for many of you to get here from your homes.' He paused, noting with satisfaction the expectant look on Cabeza's face, before continuing. 'Nevertheless, I must inform you, Señores Hontar and Cabeza, that I am less decided now than I was before I started out. Accordingly, I have resolved to visit at least one of the missions in question before making up my mind. I am sure that from his vast experience Senhor Hontar will agree with me,' he said, turning to his adversary with the gravest possible face, 'that in dealing with a matter which involves such major issues, the *sine qua non* is modest patience.'

Impatiently Cabeza said, 'If it please you, Reverend Father, there is a little mission not above forty miles from here which we could easily visit. What good such a visit might do I can't imagine, but this one will surely do as well as any.'

'No,' Altamirano answered blandly. 'It pleases me to visit the Mission of San Miguel.'

Hubbub swelled in the hall. 'But Reverend Visitor-General,' Cabeza protested in consternation, 'you do not understand what that involves. That mission is more than two hundred miles away, upstream, and all the other members of this conference will have to accompany you, to see what you see. The number of boats required will be enormous. Besides, it will be a very arduous journey.'

Altamirano's eyes were fixed on Father Gabriel as he said, 'That is, however, where I have decided I shall go. Is my proposal agreeable to you, Father Gabriel?'

'Emphatically,' agreed Gabriel, 'but it will take time to collect the boats.'

'The Christian amity between the two Catholic empires,' Altamirano said, with his face turned solemnly to Don Cabeza, 'surely deserves our highest endeavours.'

'It is also an issue too important to be postponed until the crack of doom,' Cabeza replied.

The considerations that had forced Altamirano to decide to visit one of the missions were political. Hontar's public confidence in his cooperation required him now to make a gesture to suggest the missions' fate was not yet sealed. The choice of San Miguel, however, was a case of yielding to a personal inclination – above all, as he acknowledged to himself, to a simple desire to please the disconcerting Gabriel. He had learnt from Gabriel's story that San Miguel was the mission from which he had started on his work above the falls.

So it came about that one month later, towards evening, a fleet of boats was approaching the Mission of San Miguel. The three ahead were full of soldiers, with a guard of honour for the dignitaries following. The next boat contained Hontar and Cabeza, their relationship considerably strained by two weeks of voyaging together. Behind them came some half a dozen settlers who had followed them up the river in a worsening temper and without their wives. The boats of the Jesuits followed, in the middle of the fleet, and last of all came barge-loads of Guarani, servants, tents and baggage.

The further they had proceeded upriver the narrower had grown the gap of light above their heads, while on either bank black trees were densely tangled in a confusion where dusk reigned even at midday, save where a random shaft of light shot down through a gap in the foliage. An eery silence invaded the river from its overgrown banks, broken only by occasional forlorn howls, repeated a second later in the distance, only to be followed by silence again.

But now, in the falling dusk, a very different note was heard as three trumpets from the leading boat sounded in unison to announce their arrival. A few moments later, round the next bend in the river, a massive timber jetty swung into sight, with a group of Jesuits gathered on it in readiness to receive them, while from the tower of a great church nearby the bells began to peal.

Once ashore they were welcomed by the waiting Superior of San Miguel. His formal greetings completed, he immediately added, without the slightest shift of tone, 'And finally, Reverend Visitor-General, I apologize for the colour of my skin.'

Altamirano found it impossible to tell whether this was a joke, for the speaker's face was expressionless. He replied, 'In case you are serious, let me assure you no apology is called for. We are all one colour in the sight of God.'

'Reverend Visitor-General, it was to you alone I was apologizing.'

Again he could not tell whether this was a joke. 'Are there many fathers in the mission such as you?' he asked.

'No, Reverend Father. But then neither are there many such as Gabriel.' So saying, Ibaye seized his old Superior in a fierce embrace.

Cabeza watched gimlet-eyed. Hontar, after a pause, came up and formally greeted his host. This time it was Ibaye who looked taken aback. Hontar smiled.

Mendoza kept to the rear, behind the dignitaries; the long line of visitors formed up in procession, and his own face, when he raised his head, was expressionless too. At his right hand walked Babuie with the monkey and at his left Hacugh.

In the failing light, the procession crossed the square to the enormous church. Altamirano, keenly observing everything, took note of the neatly ordered stone huts on either side, each raised upon a plinth, and each with a wooden roof and five doorways. The occupants, however, were not to be seen. They were all in the vast church, awaiting him. Save for hens and goats, the only signs of life in the vicinity were a couple of old women. They were lying in hammocks and gave no sign of noticing the grand procession. Gabriel, however, went over and greeted them.

Meanwhile the clamorous summons of the bells became more urgent. Rearing itself high above them, the shadowy tower seemed menacing to Altamirano, crowded as it was with unrecognizable winged creatures, half angels, half demons, executed long ago by sculptors from the jungle. Once through the wide doorway, however, and in the dim coolness of the lofty, candlelit interior, he was greeted by a reverential hush. A second later the Te Deum sounded from four thousand throats in unison, thundering down from the distant roof. At the front of the choir an orchestra of viols, clarinets and trumpets sounded a strong accompaniment. Outside the music pouring forth from the church inundated the entire settlement and spread out and away through the darkening trees.

As he knelt at the altar rail, and his eyes adjusted themselves to the dimness, Altamirano was amazed by the spectacle of that vast Guarani congregation, all wide-mouthed in praise, packing the full space, nave and transept. Hontar, for his part, found the presence of so many Guarani made him cough with unaccustomed awkwardness.

Next day, mounted on a white mule, Altamirano was led by Ibaye, together with Ribero, Cabeza and Hontar, through miles of farmland. Gabriel walked beside him and the rest of the Jesuits followed thirty paces to the rear.

To the left and right the Guarani labourers went silently on with their work, unless he halted and faced them, whereupon they all knelt as one man. So it came about that eventually he found himself seated on a rise, where he had stopped to rest in an orange grove, surrounded by kneeling Guarani.

Looking Hontar directly in the eye, he said, 'I find this place impressive, don't you?'

'Yes, very impressive,' the diplomat agreed.

Cabeza, however, was resentful at having been called at six in the morning to trail around on an ambling nag in the retinue of a treacherous cleric. Moreover, he had a headache. 'I may be blind,' he commented, 'but to tell the truth I don't see any difference between this lot and the ones I use on my own trees back in Asunción.'

'There is this difference,' Ibaye said softly, 'that here at San Miguel the trees are theirs.'

'Theirs?' Altamirano exclaimed. 'In what way theirs?'

Mendoza came a few paces forward from the procession and replied, 'Nine-tenths of the produce goes to them; we receive only one tenth.' He turned to a labourer who was kneeling close by, and asked him a question in Guarani. A score of other labourers took up the answer which this one gave, and then more, until the grove resounded with it. 'Yes, they all say yes, the grove is theirs,' reported Ibaye.

Altamirano, watching Cabeza wipe his forehead, went on, 'They certainly seem contented.'

'Indeed, Father Visitor-General, I would say they seem no less contented than my own Guarani do.'

'Reverend Father, there is another difference, by your leave,' declared Mendoza, returning to the group of visitors and leading a labourer by the hand. He stripped the Guarani's thin clothing off his back, revealing a welter of old scars. 'As you can see, this man has been living here at the mission long enough for the wounds he received from his owner's whip to heal. Before he escaped, however, they rarely stopped bleeding. He tells me he used to belong to a Spaniard, who bought him from a Portuguese.'

At first nobody spoke. Then Ribero broke the silence. 'There is a very fine plantation along this way, Reverend Father. Would you care to see it?'

Mendoza raised his eyes to Altamirano's face. The latter hesitated. Then he turned on Cabeza. 'Captain-General, tell me, is such a thing lawful?'

Cabeza's face was dark with rage. 'What meets a public demand is surely lawful!' Then he did what he had been longing to do all day. He drove spurs into his startled mount and left the whole lot of them at a gallop.

Altamirano followed him with his eye and then looked at Mendoza. 'Father Ribero,' he then said, 'which way is it to the plantation you were speaking of?' and he urged his mule forward.

There were many plantations to be visited – orchards of pears and apples, groves of apricots and lemons – and he was taken to each in turn. Devout labourers crowded round his mule and knelt to receive his blessing. Accustomed to mass piety, at first he suffered these demonstrations with a fixed expression of indifference, but at last they began to irritate him. These flat, alien faces with their burning eyes seemed to make him irritable. When they reached the lemon grove, he reined in his mule and said, 'I have seen enough fields. Show me something else.'

Ibaye said, 'But you haven't seen the clearing yet. That's where we keep the cattle. I beg you to inspect our cattle, Reverend Father. They have been cleaning up the steers since yesterday.'

'I have seen sufficient,' Altamirano repeated, and it was he who led the departure.

Hontar looked after him thoughtfully, and gently turned his horse to follow at the head of the accompanying notables. The crowd of Guarani trailed faithfully along behind. Last of all came Mendoza, staying with Babuie apart from the rest.

They took Altamirano next to the carpenter's shop. Here Ibaye took the two halves of a flute and fitted them together. A hair line was running the length of the flute. 'Like the blow-pipe,' he explained.

'Yes. Indeed,' Altamirano agreed, 'I see.' He looked round the commodious shop at the viols, violoncellos and other instruments being fashioned there, and at the dignified carpenters standing by. He stroked the strings of a guitar and was surprised by the murmur of sound that came from it. He made his way out.

Still accompanied by the crowd, he was then taken to a vast, open shed, with some forty women in it who stood up at his arrival. Carpets were made there, and he was conducted round the shed, invited to finger, one after the other, the half-completed works still strung up to be woven. He turned, and there was a whirr of wings; he glimpsed a bird flying right through the place and out into the bush beyond, where it emitted cries of warning.

He saw the schoolroom, empty now. Drawn on a slate were the figures of a mother and father with three strong children; it could have been the work of any child anywhere.

He frowned and came to the living quarters. In a Guarani dwelling, containing rolled up bedding whose gaudy pattern was reflected on the white-washed walls, Altamirano found a mandolin leaning against the wall on which a picture of the Virgin hung. When they visited the cells of the Jesuit fathers, an elderly priest showed them a case of Guarani bows and arrows. Each item was neatly labelled, and the collection was displayed on the wall. To Altamirano he seemed proud of these primitive weapons, though Ibaye looked away. 'There . . . you see . . . beautiful . . . how beautiful!'

'But surely they don't make them still?' Altamirano asked.

'Oh no, not nowadays.' He replaced the bow he had been handling and swung round to face him. 'I hope they never regret that, Reverend Father.'

Altamirano noted all this but kept his thoughts to himself. So did Mendoza. Like all the brothers, they could only wait.

Later, when evening began to fall, Gabriel and Mendoza sat with the other Jesuits outside the mission storehouse. The eaves of the pantiled roof served them as a veranda. The Guarani sat quietly outside their own dwellings. All eyes were on the refectory, whose interior was already illuminated by a lamp, where the Visitor-General was interviewing the Superior of the mission. The Provincial Superior too was there.

Altamirano shut the account book he had been examining. He looked at Ribero, but the look he received in return said nothing. Outside he could hear the breeze in the trees, the croak of frogs, the soft, indecipherable utterances of the distant forest. He rubbed his face, and for the first time he felt cornered by his responsibilities.

'Father Ibaye,' he asked, 'are all the other missions much like this one?'

'Yes, Reverend Father. Why not?'

'There is no gold, then?'

'None.'

He said to Ribero, 'How many Guarani are you responsible for, in all?'

'All told, three hundred thousand.'

'These figures are good, Father Ibaye.'

'I know, father.'

'One-tenth of what is produced you take on behalf of the Order?'

'Neither more nor less, Reverend Father.'

'And how is the rest distributed?'

'By families, in equal shares. By this arrangement we avoid the sin of envy.'

'That is the doctrine of some modern French thinkers. Did you know?'

'No, Reverend Father, but I do know it is the doctrine of the founding fathers of Holy Church.'

'And are all who live here brought up in the practice of true worship?'

'As you have seen them, Reverend Father.'

Then Altamirano said to Ibaye, 'I am inexpressibly impressed by your work, father.' He said it dutifully but formally.

'Father, will the good impression you have formed suffice to save us?'

Altamirano turned away. 'Request His Excellency to attend me here.'

Ibaye went out without a word. He passed by the Jesuit fathers sitting beneath the eaves of the storehouse and through the Guarani lines to the guest-house on the far side, where Cabeza, drinking, and Hontar sat waiting, while their guards lolled outside, yawning or playing cards.

Cabeza's drinking showed. When he heard Altamirano's request, he slapped the table with his hand and replied, 'Present my compliments to the Reverend Visitor-General, and tell him I await him here.' Ibaye looked at him but, receiving no addition to this message, went out without a word to deliver it.

'Softly,' said Hontar. 'Don Cabeza, softly now!'

'No. Not softly.'

Watching from under the eaves of the storehouse, Gabriel and Mendoza saw all that was happening. In common with the rest, they rose to their feet as the Visitor-General passed by them, guided by Ibaye, on his way to what they all expected would be the conclusive consultation.

On arrival, without waiting to be invited, he seated himself and said at once, 'Don Cabeza, I address you as a true son of Mother Church. The royal house of Portugal, for all its seeming confidence and greatness, is lost and desperate because it is faithless and godless, whereas you, my son, are a joyous believer in the life everlasting in the company of Christ and all His saints, to which, as a member of our Holy Church . . .'

Hontar, appearing deeply shocked, held up a protesting hand. 'His Catholic Majesty, the King of Portugal whom I serve . . .' he started.

Altamirano turned to him and said flatly, 'The man you serve is Senhor Sebastião José de Carvalho e Mello, the sworn enemy of Holy Church, and most unhappily he rules your King as well as you.'

The surprise on Hontar's face was genuine. As an experienced negotiator he had patiently thought out his opponent's possible moves and this direct onslaught had not been one of them. What devil had got into him? The Jesuit was leaning forward in his chair, crowned with an evil or a seraphic pair of wings that had been carved by the Guarani. 'Which being so,' he went on, 'I cannot advise the transfer of mission territories to Portuguese administration. At the same time,' he concluded, forestalling protest, 'the Treaty clearly does cover those territories so Portugal is not to be deprived of them.'

'What other way is there?' Cabeza demanded.

'You can advise your King, and I, His Holiness, that Portugal should guarantee survival of the missions, pending which guarantee any operation of the Treaty in respect of mission territories will be postponed. This I call upon you to do together with me, as you have hope of Heaven through the intercession of our Merciful Redeemer.'

Hontar was thoroughly alarmed now, but the heavy features of Cabeza, thus appealed to, swelled into those of a bullying hooligan. 'In my opinion,' he said with hatred, 'and most truthfully as I have hope of Heaven, which I do – in my opinion, which is that of one whose family has been here for generations, the work of the missions is the Devil's work!'

His sincerity too astonished Hontar. What astonished Altamirano now was his own naïvety. Because Cabeza obviously accepted whatever he had been told in the name of religion during childhood, he had expected him to be obedient now. He opened his mouth to protest, but Cabeza rose to his feet to deliver a further thrust. 'Let me tell you something. Even I, myself, the Captain-General in person, have to ask Father Ribero for permission – permission, do you hear – to enter a mission in my own territory.'

'Not yours. Only your King –'

'His Majesty's and mine. He's made it all the same now.'

'Not at all –'

'The same, the same.' He loomed threateningly over the table. 'And where are the gold mines?'

'In the imaginations of the settlers.'

'Yes?' The word hung heavy; it was the first time Cabeza had questioned his integrity. Altamirano raised his eyebrows. There was an awkward silence for the time it took Cabeza to realize how far he had gone, and he added, 'Well, maybe, maybe you're right. Who knows?' He walked to the window and looked at his soldiers resting outside beneath the overhanging roof. Beyond them, in the darkness, he sensed hundreds of Guarani faces turned to watch.

Altamirano smoothed his brow and began again. 'What I find true is that they teach these people . . .'

Cabeza flung himself round to interrupt. 'What they teach them is that they are equal to ourselves. They also teach contempt for property and lawful profit –'

'And slave-owning?' Altamirano asked in a level voice.

'I have explained that. I'm tired of explaining it. The point is that they teach contempt for lawful trade. They scorn civil authority and those who have been appointed to rule over them –'

'Not so. The paramount vow of the Jesuit Order is the vow of obedience –'

'Then let Jesuits obey!' Cabeza struck the table. 'Tell them to obey. Or on your own head be it, Reverend Father!'

Altamirano said, 'Consequences will be on your own head too, from your own doings, Don Cabeza.' He pushed back his chair and added, 'For my part, I will obey my conscience.'

When they were alone, Hontar gave Cabeza a profound sigh. 'I fear you have been foolish, Captain-General.'

Cabeza glowered, shifted his heavy buttocks and sat down. 'It's time he heard the official view in these parts.'

'Ah, so that is what he heard, is it?'

As Altamirano made his stormy, fluttering way across the square, he thought, 'So, I am to consult my conscience! Conscience, are you there? My pride is there, certainly, and it has a lot to –' He pulled up, finding himself face to face again with Gabriel and Mendoza; he veered off towards the river.

'Shall I go after him?' Cabeza offered.

But Hontar said quite sharply, 'No. Not you.' In the soft

shoes he persisted in wearing despite the climate and the sand, Hontar went out of the guest-house and, watched by hundreds of Guarani eyes, strode through the gathering dusk, across the square in pursuit of his opponent.

Ignoring the mindless thudding which Babuie was conjuring from a guitar left lying on the table, Mendoza sensed Gabriel's uncertainty at this development, and ordered the boy to stop his noise. He was obeyed at once and then, aware of the boy's look of speculation, he apologized, at which Babuie stretched out his hand to touch his arm.

Altamirano walked out on to the jetty. The river looked leaden and the trees, from which night noises now emerged, were darkening fast. A short distance downstream half a dozen empty barges had lost their reflections, but children were still scampering on them. An older girl, posted to watch them, gazed dreamily at the water. He took no notice of their shrill cries and when Hontar came up behind him he did not stir.

'I fear that I bear bad tidings from Senhor Carvalho.'

'Give it to me,' Altamirano said, holding out a hand.

'What?'

'The letter, in which he threatens to expel the Jesuit Order from Portugal if I decide in favour of the missions here.'

Hontar said, giving it to him from his inside pocket, 'And Spain and France.'

'And throughout the world,' said Altamirano. He took it and read it attentively.

'He will do it.'

'Of course,' he said, returning the letter to its owner. His gaze went back to the half a dozen children now straggling home. It would be completely dark soon.

'I should like to express my personal regret; I did not expect to see what we have seen; I had expected to find the Jesuits ready to compromise.'

'So had I.' He turned to face Hontar. 'But you see what they are like.'

'I did not expect to see such rigorous application of the saying "Love thy neighbour". It is quite refreshing to see people being nice to one another.'

'That too.'

'Anyway you can still have a noble failure. You see, your Christian community has its uses. Settle for a noble failure; there is something admirable in that.'

Altamirano stared at him, for he was using the exact words he would have used himself before coming out here. Then, without answering, he strode off the jetty and back to the mission.

'Well, what is the upshot?' called Hontar after him, but he ignored the question. No less resolutely Father Gabriel intercepted him. Their eyes met, and for the first time since he had been involved in this affair something like fear appeared in the Visitor-General's eyes. Without disguising his evasion, he changed direction. The cross on the church seemed to beckon to him, and he went towards it.

Gabriel rejoined Mendoza and the others. He stood there in silence for fifteen minutes. Then he went after Altamirano into the church. The sound of the door closing behind him reverberated through the gloom. Only a few candles had been lit. Watched by some Guarani worshippers, Altamirano was kneeling at the altar rails. Seating himself at a distance, Gabriel said nothing until the kneeling figure rose with a sigh and, peering through the shadows, asked, 'Is that you, Father Gabriel?'

'Yes, Reverend Visitor-General.'

Altamirano came and sat down next to him. 'I cannot. Cannot pray.'

Then Gabriel said, 'Come with me beyond the falls to see the Mission of San Carlos.'

There was another prolonged pause and then Altamirano said, 'Why should I do that?'

'It's very much easier to see there.'

'And you invite me?'

'Yes, Reverend Father.'

'How long would it take?'

'A month. And it would be a hard journey.'

'I'll come.'

———————

Two days later the visiting notables, with Cabeza and Hontar at their head, stood on the jetty watching a few dug-out canoes paddling upstream. When they were out of earshot, Cabeza observed, '*Hostia!* There goes a traitor,' and stamped his foot on the resounding timber.

'A traitor?' queried Hontar.

'A traitor – the Jesuits make their own false church within the true one.'

'Don Cabeza, your motives do you credit.'

'Confound your impudence,' said Cabeza. 'I speak in all sincerity. I am the Catholic son of a Catholic Church.'

'Then you alarm me.'

'Why? I am saying that I am a good Catholic, why is that alarming?'

'If you regard yourself as a good Catholic, perhaps Altamirano regards the Catholic Church as Christian; in which event,' he said waving after the dug-out canoes, 'there's no guessing what he'll do.'

Altamirano, in a pair of hessian boots and a wide straw-hat, despite his fine black cassock, sat trailing his hands in the water beside the canoe, and found that he could not guess either.

Ahead of him in the leading canoe he could see the back of the stern paddler, Mendoza, a back that seemed militarily hard even in its cassock. Mendoza's face, however, when from time to time he turned to stare back over his shoulder, looked more and more relieved as the Mission of San Miguel, with its garrison, was left behind. He began to crack jokes with Sebastian, Hacugh and the boy, who were in the boat with him. The words must have been Guarani. Altamirano could not catch them, although he heard the laughter. His own companion sat hunched and silent as though he were beneath a burden that it took all his strength to bear. This was Gabriel.

On both sides he saw the jungle closing in: sometimes with high, dark, tangled branches, sometimes with a wilderness of flowering bushes that stretched away over acres, blazing in the sun. Once he suddenly found himself staring into a predatory eye. It belonged to a monstrous creature with the hard, unnatural skin of a fiend or dragon in a medieval painting: an alligator. Day followed day and he began to forget why he was there. No longer mindful of responsibilities to the Holy See, the thrones of Spain and Portugal, the Order, he found his judgement reverting to the simplicities of childish liking, and wanted Gabriel for a friend.

Each night they camped on a muddy bank. The Visitor-General's boots grew caked with mud, but he shaved his face scrupulously every morning in hot water which Mendoza fetched for him, without being told. It was also Mendoza who unpacked his things for him each night and packed them up again each morning, rendering the same service for Gabriel too, unasked. He washed their clothes as well, but rarely spoke with them. He kept his conversation for the Guarani.

Hardship started when they disembarked at the rapids. The elemental smash of water over rock alarmed Altamirano. It was too wild. The canoes were dragged up the bank, turned upside down and covered in branches. They camped for the night. In the morning Mendoza took Altamirano's bedding and rolled it with his own, setting off uphill with the bulky bundle, without a word, to lead the way. Altamirano followed. The rest of the party, Guarani included, followed after him. On that day, and on several of the days that followed, from time to time an obstacle or incline compelled him to stop. He could not go on until Mendoza turned back to help him. On the fourth night, while Mendoza was spreading his bedding, he asked, 'Was it up here you carried all your weapons?'

'Yes, Reverend Father.'

'You must be very strong.'

'I used to be, but I was rescued.'

'By whom?'

'By him.' He pointed at Hacugh. 'Goodnight, and God be with you, Reverend Father.'

Before noon on the seventh day they were back beside the river at the place where, on their journey to Asunción to attend the conference, the delegation from San Carlos had beached their raft. On this they now resumed their voyage. Five days later, when they had camped for the night, Altamirano became aware that the darkness was filled with a low, dull, inescapable roar. 'What's that?' he asked, although he knew what it must be, and it was only after a pause that Gabriel answered that it was the falls.

Throughout the next day's journey the roar grew louder and

more ominous. After they camped, Gabriel led Altamirano to a high promontory from which the falls could be seen above the intervening roof of the forest. Fascinated, he stayed there to gaze until it grew dark, and kept waking throughout the night to hear the irresistible flow. By morning the sense of threatening catastrophe that had gripped him when he first heard the din had given way to one of inevitability, so that next day he completed the ascent of the heights in a state of numbness, although his body trembled with the general vibration. When they came out at the top at last, Gabriel said, 'If it please you, wait here for an hour.' As if in a dream, he watched the darkness gathering, stars coming out and, rising from below to mount above him, the still iridescent spray that changed from saffron colour to rose and finally, as it fell upon the forest below, to crimson. Gabriel waited until it was completely dark before touching his sleeve and saying, 'Now let us go. It is time to sleep.' That night the sound of falling water, behind them now, was peaceful.

'Father,' Gabriel announced next morning, 'now you are about to see the Garden of Eden.' His taciturnity had gone. In high good humour he pointed to a couple of dug-out canoes, each with a crew of two Guarani, that had come to fetch them. Soon the sound of the falls died away, and all was silent as they floated through the liquid calm, save for the pluck of the paddles and the grunt of the prow. Long, bending branches with dripping leaves stretched out like arms over the water. There came a sudden shriek and splash at which Altamirano sharply turned his head. A rotting branch had fallen under its own weight into the stream. Gabriel sensed his guest's uneasiness. 'The Garden of Eden is thinning itself out,' he said cheerfully. But it was not the strangeness or the silence or the unexpectedness that alarmed Altamirano. It was the absence of anything within himself to set against these things, now that he had left familiar surroundings.

The silence did not last all day, however. There had been no sign of Babuie when they awoke, for he had already gone ahead to prepare for their arrival. Towards noon Gabriel suddenly raised his head. 'Ah, Reverend Visitor-General, hear!' And then he immediately fell silent, himself listening.

There was no discernible change as yet in view, but faintly, like some hallucination conjured up in reaction to the wilderness, the opening strains of the Spem in Alium could be heard. Then the canoe rounded a bend in the river, and Altamirano saw a complete tribe of Guarani standing motionless on the edge of a deep clearing, all joining in the chant. Some were at the water's edge, others knee-deep in it. Those to the rear were stationed at the openings of the pathways between the huts of the village. Above it all rose a high church tower on which a plain wooden cross had been mounted.

They put in to land, while the chant swelled in magnificence and beauty. As he drew near he could see the concentration on the faces of the singers – men, women and gold-skinned children – and recognized a choir fit to grace Saint Peter's. The chant soared to its conclusion. In the silence Hacugh looked at him, and he acknowledged to himself the justice of the pride he could see in the Guarani's face. Then, without speaking, he signalled with a gesture that he wished to be alone and followed a path into the forest.

Almost immediately the village was completely hidden from him by foliage. There was no sign of human life. He had cut himself off, as he intended, but the separation was alarming. He heard stealthy rustlings, first in one direction, then in another. There were sudden rattling sounds, harsh cries of unknown birds and abrupt eery cries that seemed to mock one another. At the foot of a sublime tree that rose straight and true, like a ceremonial pillar decorated with gold and ivory flowers, he stumbled on the carcase of a monkey, alive with maggots. A six-inch spider glanced at him with lively eyes from the summit of the fungus on which it was squatting, while near by orchids of the most intricate symmetry sprouted on a mouldering branch. A brilliant cloud of butterflies revelled around a stagnant pool. He had come away to seek strength and direction, but now stood, confused, in a grotesque world where the works of God and of the Devil seemed to grow in and out of each other. He sank to his knees. Once again, however, prayer proved impossible. It was a long time before he rose to his feet in despair. From now on he would be resolute enough. He would do what he had always known he would have to do.

That night he told them. He was sitting in the largest hut. Outside, the tribe surrounded it in the deepening twilight. The braves stood close. Behind them were the women and then the children. Inside the Jesuit fathers sat silently against the walls. Hacugh, backed by two elders, was seated facing him. Beside him was Gabriel, serving as interpreter. 'You must understand that you have a new ruler – no longer the King of Spain but the King of Portugal.' As he spoke, he knew he would never forget the thoughtful eyes of Hacugh watching him from his flat, taut Guarani face, but he did not flinch. 'Tell him,' he said to Gabriel. 'Make sure he understands.'

Altamirano could not make out Gabriel's expression, because even when it came to translating Hacugh's answer, Gabriel kept staring straight ahead. 'He wants to know what that means. "What will we have to do?" he asked.'

'Whatever the King of Portugal orders.'

'And if he orders us to leave the mission, what do we do then?' was the next translation.

Altamirano wished Hacugh would look at Gabriel instead of at him, but still he did not flinch as he replied, 'Obey.'

At this Mendoza, seated against the wall with the other fathers, raised his head to watch and listen, while Hacugh and the two old braves discussed it. 'This mission is our home now, not the forest. We have no wish to go back to the forest,' came their answer.

To which the response was, 'Submit yourselves to the will of God.'

But he saw it did not suffice. Hacugh replied without strong emphasis but with a connected flow of speech, spelling out an argument. 'It was by the will of God we left the forest and built this mission. For what reason has He now changed His mind?'

'I do not know God's reasons.' Altamirano found comfort in the orthodoxy of his evasion. It was, he reflected, also Socratic. He did not know and he knew he did not know.

But Hacugh's answer was, 'I do not believe you speak for God. It is for the Portuguese that you speak.'

'I speak for the Church.'

'Then speak for the Church to the King of Portugal.'

'I have already spoken, but he has not heard.'

'Then make him listen.'

'When a king will not listen, I cannot make him listen.'

Hacugh looked satisfied. This time he nodded directly to Gabriel. 'I too am a king and I will not listen,' he said. Courteously he waited for this final declaration to be translated and then, followed by his two advisors, left the building. They could hear him addressing the crowd outside. Then the whole tribe went down to the river and sat on the bank. One of his advisors started speaking to them in a low, thoughtful voice.

'What is happening?' asked Altamirano. 'What will they do?'

'They are going to fight,' Gabriel informed him. 'They mean to defend themselves.'

'Try to persuade them not to. Have you not the power?'

Gabriel said, 'But I have already failed to persuade Your Reverence.'

'To do what?'

'To fight for them, to fight on their behalf, Reverend Father in God.'

Without replying to this, Altamirano stood and addressed the assembled Jesuits. 'If they do fight,' he informed them, 'for the sake of the Order you must make absolutely sure that nobody can say that you encouraged them to do so.' He avoided Gabriel's eye. He looked admonishingly towards Mendoza, but the latter was staring into a corner. 'For this reason, you will all return with me tomorrow to Asunción.' He was aware of Mendoza's eyes turned suddenly upon him, as if making sure he meant what he said. 'Whoever disobeys will be cast off,' he continued. 'He will be cast out of the Order. He will lose the succour of the Blessed Sacraments. He will be expelled from the consecrated body of the Church. In short, he will be denied all hope of Redemption. And so, may God be with you, my brethren! May He be with us all!'

'God be with thee!' echoed the brethren as they departed, but Mendoza did not so much as exchange a glance with any of them. Alone and silently he went to his hut and dropped the screen. But even beyond his screen, except for the irrepressible forest noises, he heard only silence.

In the cloisters of the church, however, Altamirano consulted with Gabriel, who calmly inquired, 'Did you know that this would be your decision from the beginning?'

'Of course,' said Altamirano. 'Didn't you?'

'No,' Gabriel admitted.

'The only reason I postponed it and came here first,' Altamirano explained, 'was to teach the Captain-General that he must never take the Church – take me, in fact – for granted.'

'I see,' said Gabriel. 'I did not understand,' he confessed.

That was all he said. To Altamirano it sounded like an accusation. 'That is not completely true,' he admitted. He had never spoken to anyone like this since that distant childhood which his visit to America had unaccountably resurrected. 'It came to me,' he confessed, 'at one time not so long ago – indeed, quite recently – that God might speak a different word to me, if He ever spoke to me at all. God speaks to some,' he seemed to apologize, 'but not to me. There was no answer. There was no answer at all.'

'I see,' said Gabriel. 'Is it settled, then?'

In reply Altamirano explained what would become of the Order if Carvalho did not get his way.

'The annihilation of the Order!' Gabriel seemed to contemplate the catastrophe. 'Yes,' he concurred, 'it would be grievous. But it is more grievous,' he continued, 'for the Order to join in the Devil's work.'

'But the death of the Order,' said Altamirano. 'Surely, that is the worst thing of all.'

'Perhaps death is not as it seems to us,' said Gabriel. 'But the work of the Devil is unmistakable, even to the damned.'

'Father Gabriel,' Altamirano told him, 'they chose wisely who appointed you to guard these savages. Nevertheless, what I have said must be.'

A crouching figure emerged from the shadows and flung

itself at Gabriel's feet, clutching his robe. Altamirano recognized the boy who had sung at the conference at Asunción, who idolized Mendoza. Words poured from him in a passionate plea. There came a pause. Gabriel gave some sort of answer, but no sooner had it ceased than the plea was renewed. 'He is afraid,' Gabriel explained, 'He fears to be left alone. He wants help. He says that the Devil is waiting out there, in the forest. He says he has seen him. He begs me not to abandon him. He begs me to stay tomorrow, Reverend Visitor-General.'

'You know better than I do, Father Gabriel, what will become of anyone who stays here,' Altamirano said.

'This is not what I brought them out of the forest for,' Gabriel answered heavily. Then he spoke to the boy, consolingly but not encouragingly, until at last the child obediently went away, pausing at the end of the pathway for a last look at Altamirano, who, in his own turn, said, 'Father Gabriel, I beg to be remembered in your prayers.'

But he had not forbidden him to stay.

'And much good may my prayers do you!' Gabriel muttered, when he had left Altamirano at his allotted cell. But upon entering his own cell, he found Mendoza waiting for him. 'What do *you* want?' he growled.

'What do I lose,' asked Mendoza, 'if I break my vow – my vow of obedience?'

'Leave me,' was Gabriel's answer. 'Disobedience is a thing I will not discuss.' But Mendoza made to speak to him again. 'Get out!' he ordered. 'Leave me! I refuse to hear.' At the same time, without knowing why, he pulled off his cassock to reveal a nondescript, skinny body, with grizzled pectoral hairs. 'Just you, by yourself?' he asked. 'What do you hope to achieve, Captain? Death with honour, is that it?'

'We undertook to protect them.'

'Remember this, Mendoza,' Gabriel said hoarsely, delivering each word like a blow. 'If you die with new blood on your hands, you will die a traitor. You swore to give your life to God, and God is love.'

The back of the Captain-General's residence in Asunción overlooked the parade ground where, in the swirling rain that had gone on all day, the expeditionary force was mustering to the accompaniment of kettle-drums. Through a window Altamirano watched in comfort as they were inspected by their commanders. He had deputed his secretary to pronounce the necessary final blessing on the lot of them: Spanish troops, Portuguese troops, mercenary musketeers, bands of conquistadores and a party of Chaco Guarani, lost and drunk.

One of the conquistadores, a black man, had a racking cough and the inspection party paused to question him about his condition before passing down the line to check the artillery train: cannon loaded on to mules. Last of all the joint commanders, one Spanish and one Portuguese, came to where Cabeza stood with Hontar, to report to the representatives of their royal masters.

'No more force is to be used than you find necessary to carry out your lawful duties. Is that understood?'

'Perfectly, Excellency.'

On the parade ground a priest stepped forward, and all the assembled men of war, except the Chaco Guarani, fell to their knees. Altamirano, however, was no longer at the window to see this, or to watch his secretary proceed to invoke God's blessing on the enterprise. He had slipped away.

The boy was alone in the canoe. He paddled downstream, towards the falls, until he reached the legendary place. Every Guarani at the mission knew the story of how Mendoza had come to live among them, and how Hacugh had freed him from his burden of steel. They also knew exactly where that burden had disappeared into the water. Beaching his craft, Babuie now crouched and peered into it. He dived and surfaced, again and again, until at last, gasping and exhausted, he emerged dragging what looked like a weed-infested piece of sodden wood.

Again he crouched, this time to scrape what he had found; a scabbard was revealed. Then, with a pull, he drew forth the sword. He examined it carefully, and fell to cleaning it, until it shone nakedly. Stowing it in his canoe, he went back upstream.

Following Altamirano's instructions to the letter, Gabriel told the tribe that they must abandon the mission. God would go with them and so would he. Deep in the jungle they would found another mission.

When he had finished, Hacugh stood up. 'You are a man of God,' he said. 'But now God has abandoned us, as He did His Son. We will stay in the home that we have built, and we will fight. That is my word.' And it was evident that he spoke for the rest of the tribe.

Gabriel, lying awake at night, wondered at the cunning of the Devil who had persuaded clever men in Europe that greed left to its own devices brought prosperity and peace. Staring up at the brushwood ceiling, he found that the old impulse to bring his difficulties to Christ had left him.

Mendoza too kept to his cell. It was there Babuie brought him back his sword. He knew it at once, stretching out his hand instinctively to heft its familiar weight, but just in time withdrew before he had touched it. There was a bundle of faggots in the corner of the room. He told the boy to lean the sword against it and go away. Nevertheless, his eyes were fixed on it and it never left his thoughts that day. Towards evening a text repeated in his mind: 'Finally, my brethren, be strong in the Lord and the power of His might. Put on the whole armour of God, that ye may be able to stand against the wiles of the Devil; for we wrestle not against flesh and blood, but against principalities, against powers, against the rulers of darkness of this world.'

Calmly he stood up and took the sword, which once again felt like an extension of his own body, and went to Hacugh with it in his hand. 'I bring no message from Christ,' he told him. 'If you wish to hear from Christ, go to Father Gabriel. But I am joining you.' Hacugh thanked him, adding frankly, 'For, of ourselves, we have no idea how to defend this place.'

By this time the expeditionary force was proceeding upriver on three barges. It was approaching the Mission of San Miguel. Within striking distance they camped. They were irresistible; they were jaguars. Next morning, as they sailed round the bend and the jetty heaved into sight, they found the whole population of the mission assembled to receive them, armed only with banners on which the last moments of dying martyrs were portrayed. The soldiers and their two commanders, one Spanish and one Portuguese, swarmed ashore. The Guarani knelt and offered their pictures of the dying moments of the dying martyrs. The soldiers, conquistadores, fell upon them with fire and sword. By nightfall the leaping flames of the great church, stores and dwelling places were already dying down. The glowing remains spluttered and crackled as if in protest. Corpses of Guarani littered the square where, not so long ago, Altamirano had processed. Some of them had escaped into the forest.

Enough, however, had been captured to make up six barge-loads of slaves. The mission's barges were used to carry them down to Asunción for sale. They were carried away, keening, under the minimum guard. For the soldiers, conquistadores and Chaco Guarani still had to ascend the falls and to take the Mission of San Carlos.

In his retreat close by the village, Tanretopra learnt that the day he had long been promising them had come. The spirits themselves now summoned him. In a quiet place in his mind he prepared himself for this. To stay close to them he went without sleep and food. He renewed the ornate feathers in his huge head-dress, so that when the time came for him to die he would pass on this symbol of more than earthly power to another person intact.

Now he painted his face and body with the correct lines and marks and, carrying the head-dress, returned to the people. He watched and when Mendoza had gone out into the forest, he donned the head-dress and revealed himself to them, standing on a heap of earth. Slowly they gathered round to hear what he had to say.

'See, what I have foretold, it has come to pass. You accept the men of Christ, and then you must accept the men of rapine.'

'It is so,' said one of the old braves to Hacugh. 'He foretold it. Now hear him.'

'You have built a fine village for Christ; and behold Christ has let the conquistadores into it.'

'Oh, that is true. Hear him,' said the white-haired old brave.

'You have insulted the spirits by your doings.'

'Then tell us, what should we do?' said the old brave.

Hacugh looked at the earth and knitted his brow. He did not know what to do. And now Gabriel, realizing from the sudden silence that something was occurring, emerged from his hut. Seeing the tribe gathered round the farouche figure, he went down and said, 'No, no, now hear me . . .'

'They do not hear you,' said Tanretopra with a shake of his head. 'You are a man of Christ. A man with the goodness of Christ. But where is that power with the unchastised parts of the forest?' He turned to the tribe and said, 'Let Christ depart. Let you return to the spirits.'

'Yes, yes,' cried the elderly brave. 'It is true, Hacugh.'

Mendoza stepped out of the forest, having heard Tanretopra's question, and the tribe grew utterly quiet. With long, slow strides he went up to the shaman and paused there. He could see the wild eyes peering out of the head-piece, and he leant on the stick which he had cut in the forest. 'What you speak is a lie,' he said, passed the staff he was holding to the boy and stepped still closer to the shaman so he could feel the breath coming out of the head-piece. 'Give me that,' he said, but Tanretopra took a spear from the white-haired brave and levelled it at Mendoza's face, leaning back, poised for the thrust. Mendoza moved to the left and forward and seized the spear with a wrench that sent his assailant sprawling. Now it was Tanretopra's turn to gaze upwards into his opponent's face. The point of the spear descended and levered off the head-piece, revealing a scowling man with his head painted in red and yellow stripes. He rose to his feet and looked at the tribe; then he turned about and was swallowed up into the forest.

Babuie gave a cat call which was taken up by several braves, but they were rebuked by Mendoza, who was watching Gabriel. But he turned, went back into his hut and shut the door.

'My ways are not the ways of Christ,' Mendoza repeated to Hacugh. 'If you want the ways of Christ, go to Father Gabriel.'

'I have said that we follow you.'

'Then,' said Mendoza, taking the staff off the little boy and showing it, 'you can get me three logs of this, as thick as your chest and as long as this, but they must be of hard wood, like this.'

Hacugh took the staff. 'Of copper-wood, yes, we can do it. But why?'

'Perhaps we shall be able to return the fire of their cannons.'

'Good. But where shall you get the cannon balls and gun-powder?'

'Down there,' he answered.

'I see,' said Hacugh. They went and presently brought him three large logs from the forest. He made them split them in two, and then they bored a tunnel through each one.

Down at the foot of the falls the Spanish and Portuguese commanders stood gazing upwards. Their forces were strung out behind them further than a day's march. 'Have you been here before?' asked the Portuguese.

'No,' said the Spaniard. He was a man who had acquired the new taste for the picturesque. 'What a spectacle. It is sublime.'

'Yes? Possibly. We have to go up there,' he said, indicating the ascending spiral of water vapour, 'to hunt down a tribe of half-tamed Guarani and a couple of priests?'

'To prove that we can.'

Tanretopra stood on a jutting rock at the head of the falls, facing the darkening water. He took the head-piece from the grasses at his feet. He flung it far above the surface of the river and it floated quietly towards the falls. For a long time he stood there, naked. Then he picked up three spears and vanished in the direction of the invaders' camp. He made no effort to conceal his approach. A sergeant saw the painted, naked figure coming towards him. With an oath he cocked his gun and fired. Tanretopra fell, then rose to his feet again and began to throw his spears. 'Fire,' screamed the sergeant, panic-stricken, 'fire, damn you, fire!'

The whole camp came to see the exotic corpse. 'It was a noble savage,' said the Spanish commander. 'Look at it. The proportions are truly classical.'

At the village they bound the cannon round with lengths of running root to minimize the effects of their bursting. They were mounted on wooden blocks. Mendoza said to Hacugh, 'I want six men to come with me below the falls to fetch the powder and the balls.' Hacugh chose five. 'I will be the sixth,' he declared.

'No. You must stay here. You are the commander in chief. You must lead your people if we fail to return.'

'I understand.' He appointed the old white-haired brave to stand in for him.

The two sentries, half asleep, did not notice the seven figures who cautiously made their way among the rocks in the early hours of the following morning. Picking his way from one group to another, Mendoza came at last upon the ammunition train. Cannon balls, kegs of powder, ram-rods, wads and bundles of fuse were all strewn anyhow upon the ground, with the sleeping forms of tired men scattered among them wherever they had succeeded in finding comfort among the rocks. Mendoza could see everything he wanted within twelve paces of where he crouched, with the others pressing behind him, but a conquistador with a cough that kept him half awake was huddled in the midst of it all.

With his knife ready in his hand, he crawled towards him. When he was almost on top of him a cough roused the sleeper. He raised his head and Mendoza saw he was a negro. The next second his knife pricked his victim's throat and he recognized Gaspacho's face staring up at him. They stared across the knife. Then, cautiously, the veteran conquistador shook his head to signify that he would make no sound and let his head drop waiting.

Mendoza was bewildered. Had it been anybody else he would have pressed his knife home on behalf of his Guarani brothers, but this man was his private enemy. Removing the knife, Mendoza signalled him to get to his feet and accompany him. With a mute gesture Gaspacho inquired whether he should bring his weapons with him. Mendoza shook his head and then, turning to the Guarani, pointed out to them what they were to take: some small cannon balls, three kegs of powder, ram-rods and wads and fuse. They vanished as silently as they had come, only now they were eight.

When they reached the shadow of the falls, the white-haired brave asked, 'Why have you brought this man? Why did you not kill him?'

'He is an enemy of mine from the old days.'

'So?'

'I cannot do it.'

'Then I will do it for you.'

'No,' Mendoza said, stretching his arm to protect Gaspacho. And then Gaspacho smiled. '*Hola*, father.'

276

'Do not call me "father".'

'I am forgiven, is that it?'

Mendoza looked at him and took in his decision. 'Yes,' he said.

'*Poco del mundo*,' came the reply. 'When I heard about your conversion, I told the others it would be complete.'

'You have only to raise your voice a little to see how little complete it was.' Apart from his coughing, Gaspacho made the ascent without a sound.

The disorder in the camp was such that the stores he had taken were not noticed in the morning – but the absence of Gaspacho was.

'He must have deserted,' said the Spanish commander.

'Or else he has fallen into the water. See. He has not taken his weapons.'

Mendoza widened the cannon holes to take the cannon balls; then, with the cross-woods running the other way and with the running twine, he bound them up. He made the braves stand well back and fired one of the cannon. The explosion was impressive and to the jubilation of the onlookers the cannon ball went whizzing among the trees on the far side of the clearing. He reloaded it and fired again. The second shot barely cleared the open space. At the third shot the cannon disintegrated, sending slivers of wood over their heads. 'Now we know,' said Mendoza, 'what to expect. Two rounds from each cannon. After that we are back to the weapons we are used to.'

'Yes,' Hacugh said. He went and examined the powder. 'It is a trick.'

'Yes, but a trick of a terrible kind.'

'Good,' observed Gaspacho. 'You could start an empire of your own now.'

Mendoza looked at him keenly and said to the Guarani who

had him in charge, 'Keep a close watch on this one. He is tricky; kill him if you think fit.'

He placed the cannon, loaded them up, and put a piece of matting over their holes.

Filthy and stinking, the ragged army of the Spanish and Portuguese commanders was assembled at the head of the falls. The Spaniard took his stand above the falls and exclaimed at the view. They fitted together the barrels and the wheels of the two large and four small guns; they made rafts on which they tied the two large guns, as well as a couple of rafts for the Portuguese soldiers.

Mendoza saw all this from the forest where the scouts he had posted came to report.

Towards the close of that day Gabriel repaired to his hut. He would not speak a single word to Mendoza. But on this evening he looked for a long time at the shaft of sunlight which slanted in through the tiles; and when it turned red and then disappeared, he received a message from the braves: a high-pitched war cry, taken up by the others, a word of caution and a laugh. That night he said no prayers; the morning found him on his bed without having slept.

There was a knock at the door. He issued the invitation. Mendoza opened the door and stood there like a shadow in the sunlight, carrying his sword in his hand and wearing a knife in his belt which kilted up his cassock. He shut the door behind him and knelt at Gabriel's feet.

'Well,' Gabriel asked, 'what is it?'

'Bless me, father.'

The pale ghost of a smile flickered on Gabriel's lips. 'No,' he said. 'If you are right, God's blessing will be on you. But if you are wrong, my blessing isn't relevant.' He paused for a moment. 'If might is right, love has nothing to do in the world.

And it may be so,' he reflected heavily. 'It may be so. But I haven't the fortitude to live in a world like that, Mendoza. No, I won't bless you.'

Mendoza rose and was turning away, impassively, when suddenly Gabriel called him back and gave him a cross, from his own neck to his. He embraced and kissed him.

Shortly after this Mendoza's scouts brought him word that the enemy had begun the advance on the mission. The Portuguese detachment was approaching on the now completed rafts along the river. The Spanish contingent, the Chaco Guarani and the conquistadores were coming through the forest, dragging the three pieces of light artillery with them.

Mendoza turned to Hacugh. 'Go and may Christ go with you.'

Hacugh led the archers at a trot to a place three miles nearer to the falls, where they had hidden their canoes in a backwater. When the Portuguese poled their rafts laboriously past them, they shot out into midstream and sped their first volley of arrows upon them, hitting five. The Portuguese commander cursed, commanding his men to fire on the Guarani. The Guarani slewed their little dug-out canoes to the right and the left so that only two of them were hit, and then discharged another flight of arrows. The Portuguese had to leave off poling their rafts and reply while the current got hold of their rafts and began to make them drift towards the falls.

The Spanish hacked their way through the jungle and came out on the open glade, which barred their way to the mission. They were half-way across when the first flight of arrows struck them. They turned and fled back to the undergrowth, leaving a quarter of their number wounded or dead in the open.

The sight of the Spaniards and conquistadores fleeing from

them was overwhelming to Mendoza's Guarani. They broke cover, ignoring Mendoza's command to stay where they were. The Spanish commander waited till the yelling pack were at full scale in the mouths of the muskets, then gave the order to fire. A third of Mendoza's force was obliterated, while the rest did what they all ought to have done and took refuge in the undergrowth. The Spanish commander kept silence for twenty minutes, save for the groans from the wounded, and then signalled to two of his soldiers to cross. They crossed; finding no sign of the Guarani there, he sent the rest across in twos and threes, formed them up and resumed his advance upon the village.

In the mission church Gabriel had gathered the women, children and elderly, who waited passively, their eyes fixed upon him. He read to them about Christ in his mercy, seated at the right hand of God, who will upon the Last Day of Judgement rectify all the miscarriages of justice. He got up and went to the porch. Never before had he seen the clearing totally empty.

On the river the Guarani acquitted themselves well. Those who survived the fire of the Portuguese aimed their arrows truly, and many of the uniformed soldiers were dead. Other invaders had poled their rafts up to the side of the river, where they waited for orders. These were not given by the Portuguese commander, who was dead, and so was Hacugh. There was a mantle of dug-out canoes with their occupants dead or alive, and two rafts floating after them towards the distant thunder of the falls.

Mendoza's cannons were placed in a thicket, where he knew the enemy must come. He made the Guarani stand back again, and again Gaspacho's face wore that thoughtful expression as he watched him. Mendoza could sense the Spaniards reaching the target area, and he thrust the glowing wick into the touch-hole of the cannon at his side. He leapt away. The cannon roared. He glimpsed the havoc it caused and went beside the other cannon. Another roar and the mangled shapes of the Spaniards fell at the far side of the clearing. He began to reload it methodically and set it up; it fired and collapsed outwardly, sending its splinters among the Guarani.

The fleet of dug-out canoes was crewed by dead men now, and the men on the rafts were working desperately to reach the side of the river. One did, and one didn't; the raft followed the dug-out canoes with their dead men over the falls, its three soldiers flung far into the cavernous upsurge of the water.

The Spanish commander spied the thatched roof of the mission church. He ordered the Chaco Guarani to tie strips of cotton to their arrows and then to get down on their haunches; the strips were set alight and they fired from a prone position.

Smoke began to billow from the church roof and there was the sound of crackling flames. The old and young folk wailed at Gabriel, who seized the ciborium and pushed open the door. As soon as he reached the top of the steps, he began to chant, 'In thee, O Lord, have I put my trust; let me never be ashamed; deliver me, in my righteousness.' The Guarani poured out after him, clinging to his cassock, and began, 'Bow down thine ear to me; deliver me speedily; be thou a strong house of defence for me.' Slowly he led them out of the shadow of the church and towards the Spanish soldiers.

Babuie was choked by the fumes and by fear; he left the hubbub round Gabriel and dashed to the far side of the clearing. There he saw Mendoza and went gladly towards him.

With the remainder of his gunpowder Mendoza had mined

the bridge which the Spaniards would have to cross; he was now bending over the long fuse.

'Look,' said Gaspacho, and Mendoza saw the boy.

'Go back,' he yelled desperately. 'Go back.' Babuie came to a halt in full view of the Spanish commander. Mendoza ran to him and turned him round and pushed him. 'Now, go,' he yelled, and the boy started at a jog trot and then went hurtling into the forest.

Mendoza looked, and saw that Gaspacho was standing in the middle of the bridge by the kegs, holding the end of his fuse in his hands. He looked at Mendoza and then slowly shook his head.

Mendoza drew his sword and rushed at him, but he fled to the other side, where Mendoza was met by the Spanish musketeers. He attacked them fiendishly, as in his old con- quistador days. It was then that the Spanish commander, astounded, drew his pistol and shot him.

Mendoza thought, 'How is Felipe, and my mother?' and then turned his misty eyes towards Gabriel, who was coming towards him from amidst the Guarani, leading them on. 'Pull me out of the net that they have laid privily for me; for Thou art my strength.' The sergeant major took careful aim and executed him; for that, as he was never tired of telling, was a priest who had made the Garden of Eden in his mission. Gabriel had a swift dream of the coast of Kerry. 'Father, forgive me.' Through this he could see the set face of Mendoza. 'My son.'

With a pale face Altamirano read the three-page report which the Spanish commander had prepared for him. It was night, and huge moths were flying in and out of the windows of the Captain-General's residence.

Cabeza looked at his other guest and shrugged, but Hontar looked away.

'Have you the effrontery to call this slaughter "necessary"?' Altamirano asked in a low voice.

Cabeza stared back at him. 'Given our legitimate purpose, duly sanctioned by the Reverend Visitor-General, yes.'

Altamirano made no reply. He walked to the window and looked out on to the cool night sky.

Hontar gave a cough. 'You had no choice. You must work in the real world. And the real world is thus.'

'Oh no,' said Altamirano. 'Thus have we made it.'